Carrots at

(or Fifty Shades – with

By Craven Morehead

Warning;

Contains colourful language, graphic scenes of a sexual nature, strobe lighting and nuts!

(Some) Genuine Reviews!

"I thoroughly enjoyed it. It's a book that I can really recommend."

Medwyn Williams,

President of The National Vegetable Society.

"See you Jimmy, this book is nae but utter bollocks."

Angus McShite,

BBC Scotland's Outer Hebrides Horticultural Correspondent.

"Fatwah!"

Abu Hamza.

"Fuck me! Not quite what I was expecting!"

Prudence Prim

Chair of The Mary Whitehouse Society.

"If you've finished writing that crap can you put the bins out please?"

My wife.

The main characters.

Jim Lightfoot – 49 years old, latterly an engineer, who has recently settled into rural life. An enigma.

Harry Ecklethwaite – 68, ex-drayman, village show champion many times over and Olympic standard moaning bastard.

Bill Grudge – 66, ex-policeman, quite fat but otherwise an all-round good egg.

Mrs. Dibble – 72, no bother to anyone but always has a strong opinion.

Bob Dillage – 56, local inn-keeper. Keeps a good pint but otherwise one of life's twats.

Deirdre Dillage – 39 if asked, actually 58. Bob's wife. Slag.

Pete Greensleave – 44, local farmhand. Village stud. Thick as pig swill.

Mary Ecklethwaite – 42, Harry's sexually frustrated housekeeper, and his daughter.

Molly Greensleave – 42, Pete's long suffering wife, Mary's friend and a lass with a plan.

John Simmons – 66, bachelor, secretary of the village horticultural society, ex-university lecturer.

Jane Tallboys – 24, blond, attractive, otherwise a village lass of little consequence.

George – 74, a man who nods. A lot.

Reverend Arsley – 60, local vicar, probably partial to young boys.

Ted Grangeworthy – 63, semi-retired, school bus driver.

Lady Belton – 81, wheeled out for village functions and presentations. Almost dead.

Dick Tallboys – 76, definitely dead.

And assorted farmhands, pub regulars and large vegetables often of a phallic nature.

ONE

Oh to be in England.....

"You can fuck right off" shouted Harry Ecklethwaite as the Chairman struggled to restore order to the annual general meeting of the Allaways-on-Cock Horticultural Society held in the small but well-used village hall. "Big marrers have been on the show schedule of classes since my dad were winning everything afore me and the public like to see 'em, and you aint gonna delete 'em as long as I'm around! Am I right George or am I right?" he said gazing down to a rather feeble looking chap in a trilby hat sat next to him, and who was nodding compliantly.

"But Harry," interrupted John Simmons, the Society Secretary "for the past ten years you've been the only entry in the marrow class and we need to make some changes. We can't keep asking local residents to sponsor classes of vegetables that no-one is interested in growing except you."

"Bollocks," screamed Harry again. "Take some o't domestic classes out of the fucker then. There's way too many of them twattin' things. Who wants to see fuckin' cakes and jams anyways?"

"Actually Mr Ecklethwaite," piped up Mrs. Dibble, former village postmistress and local baking goddess par excellence, a slim lady of advancing years with grey hair in an immaculate bun (what else?), "all cookery and preserve classes have been well supported with many entries for several years, unlike some of the horticultural classes. They attract entrants from WI members from many miles around and Show day is their biggest event on their calendar. We always have to bunch up the jams and wines to make room for your enormous marrow and no-one can read the labels properly because they're all so close together. And might I remind you yet again to moderate your language?" she said with her customary grace and elegance, but firmly and directly.

The Chairman, Bill Grudge, a tall, rotund man formerly the local beat bobby finally managed to make himself heard. "Okay, okay, Harry, we'll keep the marrow class, purely for educational purposes. But something has got to give so instead I propose that we ditch the class for three onions as grown....."

"Fuuuuuck ooooff," roared Harry, standing to his feet and pointing excitedly at the committee on the top table. Papers went flying from laps onto the floor as several others stood up among the assembled membership wishing to make their point. Bill Grudge banged the table furiously calling for quiet, and school bus driver Ted Grangeworthy's faithful Labrador barked and howled with a loudness that was totally out of character.

Towards the back of the crowded room Jim Lightfoot sat quietly in staggered bemusement at the proceedings cracking off in front of him. He had settled in the village over the winter after several years working in the Emirates project managing large building constructions. Having made a small fortune and now in his late forties, he had decided to move to a quintessentially English village in the Midlands to indulge his passion for growing vegetables and flowers, walk idly in the surrounding countryside and maybe, just maybe find a little light romance. As a teenager he had spent many happy hours during summer holidays helping his granddad out in his back garden up in Yorkshire, and had accompanied him when his granddad entered his own prize vegetables in the local town show some thirty years before. It had not been like this as far as he could recall. He could only remember shiny cups on the presentation table, the smell of newly cut grass in the marquee, a brass band playing and friendly, smiley faces as the winners (often his granddad it has to be said) were politely congratulated on their achievement.

Thus far he had managed to settle into the village with the minimum of fuss and only some mildly annoying interrogation from his immediate neighbours and the landlord of the local pub where he retired each night for a couple of pints of the house ale. He had spent the long winter months renovating 'Peony Cottage' which had suffered several decades of decay. The previous incumbent had died the year before, a Mr. Tallboys, for a long time Harry Ecklethwaite's only serious competition in the annual show. But even he had tired of Harry's constant moaning and belligerence. Poor health had led to him being unable to keep his garden tidy many years ago which subsequently left the coast clear for Harry to sweep the board ever since.

One evening in late January after finishing decorating the final room to be tackled, the kitchen, Jim's eyes had alighted on the poster on the pub notice board announcing the AGM of the local 'hort soc' and so he thought he might pop along to see what it was all about. Having been made very welcome by Bill Grudge and the other committee members, Jim had settled down at the back of the village hall expecting friendship and camaraderie to flow forth from this assembled group of pensioners, housewives and local bigwigs. When the subject of the annual show was reached on the agenda Jim's mind went back nostalgically to those sweet days with his granddad and he started thinking it might be nice to wander down the road one balmy day in early September to the village green and throw a few nibbled vegetables onto the table in the horticultural marquee. Then someone had dared to venture that they might omit marrows from this year's show and the blue touch paper that was Harry had been well and truly lit!

The argument showed no sign of abating, for Harry was not to be turned. "Unyuns as grown are part and parcel o't village show. You might as well get rid of the class for five coloured tatties and that aint gonna happen 'cos Lady Belton sponsors that class in honour of her husband who won it one year when me and Dick Tallboys both had a bad dose of potatie blight and couldn't enter, warren't that right George?" George nodded.

Someone ventured to suggest that globe beetroot could be deleted instead, which prompted more expletives from an increasingly apoplectic Mr. Ecklethwaite, more frustrated and urgent table banging from the Chairman, more nodding from a seemingly mute George and just about everyone in the room to rise to their feet seeking a platform to be heard. Jim quietly slipped out of the village hall unseen, into the damp night air, a hard frost starting to creep across the perfectly clipped village green on which the show that was causing so much argument would be held in approximately eight months' time. He had decided entering vegetables into the show didn't quite fit into his idyll of blissful village life and resolved to just grow for the kitchen pot instead.

As he walked briskly over to the Dog and Gun for a nightcap he wished he had bought his overcoat as it did not take long for the cold to penetrate his lightweight jacket and start to chill his bones.

Upon entering the pub at the opposite corner of the green, landlord Bob Dillage immediately went to get Jim's pewter tankard but Jim stopped him in his tracks. "Bugger that Bob, whisky on the rocks please".

"Orty soc tonight was it then Jim?" said the publican, a knowing smile breaking out across his hairy face. "I've been here twenty two years and I've seen that same look on your face miraculously appear on many other folk after an AGM. Let me guess……they want to change the schedule and Harry Ecklethwaite threatened to stick his cock up the vicar's arse if they so much as altered a word of it? Vicar'd probably enjoy that mind!" he chortled to himself.

Bob Dillage was a typical publican, loud, brash, larger than life, a caricature almost. Blunt to the point of rudeness, locals took him in their stride but visitors passing through who had just stopped for a bite to eat had often been known to storm out in disgust at an alleged insult. It must have cost Bob thousands in lost sales over the years but he always laughed it off. He was not computer literate or else he might have taken a different view had he known how bad his online reputation was according to those websites that scored an establishment's performance. He was so tall he had to duck under the several wooden beams that crossed the bar area, his large bushy beard often betraying a morsel or two of the evening's meal that he had rushed in order to open up in time for his many regulars. Allaways- on-Cock and its environs was a farming community and the local farmers did like to fill their bellies with Bob's immaculately kept ale of an evening, often falling into the nearby River Cock on their way home. Bob didn't much care when a man had had enough, he was quite happy to take their hard earned wages until they could stand no more. He was also a nosy bastard and took great pleasure in finding out as much about the villagers as he could so that he might drop a tasty piece of gossip into a bar room argument to slap someone down. In other words, he could be a bit of a bully.

Bob liked to think he knew everything about the villagers and missed nothing, although he remained blissfully ignorant of the fact that his wife Deirdre Dillage had been shagging Pete Greensleave, a local farm labourer for the past six years. The aforementioned policeman Bill Grudge had witnessed her being nailed by Pete against a combine harvester one afternoon several years earlier when he had been on his rounds pre-retirement. Bill had jumped over a fence into the corner of a field for a crafty sleep, hiding his police issue bike in a hedgerow and was zedding away blissfully unaware that Pete's one hundred and twenty decibel combine harvester had come alarmingly close to mincing him on a couple of occasions. What had actually woken Bill were the manic cries of Deirdre's orgasm, a nightmarish noise that several villagers had since heard for themselves. Those same villagers were now keeping their secret trump card close to their chest for when the publican's verbal badinage became too much to leave unopposed.

Deirdre now came into view in the bar area from their upstairs living quarters. She never appeared downstairs until eight o'clock after her fill of the evening's television soap operas. In truth her life was a mini-soap opera on its own. Pete Greensleave was in the corner of the bar playing a very raucous game of darts with some of his farming cronies and Deirdre made her way over to collect some empty glasses, making sure she brushed against Pete's chest with her ample bosom as she did so. The other boys stopped their throwing and drinking momentarily to admire Deirdre's hard nipples stretching the thin material of her blouse several millimetres out of shape, nudging each other with their elbows like schoolboys.

One of the farmhands cheekily piped up "Oi Deirdre, did you see that quiz show on telly the other night? They got stuck on that question about chapel hat pegs," much to the amusement of the rest of the puerile agriculturalists.

The landlord remained oblivious to all this as he was too busy pressing Jim for information about his life story. Thus far he had become annoyingly frustrated at finding out any nuggets of scandal about Jim's existence prior to settling in Allaways.

"This Emirates place then Jimbo", said Bob, "sandy was it?"

Bob had insisted on calling him Jimbo almost since day one of his settlement in the village, as giving nicknames was something Bob liked to do in the hope it might pique them. Jim had let it wash over him and not shown any annoyance, but it did not stop Bob trying. "Well, it's a desert Bob, so yes there was a bit of sand about," he said sarcastically.

"Bet it got in all yer cracks and crevices when you wa' shagging all them camels eh, then Jimbo?" said Bob very loudly so that all the dart players stopped what they were doing to shout appreciation at their hero landlord.

"Well not really Bob, as a very important foreign worker I was put up in the presidential palace and had my pick of the Sheik's wives and daughters every night. We left the camels for the local publicans," said Jim drily, looking down at a bar menu as he nonchalantly took a swig of his whisky.

The pub roared. "Awwwww he's got you a good 'un there Bob" shouted Pete Greensleave, as Bob Dillage bristled and turned a shade of embarrassed red that was different to his usual ruddy complexion.

Once cornered, quick-witted comebacks were definitely not Bob's forte. "Cunt", he muttered, retreating to the other end of the bar to serve one of the horticultural crowd who were now piling in from their meeting. The voice of Harry Ecklethwaite was once more to the fore.

"I told 'em Bob, they can't go around messin wi' tradition. This show's been going for nigh on oondred year. My names graced the Cock Cup for most points in show on nineteen occasions, including the last eleven on't trot, a record I might add, and we an't messed around wit schedule in all that time so why start now? En't that right George? Eh.....where the fuck's he gone now?"

Jim did not wait around to listen to any more of Harry's triumphalism and for the second time that evening slipped out of a gathering quietly and unnoticed. Peony Cottage was off Cock Side, a cul-de-sac off the Main Street and a brisk six minute walk from the pub. Jim had placed a pin on a map of Britain when deciding where to live once he returned to England and had actually come down upon Tithampton the large town some twelve miles away. Exploring the area for property his eyes had settled on the vacant cottage in an estate agent's window which had only just come up for sale that morning. At least that's what he told Bob Dillage. The late Dick

Tallboy's niece wanted a quick sale and Jim had offered more than the asking price without even viewing it, concluding the transaction in record time before anyone else even got the chance to bid for it. It had initially caused quite a stir amongst the villagers as outsiders were viewed with serious suspicion, especially seemingly affluent ones. When he finally got to walk into the place he had been immediately captivated by it and knew this was where he wanted to see out his final years. Dick's niece, a rather slight yet exceedingly pretty girl, mid-twenties in age, had been similarly captivated by the mysterious stranger and tried flirting with him as she showed him around the dilapidated property. Jim had humoured her as they sauntered from room to room.

"Uncle lived here all his life Mr. Lightfoot, but he went downhill fast after a bout of flu winter before last. He loved his garden so much", she said as they approached a decaying garden annexe attached to the house and stared out upon a large but greatly overgrown jungle of brambles, thistles and bindweed. "I hope you'll both be very happy living here."

"Both?" enquired Jim?

"Oh, yes, Mr. Lightfoot. My uncle is still here. Only last week Jimmy Duggan the village garage owner saw uncle looking down at him from an upstairs window as he passed on his way home from work one evening. I've seen him a couple of times. He never says anything these days though, he just waves."

Jim had been thinking about acting upon the girl's flirtations and taking her upstairs for a swift knee trembler against a wall, but now hastily decided against such a plan for she was quite clearly retarded and any act of copulation would surely open an almighty can of festering worms.

TWO

Jim Lightfoot has visitors

The next day was a marvellously clear and sunny winter's day and Jim woke early as was his custom. The house was now restored, redecorated and modernised to his exacting standards. He had worked every hour possible throughout the late autumn and winter, and being a skilled handyman he had soon turned Dick Tallboys lifelong but ramshackle dwelling into a very neat and tidy home for a country gent with plenty of time on his hands. The sun was just squinting through the trees of nearby Buggery Wood that bounded the field over which Jim's cottage looked out onto. It was built on a slight promontory of land which was thus the highest part of the village so from various rooms in the house on the north and western sides Jim could look out over the rooftops of most houses in the village, but for now Jim's thoughts were in the field beyond the overgrown garden and a solitary figure creeping around the edge of it, seemingly stooping from time to time as if hiding from someone.

As the minutes ticked by Jim could tell the person acting so suspiciously was none other than the bulky and indeed scruffy figure of Harry Ecklethwaite, village show champion and opponent of all things unfamiliar. After nearly ten minutes of this strange, clandestine head-bobbing Harry clambered over a barbed wire fence and disappeared into Buggery Wood, emerging thirty seconds later with a sack that appeared to be weighing him down quite substantially. Harry then struggled around the edge of the wood away from Jim's cottage and out of sight with his mysterious booty.

Jim poured himself another coffee and turned his attention to his overgrown garden, for today was to be the day he would start to turn it into the productive oasis he had been dreaming about since the very first day in the sandy sweatbox of his desert workplace over twenty years ago. The thought of a verdant England had been his inspiration as he looked out over sand dunes under a fifty degree sun where cumuli never even got the chance to form. He had a plan in his mind's eye how he wanted the garden to look, a lush green lawn near the back door surrounded by borders overflowing with herbaceous perennials, a choice tree or two, perhaps a Robinia Pseudacacia or a Wedding Cake Tree, Cornus Controversa. Towards the eastern side of the garden and protected by a six foot wall that kept rabbits from skipping in from the adjacent field he wanted to have his fruit and vegetable plot, and he imagined serried ranks of regimental onions, leeks, lettuce, carrots and celery all standing to attention, growing large, lush and flavoursome. He was stung from his daydreaming by a loud knock at the front door. Jim went through to the hall to observe a large figure casting a shadow through the glass and upon opening it he was confronted by the presence of Horticultural Society Chairman Bill Grudge, one time rural copper and now full time village dignitary, Chairman of virtually every local committee going, parish councillor, church roof charity fundraiser and general busybody. All villages need someone of Bill's energy and tenacity to get things done.

"Jim, my dear fellow, you shot off last night without your society membership card and programme of events throughout the season." At this point Jim pathetically tried to explain that the horticultural society probably was not for him but Bill was having none of it. "Now we have some very interesting speakers booked every third Thursday in the village hall from now till October, there's the tree planting in March, annual day trip in July and of course our year culminates in the annual produce show first Saturday in September on the village green. We try and get as many people to enter, even if it's just a pot plant, a Victoria sandwich or bottle of home-made wine. Every little helps and all proceeds go toward replacing the church roof. You don't go to church do you Jim? No matter, each to their own I allus say. Also, here is the list of discounted seeds the society is purchasing this season but let me have your order no later than end of Feb okay Jim? Seed potatoes are ready from early March, but onion sets are in short supply this year so get your order in to Secretary John p-d-q!"

By this point Bill had shuffled through the house despite Jim trying to shepherd him out of it again but Bill's face dropped when he saw Jim's neglected garden through the kitchen window. "Fuck me Jim, you'd best get cracking on that if you're gonna grow anything good in it for this year's show!" And with that he turned tail, gave a hearty "toodlepip" and hot footed it out just in case Jim ventured to ask him for help clearing the forest at his back door. Bill loved hard work, but it usually involved working his hands and mouth organising events for the greater good of the village rather than actually getting his hands dirty. In short, he had a severe aversion to manual work as his avuncular figure testified. He had actually ruined three police bikes in his latter years in the force. Jim stood in his hallway, clutching a pile of seed catalogues, forms and notices as the whirlwind called Bill Grudge receded down his front path and out of the wicket gate. He wondered how he had ever managed to stay still and quiet long enough to witness Pete Greensleave manufacture Deirdre Dillage to the point of sexual ecstasy and beyond, without interrupting them mid-coitus to ask them whether they wanted red onions or white onions from the trading shed.

Jim soon snapped out of his daydream and got to work tackling the back garden. He did not mind hard work and it soon became apparent that it would take many weeks to bring it into shape, but undaunted he began by making piles of debris from the hacked back bramble stems, grubbed out sycamore and ash seedlings and old bits of rotten wooden planking that he came across as he cleared. He soon realised he would need a lot of bonfires before the winter was out. After a couple of hours of non-stop frantic activity Jim stood back to admire the result of his labours. Out of the corner of his eye he was aware of a presence and turned to see the figure of an old man in corduroys, a collarless shirt and threadbare waistcoat smiling at him but a few feet away. Jim immediately started toward him but stepped on a rake that he had carelessly left lying around which promptly shot up and thwacked him full in the face in standard TV sit-com fashion. If it had been a cartoon little birds would have been circling his head calling him a clumsy twat as he lay unconscious on the recently exposed and desperately cold soil.

****

In the village it was lunchtime and at the Dog & Gun the subject matter for gossip was the relatively new resident up at Peony Cottage. Harry Ecklethwaite for one did not think much of him.

"He's been up at Dick Tallboy's cottage banging and clattering away all winter and ruining the ambience that took decades to create", he said.

The elegant Mrs. Dibble pointed out that before Mr. Lightfoot had moved in the residence was an eyesore and in serious danger of going into terminal decay. "A village needs new ideas and input and it can only be good that he's chosen to live among us. When I moved here over thirty years ago after my dear Alfred passed on I was also viewed with suspicion and took a while to feel integrated and involved in community life. Fair play to Mr. Lightfoot I say," said the demure but forthright widow.

"Pah", retorted Ecklethwaite, "it's a shame no-one else round here got a chance to buy that property. Local homes should be sold to local folk. Dick Tallboys toiled that land for years and got the soil in perfeck condition and it'll go to waste now that poncy city boy has got the property. Dick were a good man and I miss him more than anyone". At this point several regulars coughed on their drinks because when he was living Harry Ecklethwaite never had a good word to say about the former resident of Jim Lightfoot's new home, although George did nod.

Landlord Bob now put his contribution in. "There's summat about him that don't sit right. He's been here five months and no-one's found out a damn thing about him." He started counting points of reference on his fingers, "He's had no visitors, postman Dave says he only gets bills and journals, not personal letters like most normal folk get. Lekky Dave says he insisted on no internet connection when he were up there rewiring the place in November and Dick's niece said he gave her the 'eeby jeebies lookin' her up and down like some pervert when she showed him round the place."

"I can believe that", offered the recently appeared Deirdre Dillage, "he does nothing but look at my tits when he comes in here each night." Everybody nodded in agreement, especially George, and all promptly started staring at Deirdre's ample mammaries.

After several moments of collective cleavage appreciation Bill Grudge explained that he had been up to see Jim that very morning. "Had his old clothes on and was about to set to in the garden. I do hope he's not going to just lay it all down to lawn. Worse still, a six inch top dressing o'concrete! Peony Cottage should be the quintessential English domicile with cottage garden plants floppin' over the pathways, a rambling rose over the doorway and a neat veg plot in the corner of the walled garden. I left him the seed order but he didn't seem too interested. We'll never win the title for best kept village in the county again when the most prominent house in the parish is a huge carbuncle eyesore I can tell you."

Hort soc secretary John Simmons, who was also an authority on local bylaws, had until now sat quietly in the corner of the public bar sipping his half pint of bitter. "The village constitution states that all gardens must be in keeping with the local ambience and that all erections (cue much sniggering from the darts team) and installations must not be out of keeping with the area. In short, ladies and gentlemen, if he so much as puts a single modern art monstrosity in that garden we can insist he remove it."

Conversation continued animatedly along this vein, all participants pretty much convinced that Jim Lightfoot would ruin Peony Cottage. As is often the case with these situations not one resident in that establishment had ever actually asked him what his plans were. Had they done so Jim would in all likelihood have told them to mind their own pissing business.

****

Jim started to stir. He was vaguely aware that he was cold, his back was wet and that his head hurt. He was also most definitely looking up at a cloudless sky. He struggled to his feet and felt a wet trickle on his forehead, which revealed itself as a warm red streak of blood on his hand when he rubbed it.

"Sorry I startled ye lad" said a voice behind him. Jim jumped back again, this time avoiding the rake. "Fuck me" screamed Jim. "Who the fuck are you and how the fuck did you get in here?"

The old man smiled, "Sounds like ol'Harry's rubbing off on you. Well as far as I can make out I've never been away. Dick Tallboys at your convenience." The hairs on the back of Jim's neck bristled at this revelation.

"So you're not fucking dead after all?" asked Jim.

"I most definitely am," replied the apparitional Mr. Tallboys.

"Well in that case," Jim suggested, " if I throw one of these clods of soil at you it'll go straight through you will it?" and he turned around to pick up one of the lumps of newly turned earth that he had toiled over that very morning. Upon turning back around however, the old man was nowhere to be seen. He had literally vanished into thin air. "Nice trick. Come on out you old conman," shouted Jim, but the stranger was nowhere to be seen. Jim stood there for several moments waiting for a tell-tale sound but heard absolutely nothing save a woodpigeon cooing from a rooftop and the odd clank from Duggan's garage down the road. "Fucking bang on the head's made me see things," he thought to himself.

He decided he had done enough for one day and retired to the house to find a band aid for his injury. After cleaning his wound and generally tidying himself up he poured himself a glass of water. It might have been a cold day but he had still worked up quite a thirst. He decided to have half an hour in his armchair in the front room, which was positioned in front of a large bay window. As has been previously mentioned, Peony Cottage was raised up above the road and surrounding houses. Jim enjoyed looking out over Allaways-on-Cock and watching the comings and goings, mostly mundane but sometimes suspicious bordering on the illegal. More of that later. Jim grabbed a tea cake and made his way into the living room to the aforementioned armchair.

"You've made this place quite smart young'un," a voice from the corner of the room suddenly said. Turning round Jim once again caught sight of the man purporting to be Dick Tallboys, standing next to his DVD player behind the door. Jim sprang up several inches in his chair, throwing his tea cake against the wall which subsequently bounced off it and onto the floor, leaving a butter smudge on both surfaces.

"Will you stop fucking scaring me like that," exclaimed Jim Lightfoot, picking his cake up from the floor and wiping bits of dust from it. At that point there was another knock at the door, a lighter one than that which had heralded the appearance of Bill Grudge a few hours earlier.

Jim made steps towards the hall, and had already opened the front door half way but was still straining to see his erstwhile vanishing visitor and thus did not have his face toward the new one. "Don't you fucking move an inch," he shouted back into the lounge, just as he turned to find the local vicar, Reverend Arsley standing in his porch way. "Oh, fuck!" stammered Jim, "I mean oh good, please do come in Reverend Arsehole. Bollocks. Sorry."

Jim ushered his clerical caller towards the front room and waited for him to greet his first guest with a hearty hello, perhaps with a name of one of the villagers (one who was not dead) and who was maybe playing a trick on him. He waited. Jim stayed in the hallway. The vicar looked around the room, turned, looked at Jim and smiled awkwardly. Jim edged in and looked to the corner where the old man had stood just a few moments before and observed no-one, just unoccupied space. "Oh, for f....."

"Mr. Lightfoot," started the vicar, "apologies for the intrusion but I was just wondering if you'd had any more thoughts on the new church roof?" Jim vaguely recollected a conversation he had with the vicar in the pub one evening over Christmas when he had offered to inspect the church roof with a view to using his construction knowledge to suggest a more robust roof design. "All materials simply must be in keeping with the overall look of the steeple and surrounding buildings of the church yard. Bill Grudge is having great success fundraising so we're hopeful construction might be able to start as soon as the autumn after the proceeds from the village show have been counted."

Jim apologised that he had not given the matter anymore thought since Christmas but that he would have a look that very afternoon. "Excellent!" enthused the vicar, "oh…this afternoon?" he stopped, " I wonder if I might ask you to delay until just before evensong, as we have choir practice from four and I don't like to be interrupted with the choirboys once we've started. They're such fidgety little things and I like to tie them down and keep them there." The vicar gave an awkward cough, surveying Jim over his glasses for an agreement to his plan.

The Reverend James Arthur Arsley was a tall but slender man, as bald as a buttock, with white, sinewy hands that he would rub together in Dickensian fashion. He had only been assigned to the village the previous November after the death of his predecessor in unusual circumstances, found stone dead one morning on Mrs. Dibble's front lawn. A post-mortem indicated a heart attack but milkman Dave who found him needed several shots of brandy in the pub and kept gibbering on about the terrible look of horror on his face. Jim recalled hearing the police sirens as he worked on the house that morning. As a result both men in that room were still outsiders in the village. "Of course vicar," said Jim at length, "I'll see you at 4.30."

"Spiffing," said the clergyman and bid Jim a good day.

As soon as the vicar had gone Jim raced around the house, opening doors and slamming them, whether it be bedroom, cupboard or even bathroom cabinet in an effort to try and locate the hiding place of his ethereal guest. But he found nothing. No pieces of furniture were out of place, no items of cutlery or crockery were disturbed or broken and certainly no other person or entity than Jim remained in that house. It was a mystery.

****

Jim toiled on the garden for several more weeks, until by early May things were pretty much shipshape and ready for planting out and seed sowing. He acquired a large greenhouse which he positioned on a sturdy brick base, installed a polytunnel for which he employed the willing hands of Jane Tallboys to help him hold down the polythene, laid down some grass turf, pruned back several roses to their proper shape and made a pretty patio area from reclaimed bricks in herring bone pattern. All of this passed off pretty uneventfully apart from several sightings of Dick Tallboys, for Jim now accepted that the old man who kept appearing to him could only be Dick Tallboys. If Jim was at the bottom of the garden he would be in an upstairs window waving down at him, if Jim was in the house looking out then Dick would be standing in the garden waving back at him, in all weathers. If Jim attempted to rush out and confront him, as he did do the first few times it happened, then Dick would have disappeared by the time he got out there.

During evenings in the pub Jim clandestinely tried to find out as much as he could about the former tenant at Peony Cottage. But Bob Dillage was only interested in gossiping about living folk, Harry Ecklethwaite had no interest now that Dick Tallboys could no longer challenge him for most points in show, and you needed to listen to several thousand words from Bill Grudge before you might discover one sentence that interested you. The upshot was that it was Mrs. Dibble who provided Jim with the most unlikely source of information, for it transpired that she was a great watcher and listener. One evening in late April Jim had bought Mrs. Dibble a glass of sherry and sat back to listen with interest.

"Oh Mr. Tallboys was a lovely, lovely man," she started. "When I first came here over thirty years ago to run the village post office he was the one who made me feel most welcome. He always had time to help anybody out, even his arch rival Harry, and never had a cruel word to say about anyone. He had such amazing energy as well. He was involved in everything in Allaways and you would see him everywhere in the village at all hours of the day. That the village show was such a success was largely down to him. He was the main organiser fifty years ago, before my time here, and would have won most points more often if he hadn't been so busy getting everything ready, for he really was the most wonderful gardener. Heaven knows how he found time with everything else that he got involved in however. When I had trouble with my camellias it was Dick that advised me to use sequestered iron to lower the soil pH. I wouldn't have known that. As he got older and passed the reins of organisation over to younger villagers such as Bill and John he started entering more of the classes and won most points several years running. The first time it happened Harry Ecklethwaite was positively raging, accusing him of cheating and all sorts of other nasty allegations. It upset many of the villagers but Dick just shrugged it off and carried on smiling, bless him. After winning six years running he didn't put such good quality produce in the next year so that Harry would win instead, in a bid to keep him sweet. Of course, when that duly happened, Harry was unbearably smug and condescending, and he refused Dick's hand of congratulation. Despicable." She tutted to herself and shook her head.

After a few sips of sherry Mrs. Dibble continued, "Something changed in Dick that day. He was still the same lovely man to the rest of us but from that point onwards he became very competitive and won the Cock Cup for the next eight years, which broke Harry's previous record. That was like a red rag to a bull and Harry became even more the nasty piece of work he is today. Dick's record ended when all of his vegetables and flowers were mysteriously poisoned the week before the show, meaning he couldn't enter a single thing. Of course Harry won and feigned mock disgust that someone could do such a thing, but everyone knew who the culprit was. He'd actually been trying to sabotage Dick's garden for years but Dick always seemed to be around when Harry tried to gain entry. Without proof though, absolutely nothing could be said. He never entered the show in such quantity again, just a few bits and pieces to show willing, and his garden pretty much went to rack and ruin, which was an awful shame as it's the first one the judges see when we enter the county in bloom competition."

As he sat and listened Jim found himself feeling more and more empathy with Dick Tallboys and resolved to try and engage his horticultural haunter in conversation next time he appeared. He did not have long to wait. The day after his conversation in the Dog & Gun with Mrs. Dibble he was planting out some leeks when he was aware of the familiar presence at the far end of the garden wall from where he was working. He stood upright from his dibbling and addressed the entity.

"Okay, okay, I believe it. You're a fucking ghost." At which point the sky was electrocuted with the piercing wail of a dying banshee, a screaming cataclysm of sound that emanated from the direction of Buggery Wood. The two men stood awkwardly looking at each other for a few moments. "That be Pete and Deirdre appreciating each other," said Dick Tallboys nonchalantly.

"Yes I realise that", replied Jim in equally casual manner. "So what the hell are you doing haunting my garden? Do I need to get in an exorcist or something?"

"I doubt it," said the old man. "Ye only need one of them if the ghost be malevolent."

"And you're not then I take it," supposed Jim.

"Nae lad, just taking an interest in what you're doing to the old place. Mighty good job you're a making of it too." Jim bowed slightly in appreciation of his praise. Dick continued, "You certainly seem to know what you're doing. Everything's looking very healthy. I've never seen leeks that good at planting out time since mine of '66 or '67 I believe." Jim's back straightened proudly. "Will ye be entering the show this year lad?"

"Oh no, that sort of thing isn't for me. Besides my stuff wouldn't be nearly good enough," replied Jim apologetically, his modesty belying his real need to hear more words of encouragement from the old man. "Don't you believe a word of that," countered Dick Tallboys. "From what I can see you're going to do very well. Are you going to try and grow a giant marrer?"

Jim regretted that he had not managed to get hold of some giant marrow seed from a specialist supplier, and that upon enquiring of Harry Ecklethwaite if he could buy some off him a few weeks earlier he had been told that he had lost all of his seed to mice over the winter and would not even be growing any himself.

"Lying ol'beggar," chortled the old man. "He told me that four years running once. Allus managed to bench one mind. A miracle. If you look under the creaky floorboard fourth step up the stairs you'll find an old packet of seeds that should still be viable. They'll grow to sixty pounds no problem. I had to take to hiding 'em when I found Harry creeping around in my potting shed one morning. He said he reckoned he'd seen a rat go in there and he was trying to catch it to save me the bother. I knew what he were really up to though and there was only one rat in the shed that day. A mighty big 'un at that!"

Jim spent a few minutes chatting along in this manner with his newly acquired spectral friend, asking for bits of growing advice which was duly offered in the same friendly way that Mrs. Dibble had mentioned the night before. In truth, Jim was an accomplished gardener and did not need much help, his grandfather's green fingers obviously having been passed down to him.

"Do yourself a favour lad, and get a schedule for the show. You'll walk it and it'd be nice to see someone new challenge that ol'rogue again. Don't go taking no nonsense from him mind. You go and get those marrow seeds before they fall down below the footings."

Jim nodded in compliance, rushed into the house and quickly located the creaky floorboard. Luckily he had decided against carpet, preferring to sand down the stair boards and stain them for an authentic look and the plank was soon off. On a wooden ledge secured to the inside of the stringer rail was a brown paper bag, and scrawled on it were the words 'Marrow seed – large'. He raced out of the house to thank his benefactor, only to find he was no longer there.

"Thankyou", he shouted towards the sky.

Jim looked at the garden, now a large expanse of fertile looking bare earth just waiting to reward him with bountiful supply. As he stood admiring his handiwork the figure of Deirdre Dillage appeared from Buggery Wood, clambering awkwardly over the barbed wire fence and onto the footpath that skirted the wood, the same one he had observed Harry Ecklethwaite navigating a few weeks before. She waved to an unseen person obscured by the trees, proceeding to walk along the path away from his gaze and towards the village, her skirt at the back well and truly tucked into her black lacy knickers thus exposing her fat thighs and veiny calves. It was not a pretty sight. In fact it was bloody awful. But at least it reminded Jim he needed to get his turnips sown.

THREE

Harry Ecklethwaite's good news

It was now a Sunday morning in mid-May, and Harry Ecklethwaite was not a happy man. He was in his back garden on Main Street, which due to a mysterious land purchase some twenty six years before was by far the largest in the village. His next door neighbour at the time had been an elderly widower whose marbles were not all rolling about in the same box, and yet he somehow contrived to leave most of his garden to Harry leaving any future residents of his home, by this time a young couple called Jennings, surrounded by a sixteen foot tall conifer hedge that Harry planted immediately after the sale. It led to repeated requests to have the hedge hacked back to a less light-blocking eight feet, several arguments in the street about the validity of the land sale all those years ago and nine different sets of neighbours in all that time, most of whom had become fed up with Harry and his intransigent ways leading to them selling their home usually for less money in real terms than they had paid for it. Indeed, the Jennings themselves had recently had the 'for sale' sign put up.

None of this mattered to Harry at that moment in time as he reached for his tatty mobile phone, a present from his daughter Mary the Christmas before. "Pete, it's Harry, you'd best get your scrawny arse round here now if you know what's good for you!"

Pete Greensleave lived five doors down so it was only a few minutes before he appeared at Harry's side gate, for Harry's house was a corner plot. A flustered and sweaty Pete let himself in and approached Harry who had his back to him and was peering in to his large, ungainly polytunnel, a home-made monstrosity of mismatched timber, broken paving slabs and moss-covered polythene with torn bits flapping about in the breeze.

"Alright Harry? Came as fast as I could. The boys needed their breakfasts and Molly was having a lie in so I had to get her up so I could pop round here, which she weren't too happy about I can tell y............." Harry held his hand up as if to order Pete to stop talking.

At length Harry said "Notice anything, how shall I put it, out of the ordinary Pete?"

Pete, who was very flustered by now, looked around Harry's large garden at the enormous array of vegetables, fruit trees and flowers. It was still early in the season but everything looked well advanced and healthy. "Nothing springs up Harry, everything looks fantastic. Puts my stuff to shame," replied Pete.

"Not out there, you monumental twat, in here," screamed Harry as he grabbed Pete's arm and man handled him into the polytunnel where a scene of plant devastation greeted Pete Greensleave. Rows of onion plants that would normally be erect soldiers, with large waxy, green foliage, were nothing but droopy, yellowing carcasses. "Blimey," exclaimed Pete, "what you done wrong in here then Harry?"

"What I've done wrong?" raged a purple faced Ecklethwaite. "What I've done wrong is to use that chemical you got for me to kill onion thrips on 'em. This is the result. Look at 'em all. Ruined!"

And thus, dear reader, is the mystery solved of what Jim Lightfoot saw that February morning when Harry Ecklethwaite was to be seen skirting Buggery Wood. Pete Greensleave's boss kept a large lock-up at the end of a track in Buggery Wood in which he stored fertilisers, insecticides and fungicides for use on the farm. These were generally substances that are readily available to the agricultural industry in bulk quantities, but unavailable in garden centres to the ordinary home-owner, and Pete was stealing some of it for Harry's own personal use. These were serious poisons that should really only be applied with breathing apparatus and full body overalls, but Harry could often be found happily spraying away with them in a tatty string vest and shorts with his bollocks hanging out.

"But that weren't for thrip Harry," blurted a horrified Pete Greensleave, "that were weedkiller. I told you we hadn't got any thrip killer yet in the pub the week before. I'm sure I told you that!" implored Pete hopefully.

"Liar!" shouted Harry. "You definitely told me it were for thrip. Look at 'em! You're gonna pay for this."

"You can't blame me for this Harry. It's not my fault if ye don't listen."

Pete would soon be fighting a losing battle as Harry went on the offensive, in a calm but sinister tone. "Ohhhh, not your fault eh? Well it won't be my fault if them photos of you and Deirdre up against that oak tree in Buggary Wood accidentally fall through the pub letterbox, somehow marked for Bob's attention then will it?"

Pete was expecting this. "No Harry, I don't suppose it will," he replied stoically.

"Right then. Here's what's going to happen," Harry continued, "you had some onion plants by mail order back in March. You're going to dig them up with as big a root ball as possible, and carry 'em round here as careful as if you were conveyin' a newly born babe. You'll dig up these poisoned ones and transplant your onions in their place. Is that perfectly clear Pete?"

"Perfectly Harry," replied Pete despondently.

"Ok, now fuck off and get on with it."

****

"What did Pete want this morning Dad?" asked Mary Ecklethwaite, Harry's daughter, as they both sat down to Sunday dinner. As well as being Harry's daughter she was also his housekeeper for she had never left home, and after her mother had died twenty two years ago had felt a duty to stay and look after her father ever since. Not that he ever showed her any gratitude.

"Nowt to concern thee," snapped Harry as he grappled with a large Yorkshire pudding, gravy dripping down his unshaven chin and onto his shirt.

Mary sighed. She had such plans as a teenager, plans to get an education and escape the petty mindedness of village life. That village! But her mother's death had ended any plans for university as she had taken on the role of housekeeper, looking after her little brother (who had long since flown the nest), and tending to her father's every need. She was nonetheless a good woman, the kind that nobody had a bad word to say about. She always did everything that was expected of her and nothing that was not.

Harry Ecklethwaite had worked as a drayman for the large brewery in Tithampton, delivering barrels of beer the length and breadth of the county and beyond. He had always been a reasonable worker, but he was also difficult to manage, a strong union man who demanded everything he was entitled to and never gave an inch extra than he absolutely had to. He was conventional, uncompromising, intimidating and also uninspiring. A small town boy who never looked much outside the boundaries of the village despite his job often taking him many miles beyond it, for Harry did not like change. He went to the pub every evening for seven or eight pints of beer, every Saturday lunchtime, every Saturday evening, every Sunday lunchtime and of course every Sunday evening too. Without fail.

He had never taken his unstinting wife on holiday in all the years of their marriage as Harry simply could not or would not allow any time away from his garden. She bought up the children virtually single handed apart from a week's help from her mother who came to stay when each of them was born. But as a simple soul herself with no ambition she had never complained. She was amply provided for, never went hungry and if asked would have assessed her life as a happy one.

The highlight of the Ecklethwaites' year (for what was Harry's automatically became his wife's abiding memory too, whether she liked it or not) was the village show in September. On this day Harry became the champion of the area, the top dog, a warrior. As a boy and young man he had worshipped his father, who was the local blacksmith and village show champion himself on many occasions. For many years Harry helped him in his garden and on show day carrying and laying out his carefully tended produce. He served his apprenticeship and in due course his father had stepped aside and Harry had become the main man. Winning most points in show was his sole aim of the year, the only thing that mattered. To go a whole year as an also-ran did not bear thinking about. In such a small community the vicious barb of bar room mockery was something Harry could not cope with.

And at first Harry was very successful. In a seamless transition the name of Ecklethwaite was engraved onto the huge Cock Cup for a total of thirteen times in succession, six of them for the elder and seven for the younger. As has been previously stated, this was a record at the time and both men were very proud of the fact. Ecklethwaite senior passed away the year of Dick Tallboys winning it for the first time and thus ending Harry's winning run. As Mrs. Dibble had correctly informed Jim, this sent Harry into a terrible fit of rage and jealousy and all sorts of accusations came from his mouth as a result. Perhaps he was missing his father. Perhaps not. He was never exactly the life and soul of any party but after that date he became the sworn enemy of Dick Tallboys and vowed to win back what he considered to be rightly his. It was in this atmosphere that Mary Ecklethwaite had to survive.

****

After Sunday dinner Mary washed the pots whilst Harry snored in his armchair in front of the television. As usual. Harry was much too frugal to consider buying a dishwasher machine. It then suddenly struck her that she had probably not set foot past their front gate in several weeks. She had certainly not been to the pub since last autumn and tended not to get involved in village events. As Bill Grudge avoided their house like the plague she was never asked to get involved anyway. She did not exactly resent her father for she loved him dearly, but latterly she had started to wonder about all the things she had missed out on. Travel. Friends. Romance.

Of the three, romance was the one she had been thinking about most of all. Save a couple of dalliances at school there had been nothing ever since, apart from a brief fling with Pete Greensleave before he had married her friend Molly. Besides, her father had well and truly scared him off after coming home from work unexpectedly to find them cuddling up on the sofa shortly after her mum had passed away. Despite her screams of protest, Harry had pinned Pete against the wall and threatened to rip certain parts of his anatomy off if he ever found him round there again. Today was probably the first time Pete had stepped foot on their property since that day, although he would never have stepped foot in the village again if Harry had come home ten minutes earlier and found a naked Mary bent over their washing machine, an equally naked Pete steaming into her from behind. Mary had never been intimate with a man since.

It was a beautiful afternoon, if a little breezy, so she grabbed her coat, laced up her walking boots, quietly opened and closed the front door so as not to wake her father and set off briskly for a walk around the village. Being a Sunday afternoon there was a distinct lack of human activity within the village boundary so she set off toward Cock Side, the cul-de-sac on which Jim Lightfoot lived, for she knew the wooden stile at the end would take her along a footpath, out over the field and up to Bell

End Scar, a disused quarry cliff with good views back over the village roof tops in one direction, and over towards the town of Tithampton in the other. It was so-called because a bell house used to be situated at the top of the cliff to warn the villagers of an impending air raid during the war.

As of that afternoon Mary had never yet set eyes on Jim Lightfoot. For whatever reasons their paths had not yet contrived to cross, but that was about to change. Mary had heard her father talk about the new 'fella' ripping Peony Cottage to pieces, and of course he had not painted a very flattering picture. As she approached the house she was busy looking at the large yellow skip on the road that Jim had hired to fill with garden rubbish. It was almost full to the top with tree roots, a knotted mash of bramble stems, broken glass and rusty bits of iron such as a bedstead that Dick Tallboys had once used as a support for his peas to clamber over. Therefore, Mary was not really concentrating on the route ahead of her and never noticed the plank of wood emerging from the open gate in the wall surrounding Peony Cottage, and which was being carried over Jim's shoulder. Mary walked straight into it at speed, face first, her bowed forehead taking the bulk of the impact. Whilst not quite being enough to render her unconscious, for it was no garden rake, it did result in her being knocked off balance and thus falling backwards to the path as the figure of Jim finally emerged mid plank.

"Oh my God," cried Jim apologetically. "Are you ok?"

"Er, I think so," muttered Mary, rubbing her head with one hand whilst propping up her prone body with her other.

"Jesus effing Christ, there's blood," Jim blustered. "Come into the house quick and I'll get it cleaned up for you."

Mary tried to protest but before she knew it she was inside Peony Cottage for the first time in her life, deposited onto a chair, whilst Jim clucked around and about like a mother hen opening cupboards and drawers looking for items of first aid. After a few moments Jim had composed himself enough to find a box of plasters, sterilising cream and some antiseptic wipes and set about repairing the damaged head of his unexpected guest.

When calm descended in the tender but awkward moments when their faces were only a few inches from each other, both of them had time to assess the other's appearance. Jim soon realised that Mary was very attractive, if a little careworn around the edges. A full figured lady with proper English pear shaped curves, jet black tousled hair that tumbled over her shoulders, a pale complexion encompassing a face of relaxed beauty, thin lipped, blue eyed and a narrow, pretty nose.

As Jim was tending to Mary's cut she analysed him in no less detail. Sandy haired, receding slightly, a tanned, almost weathered complexion, a couple of day's stubble giving him a rugged appearance on otherwise boyish features. He was slim and strong-armed, something she particularly liked in a man. With her face turned upwards for medical convenience she felt she could almost purse her lips and kiss him. In due course she would imagine doing this a lot.

When Jim had finished his nursing role an awkward silence ensued for several moments. "Oh, I'm sorry. I've not introduced myself have I? I'm Jim. I do hope you are okay?"

Mary laughed. "I'm sure I'll be fine, serves me right for not looking where I was going. Although I guess one shouldn't expect to be accosted by a head height plank. You plank! I'm Mary." They shook hands and laughed for several moments at this breaking of the ice.

Jim decided he needed to make amends for the untimely wounding of his unanticipated but undoubtedly attractive new house guest. "Would you like a drink? Tea? Coffee? Something stronger?"

"No I'm fine, really" insisted Mary. "I just wanted to get out of the house and get some fresh air. I've heard a few things about you since you came to the village but haven't seen you around, which is strange in such a small community don't you think Jim?"

For saying Mary had little experience with male company save her father she was finding it surprisingly easy to talk to Jim Lightfoot. "I see you've made a lovely job of this old place. I'd never stepped foot in it before today but you could always see through the windows as Dick never had curtains up and I'm afraid to say it was a tatty old dump." Jim bristled at this declaration and hoped that Dick the Ghost wasn't listening in to these potentially cruel words about his former abode.

"Well thank you," said Jim, "it's been a lot of hard work but I'm very happy with how it's turned out. With that he turned towards the open back door. "My main efforts now are outside."

Mary got up from the chair Jim had sat her down in and walked out into the garden where a truly magnificent sight greeted her eyes. Jim had worked wonders. Not only had the garden been wonderfully transformed from the overgrown wilderness of a few months before, but there was a newness about it all, as if a glossy magazine had prepared it for a photo shoot that very morning. The herbaceous borders had recently sprung to life, and the large circular lawn set within them was a deep green carpet that invited you to tread on its spongy indulgence. At the bottom end in front of the sturdy brick wall that embraced the whole plot was a large expanse of cultivated soil, in the process of being planted up, and which was unmistakeably the kitchen garden. A smart UPVC greenhouse and a large and indeed brand new polytunnel lent an air of affluence to something that would have been called a vegetable plot in any other garden.

"Wow!" exclaimed Mary. "You mean business don't you?"

"Well, I plan to enjoy country life if that's what you mean. I've been working in a desert for twenty years so this is a new thing for me. I think I'm doing okay so far. I think I may have a go in the village show if I've got anything decent. Should be a giggle."

"Oh, well don't let my dad hear you say that," said Mary. "The show is his life."

"Oh?" questioned Jim. "And that is?"

"Harry Ecklethwaite." Jim's testicles pulsed as if they had been electrocuted and he looked around at her quickly, surprise etched across his face. "Don't worry. I won't tell him he has some serious competition this year. I wouldn't want a deluge of weed-killer to besiege you at the end of August!" A large and wicked smile swept across Mary's face.

Jim raised his eyebrows at this last statement, for it was interesting in light of Mrs. Dibble's story a few weeks earlier and said, "Oh I have absolutely no doubt that your dad has nothing to worry about this season," and after a short pause, "Next year though I shall wup his arse!" They both laughed loudly.

****

There was a knock at the door of the Ecklethwaite abode and Harry stirred from his slumber.

"MARY!" he shouted. "Door!" The knocking continued. "MARY!" Of course there was no reply, for Mary was still up at Peony Cottage admiring garden and owner in equal measure. "For fuck's sake, what's a man got to do to get a bit o'rest these days?" moaned Ecklethwaite senior as he pulled his bulky frame up from the chair and went to open the front door.

"Bill Grudge? What the blazing bugger do you want on a lazy Sunday afternoon? I 'ant got no money for no church roof if that's what you're a begging for!"

"Sorry to bother Harry," said Bill Grudge undaunted, "but just thought I'd pop round with some excellent news. Lady Belton has some old village records up at Cock Hall that she leant to me and John Simmons a few months back, and today we have found out something quite fabulous. Everyone has assumed that this is to be the ninety eighth annual show because there are no engravings on any of the trophies indicating a show took place during the two world wars, as you would expect of course," explained a verbally frantic Bill Grudge.

"Oh for fuck's sake Bill, get to the point before I lose the will not to slam this door in your face!"

"Yes, yes, in due course. Well, within these huge volumes we've found reports of a show taking place at the start of both wars, so you see what this means Harry? This year will be our one hundredth show!" And with that news Bill stood tall and smiled broadly at the completely underwhelmed recipient.

"Well doodyfucketydoodah!" spat Harry with poisonous sarcasm, and he prepared to close the door on Bill Grudge, but before he could Bill put his hand against it to stop him.

"No Harry, that's not the best bit."

"Isn't it? Oh deep fucking joy."

"Yes indeed," continued a visibly flustered Grudge, "for you see Lady Belton has decided this needs celebrating. She has a contact at the County Gazette and they have agreed to send a reporter on the day and are going to do a full page spread on the show, its main characters and trophy winners!"

With this news Harry's interest was now well and truly pricked.

"Really?" said Harry, his eyes suddenly giving the appearance of huge, sparkling marbles. "Well why the fuck didn't you say so in the first place you silly old twat? Well then I'd best make sure I have my best suit on for the occasion. And we need to make sure that the reporter spells my name right, you know how they get things wrong on that fucking Gazette. Which of my winning veg will they want to photy'graph me next to I wonder? Got to be my marrow I would imagine. Thank fuck you didn't delete 'em from the schedule eh Bill? You'd have looked a right marrow yerself eh? Hee heeee!"

There was no consideration in Harry's mind that anyone else but he would be the one celebrated in the County Gazette that coming September. None. Nil. Zilch. Zero. Fuck all. Nor indeed was there a remote shred of a thought that the report could actually be used to document the hard work of other luminaries in the village, people such as Bill who worked tirelessly for the greater good of the community and beyond. As Bill offered his customary and cheery "toodle pip" before trotting off down the street, Harry remained on his front door step grinning like a Cheshire cat. He noticed George walking across the road, on the way to church no doubt. "I'm gonna be in the fucking Gazette George!" George smiled back. And nodded.

****

Some ten minutes after Harry's great piece of news Mary walked in the door.

"Where the hell have you been lass?" enquired Harry.

"Just out for some air," responded Mary "bumped into that nice fella up at Peony Cottage. He really has managed to....."

"Yes, yes," interjected Harry. "Mary, I'm only going to be in the bloody Gazette!" he continued, holding his arms out wide as if he was delivering the greatest piece of news ever to visit their house. And he sat her down to tell her at length about how the two extra shows had been discovered, how Lady Belton had approached the worthy newspaper, and how Harry would be celebrated in full colour. Not once did he notice the small cut on Mary's forehead, let alone ask how she came by it. It was all about Harry.

As he told her the story several times over, Mary sighed loudly. She was about to tell him how she felt he might have competition at this year's show but now she decided on definitely keeping that particular titbit of information to herself. In common with most of the villagers she had a morbid secret desire to see someone else win the coveted Cock Cup, whilst at the same time having a dreadful fear of the catastrophic eruption that would follow from her father if such a disastrous thing ever occurred. In former times this feeling had subsided and she had cheered her father on, relieved that he would be relatively happy for another twelve months at least. However, this time it was different. She wanted Jim Lightfoot to be the village champion. And she dearly wanted him to get his hands on more than just the cup!

FOUR

Mary muses/Jim ploughs on/Harry plots

The day after Bill Grudge's excellent news Harry Ecklethwaite woke extra early in order to make sure that all his vegetables were growing as he had hoped. Now that there was a probability he would have his photograph in the local paper for all to see he needed to be absolutely sure nothing was going to go wrong between now and Show day. Pete Greensleave had already transplanted all of his own onions into Harry's polytunnel in place of the ones that had been poisoned and Harry was pleased to see how good they looked, even better than the ones he had been growing himself prior to killing them with weedkiller.

With a cup of tea to hand Harry sat down in his garden shed in a tatty old armchair and took an even tattier notebook from behind a cushion. He started to jot down some names, which were those of his fellow competitors when it came to winning the various classes at the Show. Against each of these names he made a note of what they were good at growing based on previous years, and then wrote some initials against them that nobody would be able to decipher apart from him if his notebook happened to fall into the wrong hands. Harry then examined the list of all the crops he was growing to a programme which he had timed to a fine art over the years to ensure they were at the peak of perfection come Show day, weather, insect damage and pestilence permitting. There were copious notes about when to sow each set of seeds, whether to plant indoors in pots or direct into the soil outside, when to harden off, when to plant out, when to apply a nitrogen feed for each crop, and when to give one with potash. He then exited the shed to go over each and every row of vegetables checking for any problems such as greenfly, fungal diseases, slug holes and so on. All the while thoughts were churning around in his head that necessitated a change or two to his plans. For instance, he soon discovered that his globe beetroot was a little on the small side. Knowing that John Simmons was particularly good at growing this crop Harry went back into his shed, pulled out his notebook and wrote more initials by John Simmons' name.

"Gotta make a few tweaks old lad," he mumbled to himself, "and a few repeat sowings just as a back-up I reckon. Otherwise it'll be outright victory yet again. It'd be grand if that newspaper reported one grower won every single class wouldn't it?"

There were over sixty different classes, or categories for vegetables, fruit and flowers at Allaways-on-Cock annual show, and Harry always did his best to put an entry into each and every one of them. In some classes he might be the only entrant so it all tended to add up in terms of the amount of points he won and made him near enough unbeatable. On several occasions he had come close to winning all of them, missing out by barely half a dozen classes but it remained his ambition to achieve a perfect set one day. Harry looked out over his garden and continued to daydream about his big day. The daydream was vivid, for it was mainly based on fact, Harry of course having won the Cock Cup for most points on the eleven previous occasions. A broad smile broke out across his face.

Up in the house Mary Ecklethwaite was just beginning to stir. She had fallen to sleep the night before thinking about Jim Lightfoot, his every word of that very afternoon swirling around in her head and taking on extra significance with each rotation of it around her brain. He was single and that made him the most eligible man in the village by some distance. The fact that he was handsome was a bonus. Mary drifted into slumber wondering whether Jim might be having amorous thoughts of his own toward Mary, and then had several vivid dreams about him during the course of the night.

As she lay there the very next morning, she smiled as she recalled some of them. After a while she snapped out of such reverie, realising she was somewhat premature to be thinking such thoughts yet, but she had a mind to make sure her path dissected Jim Lightfoot's as often as possible in the coming days. She got out of bed and opened her wardrobe. Of late she had taken to wearing her scruffiest clothes seeing as she had been seemingly tied to the house, but now she placed all of her best dresses on the bed and tried them all on one after the other and to make sure they still fitted. They did. In between dresses she realised it had been some time since she had shaved her legs so the next job was to take a bath and sort out that particular problem. It was a good job she had been wearing trousers when she bumped into Jim Lightfoot yesterday she thought to herself. Whilst the bath was running she phoned her best friend Molly Greensleave, Pete's wife, who was also the local hairdresser and booked herself in for a trim.

"Going anywhere nice then Mary?" Molly had asked.

"Oh, no not really," Mary had replied hesitantly. "I just thought, you know, it's been a while since I had anything done so I don't want to get into a rut."

Molly knew better. "Mmm. I know you Mary. There's something you're not telling me. Still, everything comes out in the end. Oh by the way, that plan I told you about the other day? It's all arranged and will happen on show day."

"Okay Molly, I hope you know what you're doing," said a concerned Mary. "I have to say it's probably for the best though. Right my bath's run now so I'll catch you later."

As Mary soaked in the bath she could not help herself but imagine the possibility of forming a romantic attachment with the new resident of Peony Cottage. She recalled his strong arms picking her up from the floor yesterday, the awkward tenderness with which he tended to her wound and the easy repartee they had subsequently shared. All in all she felt they had made a good start but now she needed to spruce herself up and make sure he noticed her properly.

Jim Lightfoot had already been up for several hours at Peony Cottage, and had been working away in the garden for most of them. Mary Ecklethwaite had not entered his thoughts in any way, shape or form during that time until a voice called out suddenly from the kitchen doorway behind him and raised the subject.

"You'll need to watch that lass Jim," Dick Tallboys instructed. "She'll have gone back last night and told her father all about you."

"Oh? She seemed okay," answered Jim having lifted himself up from his weeding.

"Nah. She's an Ecklethwaite. Mark my words, he'll be here snooping around before too long. I'll have to keep a close eye on the place whenever you're not at home."

Jim chuckled. "My oh my, you do take things seriously in this village over the Show don't you?"

"It's everything!" Dick retorted seriously. "Those peas need tying in by the way. Believe me lad, if you can beat Harry that would make everyone in the village very happy indeed. You'd become a local hero."

"Oh I'm not sure I can take it that seriously," Jim said flippantly which bought another frosty reply from the ghost.

"Village shows are a uniquely British thing and we need to keep 'em going young man. When you win your first class you'll be well and truly hooked believe me. Harry tries his best to make sure nobody can challenge him. He tries all sorts of underhand tactics so you'll need to be extra vigilant. For now the least that folk know about your garden the better."

"Okay Dick, calm down old chap." Jim soothed. "I shall do what I can. I must admit the thought of knocking Harry off his pedestal does appeal to my sense of mischief though."

"Now you're talking my language lad."

"Perhaps I should also go out of my way to make friends with Mary so that I can keep an eye on what Harry is up to?" Jim suggested, causing Dick Tallboys' ghost to rub his chin thoughtfully.

"Now that, young man, may well be the masterstroke we're looking for. There's a butterfly under that mesh over your cabbages. She's not had a man in years so if you could satisfy her on a regular basis there's no telling what use she might be. She's as fed up with her father as the rest of us." Dick was racing away with ideas, so much so that Jim had to hold up his hand to slow him down.

"Whoa there. I never said anything about getting romantically involved with Mary. She's nice enough but I have no plans……."

Dick was having none of it and did not appear to be listening anyway. "You'll have to go careful mind. Once Harry finds out you're having it away with his only daughter he'll be gunning for you. Best if you ask her to keep it quiet for now. I'm sure she'll agree if she finds you can fully satisfy her needs. Now then I'm going to give this some thought. Don't let me stop you. And don't forget that butterfly!"

As Dick disappeared into the house Jim smiled and turned his attention back to the garden, putting down his trowel whilst he found the offending cabbage white and squashed it between the netting. "This sure is one crazy, messed up village," he said quietly to himself.

FIVE

A village affair – or three – or four

It was the last full meeting of the village show committee before the actual event itself, the date being a Tuesday evening in early June. They liked to have it early before the main holiday season kicked in. Bill Grudge was Chair (who else?), Deirdre Dillage was minute secretary and committee members included Pete Greensleave, Jane Tallboys and Mrs. Dibble among several others. Jim Lightfoot and the Reverend Arsley had been drafted onto it at the last minute, although pressganged might have been a better word. As soon as she found out Jim had volunteered Mary Ecklethwaite also found a reason for wanting to help out. As long standing Patron Lady Belton was also in attendance, but at this precise moment was soundly asleep. In truth the show was run like a well-oiled machine. Something that has been going for over a hundred years (if you add the two wars) tended to just happen as every person knew their roles inside out and just got on with them. The old tombola machine was taken out of storage from Ted Grangeworthy's shed each summer and given a general spruce up. Bunting carefully stored in a large box under the village hall stage was taken out and checked for damage and repaired if necessary. The splat a rat game in Bill's garage was certified in A1 condition because his grandkids had been playing with it on his back lawn the weekend before. All these things and many, many more were discussed and ticked off a large checklist.

The show was actually a whole weekend of activities starting on the Friday evening with the annual bingo session in the Dog & Gun. Ted Grangeworthy had something on his mind about this.

"Will you be caller as usual Dave?"

Dave Preston was one of the farmhands who frequented the Dog & Gun nightly, a friend of Pete Greensleave and as coarse a character as they come.

"I will indeed Ted," replied Dave. "Looking forward to it."

"Well I wonder if you might be a little bit more thoughtful with some of your number terminology?" Ted continued. "As you know Lady Belton likes to attend the bingo each year, (at this he whispered her name and pointed towards her slumbering figure) and it's pretty much the only time she sets foot in the Dog and Gun. She's a lady of some refinement and sophistication so I don't think it's entirely appropriate if you insist on calling 'a meal for two with a hairy view' every time number sixty nine comes out."

Pete laughed. Deirdre smirked. Everyone else shuffled awkwardly, especially the vicar. "Errr, right you are," offered Dave, "I'll give it some consideration."

"Excellent," said Bill Grudge as he ticked the item on the agenda and made a note. "Right then, the open-air bar on showday. Gazebos available Reverend? I believe they are still in the church hall store room?"

The vicar looked visibly unaware of such a thing. "Oh I say, are they indeed? Well I'd best have a look when I get back to the vicarage and let you know," said the vicar struggling to contain his bucked teeth. He was of course a newcomer to the village, which meant he had not been present at the last show and thus knew nothing of any gazebos residing in his church hall store room. In fact he only vaguely recalled that he actually had a church hall store room.

"Mmm," murmured Bill, annoyed that he could not put a tick against the item. It was the first 'X' of the evening and it grated on his sense of order and organisation. "I trust you will be running the outside bar as always Mrs Dillage?"

"Indeed I will," said Deirdre, "with Pete's help as always." And she smiled toward the sinewy frame of Pete Greensleave.

It was during one such meeting many years ago that Pete Greensleave and Deirdre Dillage first started their illicit dalliance. In truth Deirdre had not given Pete much of a chance to say no to her, flirting with him incessantly and bombarding him with saucy texts until he more or less gave in to her demands, despite him having only been married to Molly for a few months. All of the local farmers and farm lads would make suggestions to Deirdre in the pub of an evening and she would make each and every one of them think she had a soft spot for him and him alone. It is what good landladies do. But she had settled on Pete for one reason and one reason only. He was inordinately well-endowed in the trouser snake department. She came by this information after overhearing a couple of the football team saying they felt inadequate changing next to him after a shower because he was so ridiculously large.

For his own part Pete wished he could turn the clock back for Deirdre had very demanding ways. At first her incredibly vocal orgasms had been a source of wonder to him. He had been quite flattered that she had singled him out, for at the time she was reasonably attractive for an older woman, had looked after herself quite well and was available anytime, anywhere, anyhow and at seemingly any angle. Coming at a time when Molly was becoming less inclined for intimate relations this appealed to the single brain cell in Pete's rampant phallus. However, the intervening years had taken their toll on Deirdre's figure and looks, and as a result his feelings for her now bordered on repulsion. He always tried to make sure he had a rag for her to bite on as her orgasm had become a huge embarrassment to him and the village. It is important to realise at this juncture that Pete was incredibly stupid. If he had an ounce of sense he would have realised that Deirdre was nothing but trouble, and if he had given his wife the required love and understanding at home then relations might have been better between them.

"Actually Mr. Chairman," said Pete suddenly, "I've already volunteered to help Jimmy Duggan out on the kids' bouncy castle, so you'll have to assign someone else to help out behind the bar this year."

The look on Deirdre's face at this shock departure from the usual running order was a sight to behold. She darted a look of pure poison at Pete but he was deliberately trying to avoid her stare, although he could almost feel the barbs of her toxic gaze stabbing his face.

"No matter," said Bill, "Dave, I don't suppose I can persuade you to step in?"

"Glad to," replied Dave Preston, smiling towards Deirdre (still fuming) and secretly hoping he might be the willing recipient of some of what Pete had been getting the past few years. In truth Dave had no chance, as not only was he the village idiot but he was uglier than a warthog, his face looking like it had been set on fire and then put out with a golf shoe.

As Deirdre scribbled away at the minutes, in the vain hope that having her head down thus might not betray the red rage racing across her face, Bill quickly moved onto the next item on the agenda.

"Okay. Now then, the dunking machine. Two volunteers required for this as always, one male, one female. Any offers from anyone?" enquired Bill, looking around the room eagerly for willing stooges.

The Allaways-on-Cock annual show was famous for two things, the horticultural marquee which attracted visitors from many miles around, and the dunking machine which always gathered a large crowd. A victim sat on a seat attached to a plank of wood suspended over a large pool of very cold, muddy water which was often enhanced with undesirable substances such as custard powder, flour, rotten eggs from the local battery farm and pond algae. Basically, anything that was remotely unpleasant which came to hand in the days before the show. The villagers became quite ingenious at finding stuff over the years. The fall guy would often wear a mask of someone unpopular (usually the incumbent prime minister, local MP or TV talent show judge) and members of the public would pay to throw three heavy balls at a target which, when hit plumb in the centre, would release a lever plunging the unlucky dupe into the pool of festering liquid to loud hoots of derision from the assembled throng. It was always a good money spinner. There was a long silence as people looked at the floor, the walls, their agendas, basically anything to avoid making eye contact with a very persuasive Bill Grudge. Jim Lightfoot was first to speak, probably because he had no idea what he would be letting himself in for!

"Go on then Mr. Chairman, I'll give it a go," said Jim, sat upright in his chair, his arms folded, an uneasy grin breaking out on his face.

"Excellent Jim, I knew we could rely on you," said Grudge, eagerly pencilling his name upon his spreadsheet.

Mary now became very excited and started agitating in her seat, her mind awash with a bucket load of possibilities. She had walked the length and breadth of the village since her minor accident, going out of her way many times but still had not managed to 'accidentally' bump into him again. If she volunteered likewise she imagined working side by side with Jim, taking it in turns to get dunked then retreating to the small marquee which was always provided adjacent to the attraction for the sole purpose of allowing the two volunteers to dry off between dunking shifts. They could towel each other down in their semi-naked state, for swimwear was always the order of the day. Mary would have to buy a brand new swimsuit for the occasion, she thought to herself. She imagined Jim's strong arms wrapping the towel around her, rubbing her vigorously to keep her warm before she caught his gaze and he lent down towards her, kissing her passionately as the show noisily continued outside the tent.

"I'll do it", piped up a female voice and everyone present looked up, a not inconsiderable amount of relief palpable in the air. It was however a voice that belonged not to Mary Ecklethwaite, but to Jane Tallboys. It was like a spear to Mary's heart. Not for the first time in her life she had been beaten to or denied something through her inability to act quickly and decisively. She felt a hot flush of colour on her face as she witnessed Jim and Jane nodding at each other across the room and smiling, seeming to share a private joke or two.

"Good sports the pair of you," said Bill. "Hopefully it'll be a warmer day than last year. John Simmons nearly had to be treated for hypothermia by St. John's Ambulance," he cackled

The rest of the meeting passed in a blur for Mary as more tasks were handed out. Mary ultimately found that she would be looking after the bric-a-brac stall with Mrs. Dibble, which was not the most taxing of jobs and indeed would not be the most unpleasant way of passing the day, but it was not what it could have been had she only been quicker off the mark. Bill summarised things in his usual thorough manner, going over all the decisions that they had taken that evening to the frustration of all present who just wanted to get to the pub or go home. When Bill finally wound things up Jim noticed several unhappy faces dotted around the room, not least that of Lady Belton who had to be disturbed from her peaceful slumber, much to her disgust. She had heard nothing of the meeting it seemed and contributed even less. Deirdre Dillage slammed her folder shut, startling Bill who was sat next to her, threw her handbag over her shoulder and flounced out with tightly pursed lips, her stiletto heels piercing the wooden floor of the village hall like lightning bolts. Pete waited nervously for Deirdre to depart, visibly shaking as she passed him and then lingered a while feigning an interest in the bric-a-brac stall with Mrs. Dibble. The Reverend Arsley looked worried that he had been asked to do something and yet could not quite think what it was, his large forehead perspiring, for he had already forgotten about the gazebos. And Mary Ecklethwaite was in the corner of the room, quietly gathering up the cups and saucers and taking them into the kitchen to wash, her face appearing to Jim somewhat tormented from his previous meeting for as we have heard he had not seen her since the day he had unintentionally maimed her. He followed her into the kitchen, carrying a tray of crockery himself.

"How's the head?" enquired Jim cheerily, forcing Mary to turn round in surprise.

"Oh, hi there Jim. It's fine. Look, barely a scar now," she replied as she raised the hair from her forehead for him to check. As she looked over his shoulder back into the hall she noticed a piqued look staring back at her from the girlish face of Jane Tallboys, especially when Jim gently rubbed her forehead checking for any lasting damage.

"I must say," said Jim, "it was nice seeing your friendly face when I walked in tonight. You never quite know what you're letting yourself in for when you put up for this sort of thing. Bill Grudge can be bloody persuasive when he wants to be can't he?"

"Oh, God yes," continued Mary, "you can't say no to him very easily." This was a blatant lie as Mary had frantically sought him out in the post office and asked him if she could be involved as soon as she knew of Jim's intended participation. "I must say well done on giving the dunking stool a go. People only volunteer for that once." A large smile broke out over both their faces.

Jim continued. "I was rather hoping you'd volunteer for that yourself Mary. To be honest I think young Jane has a bit of an embarrassing crush on me. Still, it's only for a few hours but it would have been nice if we could have done it together."

Mary's heart skipped at this last revelation, for she now realised Jane was no competition for Jim's affections. Jim helped her clean and dry the cups and saucers as they shared further small talk about the village and beyond. As they talked and worked, Jane slipped out quietly, now having deep regrets about volunteering for the dunking pool.

"You fancy a quick nightcap in the pub Mary?" said Jim as the last cup was placed in the cupboard, the sound of chairs and tables scraping the floor in the hall as Bill, Pete and Ted Grangeworthy finished putting things away in there.

"Erm. Why not?" said Mary. "Been a while since I stepped foot in there." As they both bid the others good night and ventured out into the warm air of an early summer evening, over the green towards the Dog & Gun, Pete Greensleave nudged Bill Grudge, who in turn clicked his fingers to rouse the attention of a busy Ted Grangeworthy. All three raised their eyebrows, huffed their cheeks out and looked at each other knowingly, before carrying on with their tidying.

****

In the pub it had been quiet, as many of the regulars were either in the aforesaid meeting in the village hall or playing in a domino league, an away match at the Red Lion in the neighbouring village of Orfton-on-Cock. Even Harry Ecklethwaite had not been in yet, which was not unexpected as it had been a warm day and he would be making sure all his plants were well watered and fed before popping over the road for last orders, which for Harry entailed throwing several pints of ale down his throat very quickly. Bob Dillage was having to content himself with the distinctly avoidable John Simmons, a conceited know-it-all of a man. Bob always tried to dodge getting into conversation with him, as his education and knowledge soon had him in knots and struggling to keep up, but due to a lack of anyone else to turn to, tonight he had to make do with John.

"Something you alluded to at the New Year Party when you were a bit tipsy has just sprung to my mind John," said Bob, "that Lady Belton had a child back in the sixties? I allus thought she had no offspring?"

John looked nervous and shocked, and nervously stroked his silver goatee. Still only in his mid-sixties he had retired some ten years before from teaching with a healthy pension on health grounds when his bad back had prevented him from lifting heavy sticks of chalk up to the blackboard. As a result he was now resigned to spending his days tending his large garden and double sized allotment. He could not remember the New Year festivities in the Dog & Gun and several folk had since reminded him about other things he had mentioned or done on that night. However, he feared he may have overstepped the mark on this one. Nearly a year ago Lady Belton had given the show committee several volumes of documents relating to the village in years gone by and he had been trawling through them in his capacity as unofficial village historian. It was in this way that he had chanced upon the two extra shows during the wars, meaning that this year's extravaganza would be the one hundredth. However, most unexpectedly he had also come upon some documents within the volumes that Lady Belton would most certainly not have wanted to become general knowledge. She had obviously long since forgotten where they were and had handed them over blissfully unaware.

"Now see here Bob," whispered John, "I must insist on deadly secrecy if I tell you this!" Bob Dillage touched the side of his nose and leaned in towards John on the bar top as if some snippet of National security was about to be divulged. "Back in the early sixties Lord Belton was getting on a bit in years and hadn't been able to father a child to carry on the family name and who would subsequently inherit Cock Hall. In fact, there was little likelihood that he would ever be able to do so because...how can I put this.......Lady Belton had no hard feelings if you catch my drift?"

Bob looked confused. "Huh?"

"He couldn't get it up!" said an exasperated John. Bob gave a knowing look as if to say he knew what he had meant really. "Anyway, it appears a deal was done with a villager, an un-named villager mind, for him to father a child with Lady Belton. A top London solicitor drew up proper papers (the ones that John had found amongst Lady Belton's volumes), and his absolute silence was bought for a tidy sum of money. It took a few years of impregnation attempts up at Cock Hall but eventually she fell with child and went away for several months presumably so that no gossip or scandal could spread round the village. That's as much as I know Bob. I don't know what happened to the child for as you quite rightly say, everyone thinks Lady Belton was childless. But she had one alright."

Bob was rubbing his chin in deep thought when Jim and Mary walked in, Mary's arm linked into Jim's as if they were a couple, which Bob could not fail to notice. From being an utterly boring night this was turning into one of major gossip for the old memory bank Bob thought to himself, as he winked at John and beckoned him to observe the two recently arrived customers. When Harry came in for his nightly constitutional it would surely become an even better night.

"What can I get you two love birds then?" sneered Bob Dillage, causing Mary to redden up and Jim to straighten his back and strike an unaccustomed look of anger at the innkeeper.

"Pint for me please Bob," said Jim. "Mary?"

"Glass of white wine please Jim," replied Mary, as she tried to feign familiarity and a complete lack of awkwardness at the situation she found herself in.

"Bring them over please Bob," ordered Jim confidently, a move designed to put the landlord firmly in his place as a servant to two paying customers, and which judging by the disdainful look on Bob's face had worked brilliantly well.

After Bob had huffily bought their drinks over to a table in the corner of the lounge, a table well chosen as being sufficiently far away from the bar that Bob could not hear their conversation Jim began, "I suppose you noticed Deirdre's ill temper during the meeting tonight?"

Mary smiled naughtily. "Indeed. Looks as if Pete's finally grown some balls, excuse my language. Pity it's come too late though."

"What do you mean by that Mary?" enquired Jim.

"Well," continued Mary, "Pete's married to my best friend from school, Molly Grangeworthy as was, Ted's daughter. She's known about him and her for several years and has just been biding her time. Pete's brother Mike always comes to help out at the show even though he lives in Tithampton. He's an accountant and a very nice chap. Single. Thinks his brother's a fool. Well, Molly and Mike have been seeing each other behind Pete's back for a while now and Molly's planning on announcing she's leaving Pete for Mike on the day of the show. Don't blame her one bit. He's treated her like dirt. Deirdre's going to get her comeuppance too. Should be fireworks."

Jim's eyes widened and he exhaled loudly. "Wow, it all happens here doesn't it?"

"Enough of the village. Tell me a bit about yourself Jim. No Mrs. Lightfoot I assume?" asked Mary wickedly.

Jim choked slightly as he took a swallow of his beer. "No Mary, I've always been a single man. After university I worked in London for a while and then this job abroad came up and I went over there intending to work a year or two and basically just stayed. The money was too good to turn down. But I always yearned to return to England one day. Live in a perfect cottage in a perfect village." As an afterthought he added "growing perfect vegetables!"

The two continued talking unaware of Bob Dillage bouncing around in the background, poking John Simmons, and waving frantically at Bill Grudge and Ted Grangeworthy who had recently popped in from their village hall clearing duties. For Bob had noticed through one of the pub windows the unmistakeable figure of Harry Ecklethwaite approaching for his nightly belly full. Bob was still smarting from Jim asking him to bring his and Mary's drinks over. In all the years of being landlord of the Dog & Gun nobody had ever asked him to do such a thing and he was now profoundly looking forward to seeing him get soundly thrashed by Harry.

The door of the inn opened wide quickly and unceremoniously as was Harry's way, no thought whatsoever being given to the risk there might be patrons just inside the door and of them possibly getting knocked sideways. A large shadow preceded Harry's portly frame and was at the bar a second before him.

"Pint please Bob," said Harry. "By eck, this mini heatwave's a challenge. No rain for a month now. Bloody glad I'm not on a meter I can tell you, the amount of water I've had to use today to keep things watered and ticking over."

This was a barbed reference to an incident several years earlier when the local water company wrote to every householder saying they were going to install water meters in the village free of charge. Pretty much everyone had accepted it without question and allowed it to go ahead, all except Harry and a few others who foresaw problems when it came to days like today. As a dedicated penny pincher he would have found it very difficult to use water as freely as he did now had he been subject to paying for every drop he used. Knowing that he would want to use much more than average, Harry had challenged the water company who admitted that they could not enforce meters on properties of a certain age and so Harry became one of the very few villagers who was not metered. On days like this he liked to rub the noses of the other villagers into the dirt and remind them as much as possible about his good fortune. Luckily for Jim Lightfoot, Dick Tallboys had been one of the few other villagers with the same farsighted prudence.

"Aye, bloody thousands of gallons I've poured on the veg today and they're responding marvellously," continued Harry, starting to notice

Bob Dillage's eyes bouncing up and down in their sockets as he tried to make Harry aware of the two customers in the corner of the lounge area. "You see, things like celery, caulis and cucumbers need to be kept moist at their feet at all times and…." Harry suddenly stopped his horticultural lecture, "….for Christ's sake Bob is there summat wrong with your fucking eyebrows, they're jumping around like a pair of demented hairy knackers?"

"I'll get that pint Bob," came the voice of Jim Lightfoot from the corner of the room, causing Harry to turn round in surprise, "Come and sit down here Harry. I need your expert advice on my tomatoes." Jim had now got up and was beckoning Harry to a chair that he was strategically planting between himself and Harry's daughter for him to sit on. Harry moved toward it with his drink in hand, a somewhat bemused look on his face.

As Harry walked towards Jim he was not aware at first of Mary who was obscured from him behind a pillar, but then she leaned forward to get her drink. "Mary? What are you doing in here lass?" he quizzed as he sat down and Jim took his pint off him and positioned it on a beer mat for him.

Before she could answer her father Jim offered an explanation, "I was just saying to Mary that I've got a problem with my greenhouse tomatoes and as you're the village champion I was enquiring of her if she'd mind asking you for me when she got back home, but no matter because you're here now. I can't say how reassuring it is to have someone of your incredible expertise in the village."

Jim was starting to play a blinder. In the desert he was well aware of the need to engage his Arab workforce carefully, often taking into account the various tribal and religious factions. In other words he had become quite a diplomat, one of the reasons he had become so successful and earned so much money. Harry was thus sweet talked with flattery and hung on Jim's every word, the need to find out what the hell his daughter was doing there with him now pushed very firmly to the back of his mind. As Jim continued to manipulate Harry's ego, in the background Bob Dillage threw his arms in the air and realised Jim had got the better of him yet again.

"Black spots on the base of the fruits you say Jim?" said Harry, rubbing his chin with a look of concentration, "Mmm, t'is blossom end rot, a calcium deficiency caused by irregular watering." Harry sat back triumphantly. "Anything else you'd like some help on?"

Jim knew full well what the non-existent problem with his tomatoes was, and decided to try a few more now he knew he was giving Harry his best disciple look. "Oh I have plenty of questions to ask you Harry if you don't mind. Would you like another pint? Yes? Bob…pint for Harry please. I was going to enter a few bits in the show this year Harry but I know I won't come close to your standard, but I'll just be a proud man seeing my veg on the same bench as the great champion Harry Ecklethwaite I don't mind admitting."

It took a while for Mary to work out what Jim was up to, for she had seen the flowers and vegetables in his garden with her own eyes and knew damn well they were even better than her father's. But then she realised that he was complimenting her father as a way of buttering him up for something. As Jim flashed several smiles across the table at her she wondered whether he was trying to soften him up before asking permission to walk out with her on an official basis. Not that they really needed Harry's permission, for they were both adults and could have done as they pleased. But she somehow felt Jim instinctively knew this was the route he would have to go down with Harry, and one which Pete Greensleave had failed to take over twenty years earlier.

Over the next hour Jim bombarded Harry with questions of a horticultural nature, massaged his bloated ego and had Bob Dillage angrily running around bringing Harry pint after pint. Eventually, a lull in the questioning arose and Mary started to make preparation for leaving. Jim got up also, "Well Harry I must say you've been an incredible help tonight and I can't thank you enough. You really ought to write a book as knowledge like yours deserves to be saved."

Harry was smiling widely, his lubricated brain not yet grasping that his one and only daughter was about to leave the building in the company of another man. "Well, I likes to do my bit and help other growers out," slurred Harry. In truth Harry had offered more advice to Jim in one hour than he had told everyone else in the village over the last forty years put together, although Jim knew pretty much everything he had been told for as we have already deduced he was a very accomplished gardener himself.

"Well Harry, I'm off myself now so I'll walk Mary to your door seeing as I'm passing. Once again, many thanks and I hope I can do all your advice justice." And with that Jim patted Harry on the back and bid everyone good night, stepping aside to let Mary walk out before him.

Harry sat alone for several minutes, grunting to himself and remembering the words of adulation that Jim had been using. At length he got up and staggered over to the bar where a disgruntled Bob Dillage was talking to Bill Grudge and John Simmons. "Fine chap, that Lightfoot fella." The publican raised his eyebrows at the other two who did likewise. "Yep, yep, yep. Absolute bloody gent. *Hic. Belch.Fart."*

****

"You crafty rogue," said Mary as soon as they exited the Dog & Gun, linking her arm into Jim's. "You had him eating out of your hand."

"Crafty? Moi?" laughed Jim, "he's not such a bad bloke if you humour him."

"You wait until the show," replied Mary, "you'll see a different side to him then, especially if you manage to beat him to most points. In fact, even if you beat him in a few of the classes he'll be like a bear with a sore head for a year. He won every one he entered in the veg section one year except for shallots and beetroot which John Simmons won. Dad insisted the classes were judged again as a mistake had obviously been made and they had to get the National Vegetable Society judge to travel back from Tithampton to review his decision. Result still stood mind. Dad stormed out of the marquee kicking over a bucket of dahlias on the way."

Jim shook his head and smirked. They walked over the green and onto the Main Street which ran adjacent to it and then out toward the Tithampton road, chatting as they did so about who lived where along the route, for Jim still did not know where most residents lived. As they approached the Ecklethwaites' house Mary slowed forcing Jim to do likewise.

"This is ours then. I'd invite you in for a coffee but dad'll be home soon and I don't think we should push things."

Jim felt a little confused at this point and tried not to let it show. As far as he was concerned he was just walking a lady home and until now it genuinely had not dawned on him that Mary might have romantic intentions toward him. Undoubtedly he found her attractive and good company but he had not been looking for love when he bumped into her that day, and was not yet ready to seek it either.

"Oh right you are," said Jim, and he leant down towards her and kissed her on the cheek, as if it was the right and proper thing to do. As soon as he did it he felt he had made a huge mistake. "Goodnight then Mary. See you soon."

As they parted and went their separate ways different emotions were coursing through both their veins. Mary flitted up the garden path to the front door as if she was floating on air, the moistness of Jim's kiss still lingering on her cheekbone. As soon as Jim was far enough away to not be heard he put his hand to his eyes and moaned, "Fuuuuuuuuuuuck!"

Neither of them had noticed a figure in the darkness walking a large dog through a clump of trees on the other side of the road to the Ecklethwaites' house. A person who had lingered as soon as the two people had been spotted walking up the road and quietly waited behind one of the trees, the obedient black dog sitting so that it too went unobserved. It was Jane Tallboys and she had witnessed the kiss if not Jim's muted expletive when he had walked away some distance. As a light came on in the house opposite, Jane saw Mary through a curtainless window examining her cheek in a mirror and tenderly stroking it.

SIX

Belton braces

It was now mid-July and early one rainy morning the Reverend Arsley was to be noticed jauntily walking under an umbrella along Cock Hall Lane, an unadopted road flanked by two fine rows of ancient beech and oak trees. At the end of the road were two heavy iron gates hanging from huge stone pillars topped by large carved spheres, a thick coating of moss and algae covering most of them. Set into the gates was a cast iron family crest. Around this was draped a metal ribbon onto which was painted a latin motto, barely legible after decades of decay.

'Aut viam inveniam aut faciam'.

(I will either find a way or make one)

The good cleric pushed one of the gates apart with not inconsiderable effort and walked into the grounds of Cock Hall, a large pond immediately present on his left hand side next to a driveway that led up to the hall. It was silent apart from the sound of a few lingering raindrops hitting the surface of the water, which was two thirds covered by a thick green layer of lily pads, the odd pink flower punctuating the verdant swathe. Here and there small fishes jumped out of the water, no doubt after a small fly that had strayed too close to the surface for its own good. After fifty yards or so a lawn sloped up towards Cock Hall, a stone staircase being cut through it at the top of which a large peacock was calling loudly. It fanned out its tail feathers as the Reverend approached, causing him to ascend on one side with his back to the stair wall as he suspiciously eyed the fickle bird on the other, fearing it would lunge at him at any moment.

Having avoided a murder most fowl, Arsley made his way to the grand if a little flaky front door of Cock Hall and pulled the bell ring. After some delay the door opened revealing the stooped figure of Lady Belton's butler, Harrison. Harrison was actually her cook, gardener and chauffeur, a man of nearly seventy eight years who had been at Cock Hall in the Beltons' service since he was a boy during the Second World War, with only a brief gap for National Service during all that time. He had been the only constant in all that time, the Beltons' lives being turned upside down on numerous occasions by many dramas, financial crashes and parliamentary scandals not to mention the various crises occurring down in the village that the folk in the big manor were expected to guide people through.

"Ah good day," said the vicar, taking off his hat, "I believe Lady Belton is expecting me."

Harrison beckoned Reverend Arsley into the house and directed him to follow with a slight wriggle of his crooked and crinkly right index finger. The vicar pursued him along a long, dark, wood panelled corridor, photographs and paintings of previous tenants of Cock Hall adorning various alcoves, where the ghosts of former balls and extravagant parties were huddled in secret trysts making plans that would be realised at the highest level of Government. At the end Harrison stopped outside a door, coughed loudly, knocked extravagantly and entered, Arsley following him in.

He found himself in a large uncluttered drawing room, Lady Belton seated in front of a roaring fire. Although it was high Summer Cock Hall was invariably cold and damp and keeping it warm a perennial problem, for it was a building that could be summed up by the words dilapidated grandeur. Bookshelves surrounded the room, and weighty tomes that had not been read in decades were covered in a thick layer of dust. Save a couple of chairs and a small occasional table that Lady Belton had been writing on there was no other furniture in the room. One can suspect that it had all been used over the decades to stoke the fires and keep Cock Hall warm.

Lady Belton sat demurely in a high backed chair, a slender woman who was barely five foot three inches tall standing up. Her clothes were once fine but now showed severe signs of age, the wool of her tweed skirt bobbling and the elbows of her jacket almost see-through. "Ah Vicar, thankyou so much for coming at such short notice. Harrison, can you go and ask Mr. Lambley-Blythe to come and join us with the paperwork?"

Lady Belton had asked Reverend Arsley to be the witness to a new will, and her lawyer had travelled up from London the evening before with the necessary documentation. He was currently in the dining room taking breakfast alone. A family friend of old, Lambley-Blythe's usual London rates were always drastically discounted for the Beltons. A month before this meeting, the house had been a scene of much consternation as Lady Belton realised she could not find her copy of the will she had made over twenty years before. As we have already been told, it was of course in the possession of John Simmons, secreted in the volume of village history that she had previously donated to him. Lady Belton had long since forgotten ever hiding the document in there. From this John Simmons had discovered the plot to get her impregnated by a local man, although much to Simmons' annoyance no names were mentioned. As such Arsley would only be required for a few moments but as he sat there in awkward silence waiting for the legal man to appear he could not help wondering if an Estella was lurking around somewhere.

"Are you looking forward to this year's show Lady Belton?" asked Arsley.

"Not really," retorted the old aristocrat, "it's such a long, tiring day and they expect me to be on hand for almost all of it, handing gymkhana prizes out, drawing raffle tickets or presenting cups to that awful Ecklethwaite man with his horrid cigarettey breath."

After some deep breaths and a period of seeming inward reflection Lady Belton continued. "My late husband used to enjoy the day enormously though. I would never see him all day after Harrison had dropped us off down in the village until later in the afternoon. Heaven knows what he found to amuse himself with all day."

He did not know why but Reverend Arsley felt a pang of embarrassment at this last statement. He certainly was not one to gossip or speculate, even inwardly, but in the darkest regions of his mind (and there were some dark ones) lurked visions of the late Lord Belton persuading himself upon one or more of the local lasses. A large oil painting hung above the fire of a man in a shooting jacket and plus fours with a faithful hound in alert pose by his side. Arsley assumed this was Lord Belton himself, a stately looking man with a mane of dark hair and a flash of blond at the front which was no doubt supposed to be a light effect but which gave him an unfortunate looking Mallen streak instead.

The door opened and in walked the slight figure of a man, quite dapper and southern European in his facial appearance, with thinning blonde hair slicked back over his head.

"Lady Belton, good morning to you, and what a fine morning it is now that the rain has cleared." He turned to the Reverend Arsley and introduced himself flamboyantly. "Reginald Artorius Lambley-Blythe at your service sir, Lady Belton's lawyer and a close family friend from way back."

The vicar shook hands with Lambley-Blythe and awaited further instruction.

"So, to business," said Lambley-Blythe loudly, before placing his briefcase on the table in front of Lady Belton and opening it. He took out a document typed on headed notepaper, the legal firm of Wickerson, Booth and Lambley-Blythe announced across the top boldly, and an address in London printed below it.

Lady Belton continued. "Reginald, perhaps I should explain to the vicar as he doesn't yet know why I've asked him here. I need you to bear witness to my signature on a will Mr. Arsley. We'll only take a few moments of your time."

"That's quite alright Lady Belton, happy to be of service," Arsley replied.

Lambley-Blythe had already laid out the documents in front of the vicar and was pointing to the first space that Lady Belton needed to sign on. After doing this the papers were then handed over to the vicar to countersign. This was done several times at various places in the documentation, Lambley-Blythe skilfully placing his hand over text that he obviously did not want the vicar to see. Within five minutes the deed was done and Lady Belton was ringing for Harrison to escort Arsley from the building.

"I'm very grateful to you for coming at such short notice vicar," she said, extending her bony hand towards him.

"My pleasure Lady Belton."

"I'd be obliged if you could keep this a private matter between us if you don't mind vicar," Lady Belton requested. "There are certain persons down in the village who would start asking awkward questions if they knew I had just signed a brand new will."

"Of course Lady Belton, mum's the word! I'll see you at the Show. Good day," said Arsley.

After Arsley had gone the lawyer pulled up a chair next to Lady Belton and put his hand over hers. The significance of the vicar's last sentence was not lost on either of them.

"How are you dear?" he asked. "I'm sorry I got in so late last night that we didn't have time to chat properly. A libel case involving a prominent politician is keeping the office very busy and I just couldn't get away any earlier. It seems so long since I saw you last, we really must make more effort to keep in touch."

"Reginald dear, I'm on borrowed time and you're not far behind me. You need to spend time with your loved ones rather than spending precious hours attending to a silly old woman like me. How is Rupert by the way?"

"Oh he's fine dear lady, although we fell out recently over his insistence on going on some gay rights march in Russia. Silly old fool but I love him dearly. And you're not a silly old woman!"

Lady Belton smiled and rocked in her chair.

"So you've left everything to him then Clarissa." Lambley-Blythe noted. "Have you seen him recently?"

"Not for a while now. He doesn't live around here. His gypsy nature takes him all over the place so he comes and goes without much warning. I don't know what will become of this place when I'm gone but I'm past worrying about it now."

"And the biological father?" asked the lawyer.

"I haven't heard from him for a while now, I suspect he's dead though," Lady Belton replied with sadness in her eyes. "We just need to wait and let the dust settle, see if anyone down there has any knowledge of our sordid pact all those years ago. It will all have to be revealed when I'm dead too I suppose."

"These are different times Clarissa," Lambley-Blythe soothed. "What may have been considered scandalous back then barely merits a mention these days, as Rupert and I now know."

"You may be right Reginald, under normal circumstances," Lady Belton continued, an air of resignation in her soft voice. "But the people down there aren't exactly normal. They're too insular and the village is like an island cut off from the World. And I know for a fact that he himself isn't happy with what I did."

As Reverend Arsely left Cock Hall and made his way back the way he had come he felt a nervous energy about the place. The wind had got up and the trees appeared to be whispering menacingly. As he reached the gates he did not realise it but only a few yards away from him a figure was hiding in the trees watching him and the comings and goings at Cock Hall, a figure who was familiar with the house and grounds but who had not been back there in quite a while.

SEVEN

Courting?

Jim and Mary saw each other semi-regularly after the committee meeting. Their parting kiss had convinced Mary they were now very much a couple and she visited Jim almost daily considering this to be the normal way a relationship would evolve. They would sit together around the kitchen table drinking coffee and eating cake and chatting away happily, Mary enjoying what she considered to be the first flush of a love affair. As a woman who was very much out of touch when it came to dating however, she was very firmly in the position of waiting for Jim to make the first move.

Despite Jim's initial horror at how Mary perceived their relationship he came to not mind her daily visits too much for they bought certain benefits after all. Mary had indeed visited Peony Cottage at every opportunity over the next few days and bought him delicious cakes, juicy bits of gossip about the village affairs and above all the latest news of how Harry's veg was progressing. Jim's ears always pricked up when she divulged such information about her father.

"I've left him in a right state today," said Mary one Sunday morning as Jim was making a cup of coffee for them both prior to a stroll up to Bell End Scar. "He's stressing that his largest marrow appears to have suddenly stopped growing so he's now hoping his back up plant will grow in time for the show. And several of his onions have developed downy mildew or something so he's been crashing around the shed this morning looking for a fungicide and moaning that he can't find it. If he tidied the damn shed and kept it that way he'd be able to find things if they were all in their right and proper place."

Jim smiled. "I must say I like to have everything organised in my shed. I'm a bit anal that way."

"Oooh, Mr. Lightfoot!" joked Mary, hoping to solicit a reaction which did not come and left her feeling embarrassed at the subsequent lack of one. She could not deny that Jim was a very organised man inside and outside the house. All kitchen utensils were tidily arranged, the furniture in the house clean, tidy and meticulously placed. In the garden every plant looked healthy and all tools were hanging up in the shed in their right and proper place. She wondered whether his bedroom might be a similarly controlled area but as yet Mary had not had the privilege of an invite, although she did not doubt that one would soon be forthcoming.

"I wonder what your father uses for downy mildew?" asked Jim. "There's nothing in the garden centres round here so he must have some REALLY old stuff?"

"Oh I don't think so. He gets all manner of weird concoctions from Pete Greensleave via the farm back door so to speak. He thinks I don't know about his clandestine dealings but I do. It's a wonder he hasn't got two heads the amount of chemicals he throws around the garden."

Mary wanted to try and steer Jim away from garden talk. "By the way Jim, you may be interested to know there's a rumour going round that Jane Tallboys is seeing one of Jimmy Duggan's mechanics so it looks like you won't be pestered by her anymore. Wonder who you'll have to fend off next?"

Jim handed her a coffee and they both sat at the kitchen table. "I'm not sure whether to be relieved or distraught then." He said, laughing as he did so. After a few moments of quiet Jim asked, "Do you know whether your father is growing globe beetroot and courgettes Mary?"

This last question caught Mary off guard. Despite her best efforts to entice Jim into talking about matters of a more bodily nature, he kept coming back to wretched vegetables. However, if the way to his heart, and ultimately his bed was to play along with him, she decided that was the route she would have to take.

"I know he's growing beetroot, always does," she answered, "and he usually grows courgettes but I can find out for sure if you wish? Is there anything else you need to know?" she asked semi-sarcastically and without any seriousness.

"Mmm, if you wouldn't mind."

Jim's persistence was unsurprising and yet unexpected all at the same time, for Mary still felt he might somehow prefer to talk about something else. He slid open a drawer from under the kitchen table and took out a sheet of paper from it. "Here's a list, if you wouldn't mind putting a tick against what he is growing and a cross against what he isn't that would be great. Bless you Mary, you're such a darling to me."

Mary looked at the pre-prepared list that Jim had written in his neatest handwriting. Kohl rabi, radish, long beetroot, white cauliflowers, coloured cauliflowers, sweetcorn, pot leeks, blanch leeks, intermediate leeks, the list seemed endless.

"Leave it with me darling and I'll endeavour to find out," agreed Mary somewhat annoyed nonetheless.

"Brilliant," responded Jim enthusiastically, "I can then judge what classes I definitely need to enter at the Show and which ones I need to shove down the list of priorities. Now then, are we going on this walk or not?"

Jim gathered up the coffee cups and placed them into a bowl in the kitchen sink before going to a cupboard under the stairs and fetching out a pair of expensive looking leather walking boots. Mary looked down at her own tatty looking clompers and sighed. However, she had been looking forward to the walk since Jim had suggested it the night before as it would be the first time they had gone anywhere together other than the Dog & Gun.

They were soon on their way to the end of the cul-de-sac, over a wooden stile and off along a track between two lines of beech trees which was the start of the mud path up to Cock Side, a mile long narrow ridge that was a natural fault in the landscape and which culminated at Bell End Quarry. It was the walk Mary had intended to do when she first bumped into Jim a few weeks before. Jim took Mary's hand to stop her slipping, for it was quite treacherous due to a recent downpour of rain. As they emerged from the trees and the gradient steepened Mary noticed a distant figure on the top of the hill next to the bell tower, as yet too far away to recognise.

"That's unusual," said Mary.

"What is?" asked Jim.

"Well, whoever that is up there has binoculars and appears to be looking down at us," Mary observed.

Jim stopped in his tracks, "So he does. Or she maybe? Come on, let's go and find out who it is."

As the track swerved to the left and then zig-zagged with the contours of the hill the summit went out of view. Consequently, by the time Jim and Mary had arrived at the top by the old Bell Tower the unknown person had left the scene. Jim bent down to pick something up in the grass next to a trig point.

"Whoever it was has left one of their lens caps," he observed, showing Mary the piece of plastic he had found before putting it in his jacket pocket. "Stunning view isn't it?" Jim continued as if he was familiar with the outlook.

"Oh, have you been up here before then?" asked Mary. "Only I got the impression it was a first for you?"

Jim looked confused. "Oh it is. My first time here that is. I was just remarking that it's a fabulous lookout. You can see why it was used as a vantage point during the war. Imagine a chap up here staring out over the valley waiting to spot Luftwaffe planes then sounding that bell to warn everyone down in the village? Not that they were in danger as they would undoubtedly have passed overhead on their way to the big industrial cities like Birmingham and Coventry."

Mary was not really listening to Jim's narrative for she was still pondering whether he had been on that spot before and who he might have been there with. There was so much she still did not know about him and every now and again he hesitated in his answers making her think there was a hidden mystery about him. Many of the other villagers had thought the same thing, for Jim Lightfoot was very secretive about his past, as Bob Dillage was still finding out much to his annoyance.

As they stared out towards the horizon they both fell silent through a sense of awkwardness more than anything. Jim suddenly realised that Mary might be expecting some form of romantic interlude, a hug perhaps followed by a lingering kiss. Whilst he was attracted to Mary and had found her recent company more than a little enjoyable, he did not yet want a relationship and was struggling within himself as to how to deal with her in the most sympathetic way. As for Mary, the kiss they had exchanged on the walk home from the Dog & Gun that night, the one that Jane Tallboys had witnessed with interest, had satisfied her that they were an item and she was now anticipating the usual progression of a relationship based on attraction. She awaited Jim's next move, wondering whether she ought to give him some encouragement but not wanting to appear as some clingy, sex starved spinster. As a result neither of them did anything.

The brick tower that used to house the bell during the war was now nothing more than a roofless shell of a building, with a steel door padlocked to prevent entry. Mary's mind wandered back in time to when the bell tower was always open. As a child she had played inside it with her school friends, climbing the spiral staircase to the top and pretended to be cops and robbers, cowboys and indians or anything else their imaginations had lead them to. On more than one occasion she recalled sneaking out of the house and coming up to the bell tower with Pete Greensleave for sex. It had not been the most romantic place for courting but they had nowhere else to go at the time. Their use of the building was embarrassingly curtailed when an official letter went up on the village noticeboard that due to the number of condoms that were being discarded in and around the bell tower a rota was being drawn up of various parish councillors to patrol the site and make sure that people were tidying up after themselves. After that episode Pete and Mary had become more daring and risked being found out at Mary's house due to Pete's house usually having at least one person home at all times.

Mary looked up at the window set in mid-height of the bell tower, and recalled a time when she was looking out through it, her skirt over her shoulders and her knickers around her ankles as Pete took her from behind so that she could keep a look-out for anyone approaching. She smiled to herself and imagined performing a similar act with Jim if only the door was not securely locked these days. At length Jim broke the silence.

"Looks like a rain storm is coming. Look at those swirly black clouds coming up from the east. The veg is going to get a right battering tonight I fear."

"Oh deep joy," exclaimed Mary, "that means Dad will be glued to the lounge window all night stressing about his veg."

"And me too!" replied Jim with a faint smile. "Come on, let's get back before we get caught up in it."

This last suggestion did not upset Mary. When Jim had proposed a walk the night before in the Dog & Gun it had been unexpected, leading

Mary to have several thoughts in the intervening hours about how they might find a secluded corner in a field during the course of their perambulations for a spot of carnal intimacy. Whilst the impending break in the recent weeks of good weather had put paid to that hope, Mary now anticipated a mere postponement until they could get back to Peony Cottage. After all, why engage in sexual intercourse in a field when there was a perfectly comfortable bed that could be used for the same purpose?

By the time Jim and Mary were half way down the incline up which they had walked a mere half hour before they were well and truly soaked to the skin.

"I'm sorry about this Mary. I should have checked the weather forecast before we came out," Jim apologised.

"It's fine Jim, really it is," Mary reassured, feeling confident that her wet clothes would soon be drying in front of the fire at Peony Cottage whilst she sampled the sensual pleasures of Jim's body upstairs, "worse things happen than a few wet clothes eh?"

"I guess so. But it's not a nice feeling is it? I'll be glad of a hot bath as soon as I get back. What are your plans for the rest of the day Mary?" Jim asked, immediately throwing all of Mary's recent aspirations into the recycle bin of life.

"Oh, erm, I don't know really. Haven't thought about it," replied Mary desperately trying not to show her disappointment.

As they skipped through the mud in the avenue of trees just before reaching the village they did not notice a figure of man with a pair of binoculars around his neck who was sheltering under one of them, and who watched them go past with more than a passing interest. He had negotiated a different route down from the top and thus managed to avoid them. As Jim and Mary climbed over the stile again and disappeared from view he said quietly to himself, "Looks like Ecklethwaite doesn't yet know his daughter's cavorting with the enemy."

Before Mary knew it Jim had hurried her past Peony Cottage without turning up his pathway and escorted her to the top of Main Street where she lived.

"Right Mary, you make sure you go and get dried up. We'll have to do that walk again when the weather's set fair. See you soon." Jim said abruptly and without ceremony, a cursory peck on the cheek Mary's only reward, before turning tail and running back in the direction they had just come.

Mary stood looking at Jim's retreating figure, unsure whether to call him back and suggest they go back to Peony Cottage and undress each other from their wet clothes and have a relaxing evening drying out in front of the fire, drinking wine and doing what came naturally (or unnaturally if the mood took them) but something in the back of her mind stopped her. Bemused and demoralised, she walked down the road until she came to her house and let herself in. Her father was sat by the lounge window surveying the storm.

"Bloody polytunnel's getting shredded in this wind. I'll need some help pinning it back down when the rain passes Mary."

"Okay dad," Mary replied, "Give me a shout when you're ready."

She hung her coat up and climbed the stairs to her room, shutting the door behind her and peeling off every one of her sodden clothes until she stood in front of a full length mirror, quite naked except for a gold necklace her mother had left her. With her dark, wet hair plastered to her neck and shoulders, and water droplets glistening over her pale yet immaculate skin she looked every inch the beguiling and mythical siren. Most men in the village would have given their right arm to be in that room with her right now, gazing upon her voluptuous form in anticipation of making love to her.

"Am I really so repulsive?" she asked herself?

EIGHT

Rumbled plans

"MARYYYYYYYYYY," shouted Harry Ecklethwaite up the stairs, "get yer arse down here young lady. You've got some explaining to do."

He stirred his morning cup of tea and sat at the kitchen table to wait for his daughter to descend. He could hear her thumping around upstairs as she struggled to find her slippers in a flustered fashion, for her father could still manage to get her ruffled and jumping to his every command even though she had long since left behind her adolescence. Harry had just returned from the village store where he had gone to buy some tobacco and had bumped into Jane Tallboys.

"Nice that Mary and that nice Mr. Lightfoot are getting on so well together Harry," she had suggested naughtily as Harry brushed past her in the biscuit aisle. It was enough to stop Harry dead in his tracks.

"What did you just say?" asked Harry, bemusement plastered over his unshaven face.

"Well they seemed very close the other night walking back from the pub. Arm in arm they were. They kissed in the street outside your gate. I assumed they were an item?" explained Jane Tallboys.

She was still smarting at Jim's rejection of her all those months ago at Peony Cottage when she had flirted with him unashamedly during the house viewing. She had gone through most of the boys in the district and fancied trying a proper man for a change so had given Jim the green light, but for some reason he had declined. She was not particularly attracted to him and certainly was not looking for a relationship but the fact that he seemed to fancy an old spinster like Mary rather than a voluptuous younger woman like herself did not sit well with her inexperienced view of the World. As a consequence she was determined to make life awkward for them both. She also shared the Tallboys family's aversion for Harry Ecklethwaite after all the things he had done to her uncle.

"Kissed?" exclaimed Harry as if his daughter was incapable of such a thing.

"Oh," said Jane feigning sympathy on their behalf, "I'm sure it was nothing, just a friendly good night gesture between two friends," naughtily adding "we've all been there I dare say," and turning to the shopkeeper, "right Ralph what do I owe you?"

Ralph Chubb the storeowner had been listening with interest. Like many of the Allaways residents he could not abide Harry and saw a rare opportunity for mischief at his expense. Unbeknown to Jim and Mary it was actually Ralph who had been the mystery figure with binoculars they had spotted stood on Bell End Scar the day before. Ralph had been viewing Jim's garden through them with more than a passing interest in the two figures approaching him, making a hasty retreat before they reached the top. "What'll you do if Mary gets hitched and takes up residence in your old enemy's cottage eh then Harry?" he said, chuckling wickedly as he did.

"Pah. You're mistaken young Jane," said Harry forcefully, "Mary wouldn't take up with anyone without my knowing about it. Least of all that fancy Dan in Peony Cottage. He aint her sort." Turning to Ralph, Harry had the upper hand of being able to mention previous battles at the annual show in order to put him in his place. "You growing some of them shitty forked parsnips again this year Ralph? Or maybe some of them cabbages that the judge felt were so small they were big brussel sprouts? Whatever, you'll only be making up the numbers as usual eh?"

And with that Harry left the shop leaving an embittered Ralph with an extra ounce or two of festering hatred for him than he had before, but he did manage to compose himself enough to shout toward the receding Harry, "Make the most of your last few weeks as village show champion?" Ralph knew full well from what he had seen through his field glasses, even at long distance that Harry was going to get more than a run for his money this year. Armed with this knowledge Ralph wanted to rub Harry's nose in it, but was wary enough to be careful not to give too much away. He had come to like Jim Lightfoot, his pleasant and polite nature at all times endearing him to the shopkeeper on his daily visit for groceries. A few weeks previously Jim had mentioned that he might have a go at the Show and was growing a few vegetables with that aim in mind and that had pricked Ralph's curiosity enough for him to take his binoculars up to the bell tower to see how good his stuff might be. He had been highly delighted at what he saw, even more so when he had seen Jim and Mary approaching with arms linked.

On the short walk home Harry also festered, for he now recalled the night in the pub a few days before when Jim had been keen to ply him with drink for a few tips on growing the best veg. All the while he was just buttering him up so that he could wriggle his way in with Mary he thought.

"If there's one thing I can't abide it's dishonesty!" Harry mumbled to himself. "What kind of a man is he, and what does he take me for?"

At length Mary descended the stairs and joined her father in the kitchen. "What on Earth is it Dad? I was having a nice lie in for a change!"

"What's all this nonsense about you seeing that Lightfoot chap behind my back then? Everyone seems to know about it except me. I won't have it, d'ya hear me?" ordered Harry.

Mary looked nonplussed for a second but soon regained her composure. "Dad, I'm forty two for crying out loud! I'm not your little girl any more. I CAN do what I want!"

"Not when you're living under my roof you can't!" spluttered Harry.

"Oh grow up Dad. I've had just about as much as I can take of your domineering ways. This is the twenty first century if you hadn't noticed. Women are pretty much the equal of men in most things and we gave up having to get permission for everything we do decades ago. If I want to jump into bed with Jim Lightfoot I'll bloody well do it and there's nothing you can do to stop me!" Mary was now bent forward over the kitchen table forcefully glaring down at her father, who in turn looked completely shocked at his daughter's sudden and unexpected defiance. At length he managed to compose himself.

"You'll do no such thing young lady. You'll be married off in good time to a gentleman who is befitting of the Ecklethwaite family's good name, and you'll be unsullied on that regard! You have me to thank for stopping you getting into trouble with that idiot Greensleave all those years ago, remember?" he pontificated.

Mary looked exasperated. "Dad, we don't have a good name. You're pretty much universally detested in the village. No man for a fifteen mile radius will come near me because of you. And for your information if you'd come home half an hour earlier that day you'd have discovered I was far from being the virginal young sweet thing you thought I was."

It took a few seconds for the penny to drop, but eventually Harry realised what Mary had just told him. He exploded like a volcano, slamming his hand down on the table, "I'll fucking kill him, the dirty little bastard!"

Mary held up a hand as if stopping traffic, "Dad, I shouldn't have told you that but it was a long while ago and it's pointless worrying about it now," she said calmly and assuredly.

"You're not what I thought you were Mary. You're dear old mother will be spinning in her grave. How could you?"

"How could I?" said Mary impishly, "well we both felt horny and we were both adults, albeit quite young ones, so we decided it would be a good idea...."

"Don't get flippant with me young lady," scolded Harry, saliva foaming at the sides of his mouth. "Where have you got this sudden rebellious nature from?"

Mary sighed, "Dad, just in case you didn't hear me the first time. I'm forty two. I can and I will do what I want. You will not say anything about this to anyone or I'll leave home and you'll be on your own like a sad lonely old man. Now, what do you want for breakfast?"

***

The rest of the day passed in awkward silence in the Ecklethwaite household. Harry spent most of it in the garden but came in every now and again to purposely ignore his daughter, deliberately making eye contact with her and shaking his head each time. But he became increasingly annoyed as she seemed utterly oblivious to his disappointment, carrying on with her daily chores without a care in the World, singing along to the radio and waving cheerily out of the front window to any passers-by.

Towards early evening Harry was planting some courgettes with more vigour than was usual or indeed good for the courgettes, mulling over in his mind why Mary had suddenly become so confrontational? Since her mother died she had been happy to be a home bird and had given up any idea of further education in order to look after her old dad, which was her duty in any case in Harry's eyes. Never in the last twenty years had they shared so much as a single cross word between them, but something had changed in Mary's thinking as far as he could make out, and all routes tended to point towards the figure of Jim Lightfoot.

Shopkeeper Chubb's last words that morning also came back to him as he wrestled with a runner bean fence that had got all tangled up in the recent winds due to him not tying it up properly in the first place.

"Make the most of my last few weeks as champion?" mused Harry thoughtfully. "What on Earth did he mean by that? What the fuck does he know that I don't I wonder?"

He was stirred from his thoughts by Mary shouting from the kitchen, "Dad, I'm just off out. Your dinner's in the oven. Don't wait up!" before hearing the door slam without giving him time to answer her, so he rushed through the house to the kitchen window to observe where she was heading. He didn't have to look far for an answer, for at the end of the road he could see Jim Lightfoot waiting for her. She linked arms and they headed off toward the direction of the Dog & Gun.

Harry's curiosity was well and truly pricked. What if it was not just Mary who was keeping something from him? Harry trusted nobody in the village, and would often get up early on regular occasions to visit all the local allotments in a ten mile radius to see what his competitors were up to, and worse. As we have already discovered Dick Tallboys once found him trespassing in his shed and other gardeners had reason to believe Harry had also sabotaged their own plants and gardens over the years. Ted Grangeworthy planted out some onions in his allotment polytunnel one evening only to come back next afternoon and find they had all mysteriously disappeared. Other growers reported that a fertiliser they had purchased via the horticultural society had started to make their plants look stunted rather than increase growth. Analysis of the offending product determined it was actually salt and Bill Grudge had to take the suppliers to task but several people suspected it had been swapped in the trading hut, and only one name was ever in the frame. Nothing could ever be proven however.

Harry popped his jacket on and took a walk out into the early evening air, dusk just beginning to descend. As he started walking over to Peony Cottage he chortled to himself as he was reminded about getting wind of a huge cabbage Dick Tallboys was growing some thirty years previous. He had scaled Dick's wall and jumped down into his garden after midnight searching for the offending brassica, eventually finding it under some cloth mesh that Dick had erected to keep the cabbage white butterflies from laying their eggs on it. It was enormous. And clean as a whistle without a mark on it. Harry found a few cabbage white caterpillars on some cauliflowers that Dick had not covered and deposited them on Dick's massive cabbage. By the time Dick discovered them a week later they had ruined the plant, and were now the largest caterpillars anyone had ever seen such was the extent to which they had gorged themselves. Dick had berated himself for somehow leaving a gap in the mesh that a butterfly had managed to fly through and lay its eggs, unaware of what had really happened.

Arriving at the wall surrounding Peony Cottage Harry first tried the gate but it was locked. No matter, he thought to himself, he had scaled that wall before and would do so again. He looked all around him to make sure there was no-one around, for he had been rumbled doing this a fair few times in the past by Dick Tallboys himself. The cabbage sabotage had been one of few occasions Harry had got the better of him, as Dick Tallboys always seemed to be around whenever he had visited and would catch him loitering outside the garden. Harry would often have to pretend to be out for a walk and he would then have to carry on over the stile at the end of the cul-de-sac so as not to raise suspicion. Dick of course was suspicious, and would stand watching him, forcing Harry to walk ever further until he was out of sight, chortling to himself as he did so. As Harry hated walking it was another reason he despised Dick.

There was an angled step in the wall about a foot off the ground which allowed him to grab the top thus enabling him to haul himself over and drop down into Jim's garden. It was many years and several pounds of weight since he had last performed this task but he had no doubt he could still do so despite his advancing years. However, it was undoubtedly much more difficult as Harry struggled to heave his bulky frame up the edifice, panting and coughing noisily. At length he was starting to succeed in inching his body upwards, feeling a surge of triumph that he would soon be able to peer over the top and see if Jim Lightfoot was likely to be any competition to him at this year's show. If the vegetables looked average he would simply drop back down onto the pavement and go back home secure in the knowledge he did not have to worry about that particular opposition corner. He was stopped dead in his ascent by a voice that he instantly recognised.

"I'm watching you Ecklethwaite!"

Harry froze to the wall like an overfed gekko that had been spotted by a hawk. It was undoubtedly the voice of Dick Tallboys, the same Dick Tallboys whose funeral Harry had attended only the year before, and at which Harry had read a very moving eulogy bemoaning the fact that he would not be seeing him at the shows any more.

"Still up to no good and cheating as always I see Harry," the voice continued.

A startled Harry lost his grip on the top of the wall and tumbled down onto his backside, twisting a knee as he landed.

"FUCK!" he squealed, "Who the fuck is that impersonating my dear old departed friend Dick Tallboys?"

"I was no friend of yours Ecklethwaite. Now clear off or I'll come and haunt you at your own house."

Harry looked around to see if he could see who was speaking to him, but there was no-one to be seen anywhere. The windows of Peony Cottage were all shut. Harry was well and truly spooked, but he did not believe in ghosts and was not about to start believing in them now.

"Oh very clever. What is it? A tape recording of Dick's voice I don't doubt?" said Harry, a tone of triumphalism creeping back into his voice. "Come on then, repeat what I say Mr. Ghost of Tallboys past. Nuh, nuh nuh, nurrrr nurrrr ni no! Harry Ecklethwaite will be the champion of the show!"

"Clear off Ecklethwaite!" the voice responded.

"Hah! I knew it," pronounced Harry. "A bloody recording!"

"Oh very well," replied the voice frustratedly, "this is not a tape recording you old prat. Nuh, nuh, nuh, nurrr nurrr ni no. You won't win this year's show."

A petrifying chill went down Harry's spine, circled his testicles for a few seconds before travelling back up his body to strangle his voice box and render him speechless. He scuttled backwards, still on the floor, eventually getting up on his legs and hobbling away quickly, looking back at Peony Cottage anxiously from time to time. When he was just a few yards from his house he had regained some level of composure and attempted to reassure himself that he had just imagined hearing the unmistakeable voice of the long dead Dick Tallboys.

"Pah. That place always did give me the 'eeby jeebies even when Dick the Prick were alive. That Lightfoot's just a bloody beginner anyways. He'll be no competition for me this year, next year nor any other damn year."

Harry opened his garden gate, turned the key in his door and went inside, oblivious to the fact that Jane Tallboys had been following him for a hundred yards or so, having seen him coming from the direction of Peony Cottage. She wondered whether he had been to warn Lightfoot away from his daughter and thus whether her devious plan had worked. It had not, but Jane didn't know that yet.

NINE

The annual day trip

Every summer Allaways-on-Cock Horticultural Society organised a coach trip to a large stately house or garden or both. The year before it had been a miserable rainy day when they had visited Kew Gardens but on the occasion of this season's jaunt to a much closer venue at Tithampton Hall the sun was beating down on the twenty five or so members who had made the short journey. As it was funded by the society and thus free to all members, Harry Ecklethwaite always went on it. He also always moaned from start to finish about the organisation, the journey, the price of sandwiches at the motorway service stops and ultimately about the place they were visiting. He usually only walked about a hundred yards to the first bench he could find and then sat reading his paper for several hours, thus actually seeing but a small percentage of each grand place they ever went, but it never stopped him bleating all the way back about what a waste of time it had all been. Mary had felt duty bound to sit next to her father, leaving Jane Tallboys to move in on Jim a mere two seats behind them. She struggled to hear their conversation above her father's open objections.

"Oh I always look forward to the annual trip Jim," Jane explained, "gets you out of the village for a day seeing as I don't drive."

"I suppose so," replied Jim, "but my travelling days are over and I'm quite happy in the village. Trust me Jane, you haven't missed much by being constrained to the area."

Mary thought this was a strange thing for Jim to say and strained her head to try and hear more but her father was being unusually loud.

"By eck, Grudge, couldn't you have hired a bus with some air conditioning for crying out loud? I'm sweating like a witch's twat back here."

Bill Grudge was sitting near the front next to his wife, and turned to look at John Simmons across the aisle from him, both of them exchanging a knowing air of resignation.

"It's only fifteen miles Harry," said Bill, "we'll be there soon enough and then you can find some shade to read your Racing Post."

A few rows back Jane was still flirting with Jim, knowing how jealous Mary must be feeling. Every jolt of the rather ageing bus that Bill Grudge had hired for penny pinching purposes sent her intentionally nestling into Jim with a little giggle. "Oh my," laughed Jane, "good job you're there to catch me otherwise I'd be falling into the aisle."

Jim's eyes rolled. He had spoken to Mary the day before and understood her reasons for needing to travel with her father but he had not reckoned on Jane making a beeline for him and insisting they sit together, thus far believing her little plan to tell Harry about Jim and Mary at the village store had worked seeing as they had not sat with each other. It was not that he did not find Jane attractive for she was certainly the village beauty by a long margin, but she had shown herself to be a little obsessive when it came to vying for Jim's affections for reasons he could not yet fathom. He hoped they might go their separate ways once they alighted from the bus but soon realised Jane had no intention of straying far from his side all afternoon if she could help it. Mary also seemed to have made certain assumptions about her standing in Jim's eyes but he felt she was reasonably under his control, whereas Jane was a complete loose cannon with hormones to match.

After Bill Grudge had given everyone their tickets, guides and instructions on when to get back to the bus for the return journey, Jane linked into Jim's right arm and dragged him away from the rest of group. "Come on Mr. Lightfoot, hothouses first for us I think."

As Jim and Jane headed off towards Tithampton Hall's famous glasshouses Harry Ecklethwaite turned to his daughter barely able to hide the glee in his face. "There you go lass, you've had a lucky escape from that one. Look at the pair of 'em, all over each other like dogs on heat."

Mary gave a wry smile, knowing what Jim had told her the night of the last committee meeting about Jane having a crush on him, although she did still suffer a small pang of jealousy seeing them wandering off together. "Where do you want to go first then dad?" she asked, resigning herself to escorting her father for the afternoon.

"Oh I'll just sit over there under that huge eucalyptus and read the paper for now. You go on ahead and I'll catch you up soon enough," replied Harry.

Mary could have screamed. "It's a redwood dad, not a eucalyptus," she said angrily, but at least it now gave her the opportunity to follow Jim and Jane and join them on their garden tour. Within a couple of minutes she had caught up with them, finding them halfway down the large glasshouse in which hothouse melons and pineapples were growing amongst several other exotics.

"Mind if I join you both?" she asked cheerfully. "Dad has done his usual and simply ensconced himself under a tree for the duration." Mary did not notice the look of relief on Jim's face, nor the one of hatred on Jane's.

"Oh, yes of course Mary. The more the merrier!" lied Jane through gritted teeth, for she was just about to shed her cardigan in the hope that her unfettered breasts would be more gratifying a sight to the hitherto disinterested Jim. The plan had formulated in her mind as she had drifted off to sleep the night before, for she saw Jim Lightfoot as a challenge. He had rejected her at Peony Cottage before but Jane convinced herself that she had not really made things obvious, so today she was determined to make sure he was in no doubt that she wanted him to give her a good seeing to somewhere in the extensive grounds of Tithampton Hall that very afternoon. And if he did not take the many hints that she was preparing to hand grenade him with then she would simply take more straightforward action and pull him into some undergrowth somewhere. Mary's unexpected appearance had put paid to all such plans and she was not happy about it one little bit.

"We were just admiring these peach trees Mary," remarked Jim. "Not a sign of pest damage anywhere, I know we struggle………," but strangely Jim stopped mid-sentence, looking outside and began waving at Bill Grudge and John Simmons who were passing by with a few others, and who duly changed course and joined them in the greenhouse. It was a warm day so temperatures inside were topping ninety fahrenheight.

"Phew! Well then people," said Bill Grudge, "what do we all think of the place? Magnificent isn't it?"

Jim, Mary and Jane concurred so Bill continued, "I tell you what young Jane, there's a magnificent maple walk here, and I know you're interested in the acer genus because of that question you asked when we had Radio Tithampton's gardening experts at the hort soc a couple of years ago. We were just off in that direction so come with us and I feel sure you won't be disappointed. Toodle-oo Jim and Mary. See you later."

Jane thus reluctantly tagged along with Bill Grudge's party, thwarted yet again in her attempts to seduce Jim Lightfoot, and annoyed that Mary now seemingly had exclusive ownership of him once again. Mary herself was pleased they were alone, rather than affording mileage to the gossip mongers of the Dog & Gun which is where they had tended to spend their few dates together thus far. Mary took Jim's arm as they wandered out of the greenhouse and along a path through some trees where a wooden signpost was pointing them in the direction of the walled vegetable garden.

"How's your veg coming along then Jim?" she asked.

"Pretty good I reckon," he replied, a satisfied smile breaking out across his face. "I'm confident of putting on a good show against your father in six weeks' time that's for sure. You do know that he tried looking over my garden wall the other day?"

The ghost of Dick Tallboys had been very quick to appear and divulge this information to Jim next morning, telling him that he had attempted to look over the wall for a snoop not long after he and Mary had gone off to the pub the evening before.

"How do you know that Jim?" asked Mary, interested only in finding out who had spotted her father spying in such a way. Of course Jim was unable to divulge the true identity of his apparitional undercover lookout and stammered momentarily over what to say next.

"Oh, just .....one .....of the village kids mentioned it next morning," Jim answered unconvincingly. "He couldn't scale the wall so he wasn't able to see anything fortunately. I think he was a bit embarrassed to be caught out if I'm honest so I doubt he'll say anything to you, and I don't think you should mention it either Mary. There was no harm done after all."

Mary thought how sweet it was that Jim did not want to humiliate her father, even though he probably deserved it. If the roles were reversed she had no doubt her father would have advertised it at every conceivable opportunity, using it to ridicule Jim in the pub especially.

"Strange that," said Mary, "your wall isn't that tall and dad has no problems clambering over the wall at the bottom of our garden to go scouting over the fields for contraband fertilisers."

"Well the wall is quite sheer and has quite a low step in it so perhaps he found it harder than he thought," offered Jim, quickly turning Mary's attention back to the purpose of the day now that they were passing through the gate of Tithampton Hall's World famous walled garden. "Wow, now this is what you call a kitchen garden isn't it Mary?"

She had to agree, as Jim marched off in front of her to admire the multitudinous plantings of fruit and vegetables. An army of gardeners appeared to be buzzing about planting, snipping and tying and over the course of the next couple of hours Jim found a reason to stop and chat to each and every one of them about the particular crop they appeared to be tending. Mary dutifully followed behind Jim and feigned an interest in what was being discussed. At first it was white fly infestations on the cabbages, then the mesh barriers erected to keep carrot fly at bay. Jim was taking a huge interest in every minute aspect of growth within those four tall walls. Ultimately though Mary dallied, and eventually deposited herself on a park type bench whilst Jim was otherwise engaged, like Jane secretly wishing that the afternoon could maybe have been put towards other uses of a more carnal nature.

Barring the occasional good night kiss on the cheek, or an endearing hug in the pub their relationship had not progressed any further than that of good friends. Mary had desires which had been reawakened since walking into Jim's plank as he emerged from Peony Cottage that fateful afternoon, and those desires had grown to urgent levels in more recent weeks as they had stepped out together on a more frequent basis. She was unsure how to play things because Jim was acting like the perfect gentleman, which was all fine and dandy in most circumstances but Mary now wanted their affiliation to become physical, on a scale widely ranging from sensual and erotic some days to wanton and bestial on others. At that moment in time she did not much care where on the scale the pointer settled, as long as something happened, and soon!

Mary nestled her back into the bench, her head resting on a wooden plinth allowing her to drift off into a state that was not quite sleep but nor was she totally awake. She could hear birdsong, the buzzing of insects and the occasional snip of a pair of secateurs in the distance as the sun warmed her rosy cheeks. She pondered various options on how to take matters into her own hands and indicate to Jim that she needed him to have sex with her. Several methods popped into her head for consideration. She thought she could simply suggest it, or start to kiss him in a far more passionate way than the polite pecks they had enjoyed thus far. Perhaps she could simply undress in front of him at Peony Cottage one evening and entice him that way? But she soon realised she was far too shy to do any of those things, for after all it had been over twenty years since she had actually been naked with a man.

She was stirred by Jim touching her on her cheek, then taking her hand and leading her out of the walled garden and through some woods, all the gardeners looking on with knowing smiles. Jim found a secluded spot, a clearing in the woods that was bathed in sunshine, the lush grass inviting them to lie down on it. Jim pulled Mary to him and kissed her hard on her lips. Mary moaned in anticipation of all the previous weeks' frustrations becoming satisfied in one fell swoop, giving no thought to the fact that any one of the horticultural society members could walk past them at any given moment. Her heartbeat escalated with each of Jim's kisses, and she suddenly felt as if she may faint through giddiness as she sensed his hand on her knee. It lingered momentarily, no doubt to see if Mary objected, but as she did not it progressed up her skirt. Mary parted her legs inviting Jim to go further and satisfy her yearnings once and for all.

"Mary! Mary. Wake up lass. The bus is leaving soon. Beggar off you dirty old mutt!"

Mary was woken from her dream by her father who had come to find her so that they could reserve their place back on the coach. In doing so he had also stopped the inquisitive cocker spaniel from progressing any further up Mary's thigh. Realising it was not actually Jim's hand between her legs and that she had fallen asleep left her feeling deflated. Looking around the walled garden she saw Jim was still in deep conversation with one of the Hall's gardeners over in the furthest corner away from them, so her father would not have known they had arrived there together. She also noticed Bill Grudge was on his way over to him, no doubt to tell him the bus would soon be leaving. She dejectedly gathered up her belongings and walked with her father back through the estate to the waiting bus.

"Dunno why you were in that bit o'garden lass," queried Harry, "some o'them vegetables were in a shocking state. Army of bleedin' gardeners to look after 'em as well. All grown organically of course, that's why they were all flea bitten old shite. You gotta throw chemicals at 'em if you want good looking veg. They won't win fuck all with 'em I'm telling ya."

"I don't think that's what they're after Dad," replied Mary with an exasperation that caught Harry by surprise, the achingly vivid daydream still agonisingly fresh in her mind.

When Bill had caught up with him to remind him about the bus's imminent leaving, Jim felt a sudden pang of guilt about leaving Mary to fend for herself for most of the afternoon. He looked at his watch and realised it had been well over two hours since he had last spoken to her such was the depth to which he had been engrossed in vegetable chatter with the walled garden employees. Turning round to try and see where Mary was he was just in time to see the back of Mary and Harry as they exited the gate.

"Ah," he mumbled in regret, and vowed to apologise as soon as he was able to.

Back on the bus most people were in raptures about the gardens they had seen that afternoon, all except Harry who would have found fault at the Alhambra, and Jane who was still smarting at having to leave Jim in the company of Mary without having had the opportunity to put her plan of seduction into operation. Consequently she was quiet on the return journey, which did not bother Jim as he was still feeling full of remorse at neglecting Mary. He tried to catch Mary's eye as he brushed past her upon boarding the bus but she was talking to Mrs. Dibble in the seat behind her.

Before alighting from the vehicle next to the village green back in Allaways, Bill Grudge stood up to make an announcement.

"Ladies and gentlemen, if I may take this opportunity to make a few announcements, this will be the last time that we're all together until just before the Show. Can we all please meet in the village hall on the Thursday evening before the Show to iron out any last minute glitches?"

"Fuck that Grudge, I need a piss," said Harry as he barged past him down the steps and off towards home, leaving Mary behind and still sitting on the bus, hugely embarrassed at her father's rudeness. Harry had no interest in how the Show was run, never offered to help out in any way, shape or form and indeed felt the Show organisers owed its success entirely to him alone.

"Mmm," mumbled Bill Grudge at the sight of Harry disappearing into the evening and rubbing his groin area, a cigarette hastily appearing from his shabby jacket, "continuing on, does everyone know what they're all doing on the day itself? If not a full programme, complete with extensive timetables for each and every person is on the village hall noticeboard and up in the pub also. I've factored in breaks for everyone during the day so no-one has to do more than a couple of hours' stint at any one time. If you're in any doubt please ask me and I'll explain."

"I've got a suggestion Bill," offered Ralph Chubb waving his hand towards the figure of Harry Ecklethwaite who had now turned a corner and was out of sight, "Can we ban that miserable old sod from the Show completely?"

A deeply embarrassed Mary sank into her seat as several people cheered or shouted 'Hear, hear."

Bill put his hands up appealing for calm, "Now, now folks. We need Harry's veg as it's all part of the appeal of the Show. You can't deny he's an expert grower."

"That's only because nearly every other decent grower in the area refuses to come to the Show because of his antics over the years. Ban him and they'll all come back," countered Ted Grangeworthy to a chorus of more 'hear, hears'.

Bill Grudge did not have the time nor the inclination to enter into this debate now. "Okay, don't forget, the Thursday evening before the Show in the village hall. Happy holidays to those of you who are going away in the meantime, I know you are Jim, so all the best everyone and I'll see you in due course no doubt."

Jim now had more cause for embarrassment for he had not yet got around to telling Mary of his plans to take a fortnight vacation in a few days' time. Jane saw the darting eyes of confusion coming from Mary and realised this was the case too, and was happy to see that Mary was still being kept very much at arm's length by the enigmatic and perplexing Mr. Lightfoot.

After everyone had alighted and said their goodbyes, Jim and Mary came together for the walk home and Jim took the opportunity to explain the recent revelation.

"Sorry, I should have mentioned about my holiday before now but it slipped my mind. It was arranged nearly a year ago. I'm going back to the desert to join up with a few colleagues that I once worked with."

"It didn't slip your mind enough not to tell Bill Grudge however," replied Mary pointedly.

Jim felt chastened. "Oh I only mentioned it to him a couple of weeks ago when I realised I needed someone to water my veg whilst I'm gone."

"You could have asked me!" spat Mary.

"Oh, I, I, didn't like to put you in a difficult situation with your father so thought it best to ask Bill," Jim stammered. "But if you're offering I'd absolutely prefer for you to do it if you'd like to Mary."

It wasn't quite the invite Mary was hoping for but she grabbed it in any case. "Of course I'd like to Jim. What on Earth do you take me for?"

"Well then that's settled," said Jim. "I'm off on Tuesday morning so if you pop round Monday afternoon I can show you what's what. You're a real sweetheart doing this for me."

Mary looked shocked. "Tuesday? That quickly?" Anger swelled inside her as they arrived at the junction of the road where Mary would invariably turn off so that her father could not see them say their usual farewells. Her ire manifested itself as a bright red tinge to her face as she turned her head sideways and Jim leant in to kiss her awkwardly, before she turned away with a cursory "Goodnight Jim."

As Jim Lightfoot crossed the road suitably humbled and embarrassed, Mary breezed up the road to her house, pushed the garden gate aside with unaccustomed force and found the front door open. Slamming it behind her she ran straight upstairs, past her father who was descending from his trip to the toilet and still buckling up his trousers, opened her bedroom door and threw herself down face first, gnashing her teeth and forcing a plaintive "Rrrragh!" between them.

"You alright lass?" shouted Harry, now from downstairs, for he had been caught by surprise as she had rushed into the house and upstairs without a word. "Mary? Don't blame me if Grudge collared you to do summat at t'Show. You should have got off the bloody bus when I did."

Mary turned onto her back and replied loudly. "I'm fine dad. Just tired that's all. I'll be down soon."

For the next hour Mary lay on her bed motionless, all manner of thoughts spinning through her agitated brain. That Jim had kept his impending holiday quiet was one thing, that he had not thought to invite her now that they were a couple was quite another. It cut her to the quick. In time however she came to realise that they had not actually been together that long really and as Jim had said the holiday had been planned for a long while. She convinced herself that it was probably too awkward to change the booking to include her now. At length she even decided that Jim had been putting off telling her because he had not wanted to upset her and indeed he probably did not even want to go himself without her, but he now had no choice as other friends were depending on him. In short, she now felt ashamed that she had reacted the way that she had, and resolved to apologise for her behaviour. She also promised herself that Jim's veg would be tended whilst he was away better than anyone else's ever had in history. She decided that when he returned he would have a nice surprise to come back to and that he would not ever want to leave her again.

TEN

<u>A strong kiss goodbye</u>

The weather broke the day after the annual trip and bought a deluge of biblical proportions to the area. Mary sat looking out through her bedroom window as the rain ran like a river down the road, the drains unable to cope with such a sudden downpour. She had got up early hoping to get all her chores done in time to get round to Peony Cottage to make a list of things Jim wanted her to do in his absence, hoping to show him how willing she was to please him. Alas, that would have to wait until the storm abated. Jim did not possess a mobile phone so she could not even text him to tell him of her plans to look after his beloved plot whilst he was away.

As lightning forked directly over the village followed by immediate thunder claps, Harry and Jim were also looking out at the dramatic squall, their hearts in their mouths as the wind whipped up and the foliage of their respective crops blew about like out of control windmills. Jim had already packed a suitcase ready for his trip tomorrow and desperately wanted to get into the garden to do some last minute jobs. He had spent the last evening in a moral dilemma, wondering whether he ought to knock Mary back and keep Bill Grudge as his holiday plant nurse for he was as yet still in the dark about Mary's new resolve, thinking her to be still deeply disappointed at him for not telling her about his impending trip.

The morning wore on interminably for all three, with no sign of a let up in the rain. Harry eventually grew tired of looking out at the bashing his vegetables were taking and decided to read the morning paper, moaning as he unfolded it for it was still dripping wet despite the poor old paperboy doing his best to keep it dry until he slotted it through the Ecklethwaites' post box. Harry resolved to complain to Ralph Chubb the next time he visited the store and haggle his paper bill down as a result. He draped the various pages over a clothes horse and put it in front of a radiator, keeping the horse racing pages and laying them out on his dining room table to read.

Over at Peony Cottage Jim busied himself taking his suitcase apart and repacking it several times, ticking off the contents against a checklist as he did so, finally becoming satisfied that all was well and lugging it downstairs ready to throw into the taxi that was booked to come and fetch him at 3am tomorrow morning. It was late afternoon by now and

Jim was now at a loss as to what he could do to occupy himself for the rest of the day, although he was still fretting about Mary being upset with him and whether she would show her face to go through what needed doing with his vegetables, especially as the rain showed no sign of letting up. Pouring himself a coffee he stood by the open back door, protected by a porch looking out at his garden longingly.

A voice now piped up from behind him. "I've seen you fretting about your veg all morning lad. Don't worry too much." It was Dick Tallboys. "The veg will take it, and if there is any damage there's still plenty of time until the show for it to recover. Bet Ecklethwaite is crapping himself mind. He's not like you. He doesn't cover things like you do. Your most susceptible veg is either in your greenhouse, polytunnels or under cloches. The brassicas will fend for themselves no bother. Aye, you're going to do 'im this season I can feel it."

"Oh, do you really think so?" replied Jim, not bothering to even turn around so accustomed had he become to hearing Dick's voice by now.

"Aye. Seen many a storm like this before. So long as they don't come the day before the show there's no problem laddie." Dick was calmly reassuring, something you could not always associate with a ghost in all probability. "Mind you, I remember we had a hailstorm the day before the show fifteen years ago I think it was. Most veg on the benches that day had massive holes in them where the hailstones had gone right through 'em!" Dick tittered.

"Not much I can do now I suppose," mulled Jim, "I'm away on holiday tomorrow morning for a couple of weeks."

"Oh? So who is looking after your garden while you're away?" asked Dick.

"Now there's a question. I did ask Bill Grudge but I think Mary Ecklethwaite is going to be doing it now." Jim didn't sound too certain.

"You can trust Mary can you?" asked a seemingly surprised Dick Tallboys.

Jim turned around and now observed his sporadic house guest sat on one of his kitchen chairs "Yes I think I can Dick. She gets a sense of morbid joy out of imagining her father getting beaten at the Show. Let's hope I can fulfil everyone's expectations."

"You need to get her upstairs and give her a good seeing to lad," suggested Dick in all seriousness, causing Jim to look down at the floor uncomfortably. "She'd look after your veg good and proper then, you mark my words. No-one's been there since Pete Greensleave when they were nippers so she must be absolutely crying out for it by now."

"I didn't know Mary and Pete had once been an item?" Jim queried.

"Oh aye, saw 'em myself once up at the bell tower. She's a vixen when her juices are stirred believe me. Whole damned village knew about it except Harry. He came home early from work one day and found Pete and Mary cuddling up on the sofa. Exploded like Krakatoa he did. Apparently you could hear him shouting over a hundred yards away. Silly old sod." Dick laughed heartily at this last recollection. "Trust me lad, you satisfy that lass and get her on board. If not she'll have that old rogue round here whilst yer away and there's no telling what he may get up to. You 'ave been warned."

Jim was just about to pester Dick for more information when a voice interrupted them, a female voice from the direction of the front door.

"Jim? Let me in please I'm absolutely soaked."

It was Mary, shouting through Jim's letter box having failed to attract his attentions by knocking, such was the noise being generated by the rainfall from outside Jim's back door which was still wide open. Mary had eventually grown tired of waiting for the rain to abate and was now stood on Jim's front doorstep, thoroughly sodden despite wearing a large rain coat and waterproof over trousers. She was clutching a notepad and pen on which she intended to dutifully write down all the instructions that Jim would tell her about his vegetables, fruit and flowers. Jim left Dick and rushed to open the door and let Mary in, water cascading from her clothes and forming a large pool of water on the flagstones of Jim's hallway.

"Oh I'm sorry about that Jim," she said apologetically, "get me a mop and I'll clean it up."

"Don't worry about that," fussed Jim, and mindful of what Dick the Ghost had just revealed, "It's really lovely to see you Mary. I've been so bored. Hasn't it been a miserable morning? Here, give me your wet things and I'll get a towel for you. Oh look your shirt is soaked too. I'll get you one of my old T-shirts. Wait there!" he said as he rushed upstairs in search of dry clothing.

Mary was somewhat taken aback by this sudden and unexpected show of affection from Jim. As she stood in Jim's hallway, steam rising from her wet hair and clothes, and waited for Jim to return from upstairs, she looked around for signs of another person, for she was sure she had initially heard two voices as she stooped and looked through Jim's letterbox before calling out to him. However, as the rain was so loud she could not be sure. Jim soon descended with a thick fleece T-shirt and a pair of jogging bottoms for Mary to wear.

"Sorry Jim, but I didn't realise you had company."

Jim looked flustered when Mary said this. Had she also seen Dick Tallboys' ghost he wondered? He was soon presented with an explanation that let him off the hook when Mary revealed that she had heard more than his voice just now.

"Oh no," Jim declared confidently, "that was just the radio. Now you get out of those wet things and pop these on and I'll light a fire to warm you up."

As Jim set about putting kindling and scrunched up newspaper on the fire he expected Mary to go upstairs to the bathroom to change, but instead she confidently stripped off down to her bra and pants, before standing in front of him with her wet clothes held out at arm's length.

"Have you got a plastic carrier bag I can put these in Jim?"

Jim looked up and having conquered his original shock, was now carefully studying her semi-naked form. She was undoubtedly a shapely woman, her pale skin still young looking, her ample breasts still supporting themselves rather than relying on a strong bra to stop them sagging. Jim could just about discern the outline of her pubic hair and nipples through the wet fabric of her undergarments, standing up promptly so as not to appear to be staring at her.

"Yes indeed Mary, I've got one in the kitchen, let me take them."

As he took Mary's clothes from her, Jim instinctively kissed her on the lips, albeit as he was moving away from her so that it was still nothing more than a fleeting contact. However, stood as she was, almost naked, it was like a lightning bolt to Mary's passions and if Jim had not now turned with his back to her he would have noticed her nipples harden demonstrably. Mary was soon aware of this physical manifestation of her wants, and although excited and energised felt sufficiently vulnerable to fold her arms in front of her chest in order to hide her rampant teats. When Jim returned with Mary's damp clothes in a carrier bag she was already dressing in the garments that he had bought down for her. Yet another moment had passed between them without action, but somehow Mary felt a definite sense of advancement, their recent kiss taking on all sorts of suggestion and implications in her overcharged mind.

"Right then Sunny Jim," she said cheerily, "you'd best show me what you want doing with all these vegetables hadn't you? From the comfort of the house I hasten to add. I'm not going out there again until it's stopped raining!"

Jim laughed as he pulled down the flap of his writing bureau and took out a couple of sheets of paper on which appeared to be some form of grid with writing in it. Upon giving the two pieces of paper to Mary she was able to determine they were actually carefully prepared and very copious notes of all the jobs that would require doing whilst he was away, one sheet for each week, thus rendering Mary's soggy piece of blank paper suddenly surplus to requirements.

"Study those please Mary," Jim said, "and let me know if there's anything you don't understand."

Mary started reading.

'Day one. Tomatoes in greenhouse, 1 litre of water per plant once a day. Use water from water butt situated in the greenhouse only. Cucumbers in polyunnel, 2 litres per plant, twice a day. Use water from water butt reference B. Leeks in garden to be sprayed with insecticide in spray gun marked number 8. Peas alongside north wall to be sprayed from gun 6 and watered along the trench, one full watering can'.

And so it went on, in such detail that Mary started to wonder how long it might all take her to complete each day. There was even a fully marked up map illustrating which was north, south, east and west, where the various letter marked water butts were, which spray guns were where and so on. She was fully prepared to do a first class job but now she was starting to become worried that things might go drastically wrong and Jim would come back to a disaster zone. What if she sprayed the wrong stuff on the wrong plants she was thinking? Jim became aware of her concern, which was now etched across her forehead in deep lines, and quickly tried to reassure her.

"It probably looks a bit daunting Mary, but trust me, everything is labelled and easy to find. I've put all feed, fungicide and insecticide sprays on show in the places marked on the map so you can't go wrong as long as you put them back where you found them."

"Oh Jim," Mary wailed, "it would be so much more comforting if you had a mobile phone so that I could contact you if I had a problem."

"I'm afraid I vowed never to have one of those infernal things when I left the desert," explained Jim. "I was a slave to the damned things ringing at all hours when I worked there. I'm sure you'll do just fine. You'll soon pick things up then it'll be an absolute doddle. Unfortunately I still work with engineering style planning hence the rather belt and braces approach to the instructions, but it's not as complicated as it looks."

They were both now knelt together in front of the fire as it cackled into life, and Mary was hunched over the two charts trying to get her head around everything. Jim's kiss and the feelings it aroused in her meant Jim's writing resembled Egyptian hieroglyphics. At length she sat up in an attempt to snap herself out of her anxiety.

"Oh don't you worry about it Jim, I'm sure I'll get the hang of it pretty quickly. This rain has just made me a bit slow witted no doubt. You go and enjoy yourself and don't worry about a thing."

They both looked at each other, Mary with a longing in her eyes betrayed by her heaving breast, Jim with a gratitude and a relief that his vegetables were going to be well cared for in his absence. But as the cessation in speech became a nervous pause and ultimately an uncomfortable silence bordering on the excruciating, Jim once more recalled Dick Tallboys' recent words. As Mary waited for something to happen, Jim was having uncomfortable visions of her letting Harry Ecklethwaite through the garden gate and his reaction to seeing Jim's wonderful vegetables. He imagined Mary laughing in revenge as her father scattered weedkiller everywhere, all for the sake of not having satisfied her flesh, or at least given her more substantial encouragement of future union, for Jim was conscious of the time ticking on as he really needed to get an early night in order to be fresh for his long journey tomorrow.

He decided to grasp the nettle and leant into Mary, kissing her still cold lips that the fire had not yet managed to reheat. Unlike their previous kisses, this one did not end as soon as it had begun, and Mary gasped as Jim continued to graze her lips with his own. She moved toward him and kissed him back ever more passionately, one hand on the back of his head and the other on his back expecting Jim to do likewise, which he did after some moments although a little awkwardly. They were now on their knees facing each other, their bodies clamped together, and Mary could almost feel Jim inside her, the trip upstairs and a frantic undressing surely no more than a formality. After a couple of minutes of noisy embrace Mary felt Jim's grasp slacken and their lips now parted.

"Wow, Mr. Lightfoot!" Mary gasped.

"Wow indeed," answered Jim, his face blushing slightly. "I'm so grateful to you Mary. I'm sorry I didn't tell you about my going away. I feel awful about it now but I'm glad we're friends again."

"More than that I hope Jim?" she implored.

"Indeed. Quite." Came Jim's unconvincing response. He hesitated before continuing. "Mary, do you mind awfully? I have a really early start and I ought to get some shut eye fairly soon."

Mary looked upset, but only at Jim's discomfort. "Oh Jim, I'm so sorry. No of course not. I'll get off now and I see you in a couple of weeks." She was utterly convinced that but for Jim's early start they would now be heading upstairs to his bed, clothes being shed on the short journey before an initially brutal coupling that would then lead to more tender lovemaking after Jim's return to the village in due course. All that would now have to wait. She was disappointed undoubtedly, but also elated at this recent and much hoped for elevation in their relationship.

Before she knew it Jim had shepherded her to the door where they exchanged one last, vaguely lingering kiss. "Bye sweetheart. Safe journey," she mouthed as she was retreating down the street, the rain having now lessened to a fine but persistent drizzle.

"Bye Mary. See you as soon as I get back," said Jim, blowing her a kiss but looking up and down the street simultaneously to make sure there were no witnesses.

Jim closed the door and leant against it with his eyes closed, and gave out a loud sigh. Opening his eyes he saw Dick Tallboys at the end of the hallway in the entrance to the kitchen.

"Well wasn't that just brilliant! You bloody useless idiot," shouted Dick. "There for the taking she was! Would it have really killed you to whisk her upstairs and rattle a few of her cobwebs away? You expect her to be satisfied with a few kisses? It's touch and go now I tell ye."

"It's not an easy thing making love to a woman when you have an audience watching your every move you know!" countered Jim angrily.

ELEVEN

Absence

The ghost of Dick Tallboys was completely wrong. Mary had no inclination whatsoever to allow her father into her lover's property. In fact, she did not even tell him what she was doing, leaving the house each day as soon as he was firmly ensconced in his own daily horticultural chores.

She dutifully followed Jim's extensive instructions to the absolute number and letter, and within three or four days was rattling through his list of tasks in next to no time, despite the weather which turned very hot and sunny almost as soon as Jim had left and meant Mary had her work cut out filling watering cans and lugging them to where they were needed. Due to the moisture in the ground from the storm of a few days ago the plants at Peony Cottage were virtually growing in front of Mary's eyes now that the warmth of the sun was upon them. She could not help but notice that they were a lot healthier looking than those of her father's in their own garden.

Jim had told her to make full use of his kitchen, including the contents of his refrigerator, so Mary always made herself coffee and some toast before she locked the house and garden back up. It was during one such coffee break that Mary's thoughts turned to Jim's bedroom. As we have seen previously, she still had not set foot inside it for the purpose of wanton indulgence and she now started to ponder what it was like in there. Did he have a reason for not wanting her to enter she wondered? Up to now the sheer volume of tasks Jim had left her meant she had been too occupied to consider exploring the parts of the house she had yet to visit, but as she sat in Jim's kitchen barely a week after he had departed she started to fight her conscience about taking a secretive snoop upstairs. The intensity of the kiss they had shared just a few days previously had played upon her mind every hour since, augmenting itself in her head to the extent she now imagined herself destined to become Mrs. Lightfoot and move into Peony Cottage, and as such she convinced herself that she had more than enough reason to check the bedroom out to see if it suited her taste in decorating. But long after her coffee had been drunk and the biscuits eaten, Mary was still unsure whether to let her curiosity get the better of her. Part of her desperately needed to know all she could about Jim's background and history, but she was also scared about what she might find up there.

Finally her indecision subsided and she bounded up the stairs after a quick glance into the street to see if anyone was approaching the cottage that might have cause to knock on the door. Although she had a legitimate reason to be there she would have felt uneasy explaining why she was upstairs all the same. At the top of the stairs a door opened into the bathroom that she had visited on a few previous occasions. Save a few bottles of aftershave there was nothing of any interest in there, for Mary had already examined the contents of Jim's cabinet on a previous visit. There were only two other doors and the first one turned out to be Jim's bedroom, where Mary was unsurprised to find that it looked out onto the back garden rather than the road at the front. She entered and stood for a few moments to take in everything she could see.

It was furnished simply. For future reference she was relieved to see that the bed, the sheets neatly folded and tucked in with hospital style precision, was a double one. In the far corner of the room was a small wardrobe and by the bed a small cupboard with a single door and a drawer, with a wicker chair against the wall next to it. Mary pulled the chair in front of the cupboard and sat staring at a small notepad next to a bedside lamp on which was drawn a heart and the words Jim and Mary. Mary put her hand to her mouth and whispered "Ahh!", smiling broadly as she touched the paper tenderly. If she had any doubt that Jim had any affection for her it had been well and truly dismissed in that instant. She wondered if Jim had written it after she had left him a few days ago, when she had to leave in order to allow Jim an early night. She imagined him lying there after the passionate kiss goodbye they had shared, perhaps playing with himself and wishing he was inside Mary, her near nakedness of that afternoon playing on his mind until he had fallen asleep, then having happy dreams about getting her into that bed as soon as he returned from his trip.

She opened the door, allowing several pairs of socks to fall out, all neatly paired and balled. With a faint curse under her breath Mary piled them all back in and shut the door to trap them again, and turned her attention to the drawer. She slid it open carefully and quietly, in case anything sprang out of it unexpectedly like the socks. As she did so she wondered why the socks were not in the drawer and whatever was about to be found in the drawer was not behind the door. This conundrum vanished from her mind as she was presented with the appearance of a couple of letters in opened envelopes, a couple of biros, a credit card, a small photo album, and what was unmistakeably a diary, all neatly arranged as was Jim's way.

Mary mused for several moments, guilt rising in her cheeks about what she was about to do, her mind trying to memorise exactly where each item was placed so that she could put them back in exactly the same position once she had finished and prevent Jim from suspecting her of snooping into his private belongings. The letters seemed like a good starting point she thought. But no, at the very last moment she decided that she could not go through with it and slid the drawer shut again.

Positioning the chair back against the wall where she had found it, Mary walked back out onto the landing and tried the door to the other room which no doubt was the one that looked out onto the road but found it firmly fastened. Yet there was no keyhole in the door so it could not be locked, meaning something was probably up against the door on the inside of the room barring entry. Try as Mary might she could not budge the door even a fraction of an inch, which she felt was strange. How could anyone get in to block it and then get out through the only door without unblocking it? After pondering this conundrum for a few moments Mary remembered that Jim was an engineer and perhaps he had installed some form of electronic locking system? This made the contents of the room even more intriguing but there was nothing she could do about that for now. She would merely have to wait until she and Jim became more legitimate lovers and partners and she had a right to enquire about what was in there.

Thwarted in this way Mary descended the stairs and after checking all was still well in the garden, made her way through the house, opened the front door and locked it behind her. As she walked away from Peony Cottage she looked up at the window of the locked room. Heavy net curtains meant she could not see into the room so she sighed and headed off home, unaware of a motionless figure in the darkened room that was watching her recede.

"Took you long enough to get inquisitive young lass. Thought you'd be up here on day one quite frankly. And judging by the cheery way you're skipping away, that heart drawing in Jim's room has turned out to be another masterstroke of mine!" laughed Dick Tallboys' ghost.

TWELVE

Detours, dead ends and wrong directions

Life was otherwise carrying on much as before in Allaways during Jim Lightfoot's absence. It was only a few weeks to the Show and many of the villagers were either too busy making various preparations for it, or tending their own prized vegetables to notice Mary making her daily jaunts to Peony Cottage. When Harry had found out from Bill Grudge one night in the pub that Jim had gone away for two weeks he felt relaxed that Jim was definitely no competition to him now, and that he did not need to make that ascent of his garden wall which was still a niggling doubt lingering in the back of his mind. Harry felt that anyone with serious aspirations to become Show Champion would not dare to go on holiday so near to the Show, with so many insects and diseases to be fended off. He laughed when Bill informed him that Jim Lightfoot had cancelled Bill's offer to water his garden for him whilst he was away, saying that he did not have much worth tending. Harry thus felt cosily safe in the knowledge that anything decent would soon succumb in this heat without judicious irrigation.

"Cancelled you say?" asked Harry to make absolutely certain.

"That's right," answered Bill Grudge, "said he only had a few cabbages and carrots growing and he was leaving 'em to their own devices. I said I didn't mind but he was most insistent. Shame, as I know he had quite a lot of seeds from the hort soc and I was hopeful he would be putting some entries in at the show. It'll be all down to you as usual Harry."

Harry waved at the sky and continued, "Well, the way the sun's been beating down this last week since that downpour he'll be lucky to come back to anything worth throwing on a show bench I reckon. I noticed blackfly on John Simmons' runner beans up the allotment the other day, and small caterpillars all over his caulis, so they'll be having a field day in the next few days. They'll be in Lightfoot's garden too no doubt."

John Simmons had also gone away for a few days and had asked Harry if he could water his allotment, much to the amazement of several in the pub, Bill Grudge and Bob Dillage among them. John Simmons was an accomplished grower, and whilst he was no danger to Harry in his annual quest to become village champion, for he didn't grow the range of flowers, fruit and vegetables that Harry did, John could still take points off Harry because everything that he did enter was usually good quality and came either first or second in its class.

"I assume you sprayed the fly and caterpillars for him then Harry?" Bill enquired.

Harry looked nonplussed. "Did I fuck!" exclaimed Harry as he put his pint of ale to his lips. "Soft cunt only asked me to water for him," he continued, beer dribbling down his chin and onto his variously soiled shirt.

Bill Grudge and Ted Grangeworthy looked at each other and shook their heads. As Harry went to the bar to order another pint, Ted Grangeworthy whispered in Bill's ear, "I bet he's spoiled anything good John has got growing as well!"

"I doubt it Ted," Grudge replied. "There are always plenty of other allotment holders down there so he daren't do anything untoward in front of 'em, and the big gates are locked at night. Besides, John told me in a quiet moment he's growing all his best stuff at home this year and asking Harry to water for him was just to throw him off the scent. I'm watering that for him whilst he's away. Harry'll see John doesn't have much of any show worthiness down the allotment and leave his garden alone. Next year John'll have to think of something different mind!"

At that point Mrs. Dibble entered the Dog and Gun, nodding elegantly to Bill, Jim and a few others, before ordering at the bar, "Dry sherry please Bob."

"You're looking very well Mrs. D," said Ralph Chubb who was seated next to Ted Grangeworthy. I was just thinking earlier today that I hadn't seen you in the shop for a few days."

"That's quite correct," said Mrs. Dibble, "I've been to visit a cousin in Shropshire and took the opportunity for a few walks in the countryside with her. Most invigorating it was indeed."

"Well you do look wonderful I must say," Chubb continued. "Amazing what a bit of strenuous exercise does I dare say."

Out of Mrs. Dibble's earshot Ralph Chubb turned to Ted Grangeworthy. "You know ever since the day she arrived in the village over thirty years ago I've been sure I know her face from somewhere. Just can't place it for the life of me though. I asked her once and she got all defensive and said she often gets mistaken for different people. She's mighty nimble for someone of her age you have to admit."

"Probably reminds you of someone you knew years ago Ralph," suggested Ted. "Right, I'm away for the evening, night all. Come on Bess." Ted's faithful Labrador, which had been at his feet all evening, obediently followed him out of the door.

A raucous game of darts was taking place in one corner of the public bar, a home match between the Dog & Gun and the Bonny Ploughman from the nearby village of Seldum-on-Cock. Pete Greensleave and Dave Preston were in the home team, and Pete was still desperately trying to avoid the clutches of Deirdre Dillage. When it was his turn to buy a round of drinks he waited until Deirdre was busy and got Bob to serve him, and had been employing this tactic ever since the committee meeting when he had informed every one of his unavailability to help out on the outside bar as usual.

For her part Deirdre had been desperately trying to attract Pete's attention since that night, but to no avail. After her initial anger had subsided she wondered if he had grown tired of her and started to worry that she was losing her allure. He usually came into the pub with Dave Preston who always flirted with Deirdre himself, but for now she only had eyes for Pete and craved his huge manhood again. Several texts to Pete's mobile for one of their usual rendezvous had gone unanswered, for unbeknown to Deirdre, Pete had destroyed his old mobile and now had a different one, telling his wife Molly that he had dropped his old one into some farm machinery.

Deirdre decided it was probably time to employ a different tactic, that of jealousy. She approached the area around the darts match under the pretence of collecting the empty glasses. Dave Preston was standing towards the back of the group of players observing the developing game. Deirdre smiled at him seductively, and after making sure Pete Greensleave was watching she gave Dave an affectionate hug, something that was not that unusual for she liked to be tactile with many of her regular customers.

"You alright there petal? How's the game going?" she asked Dave.

Dave Preston spluttered slightly on his drink, "Yes thanks Deirdre, I'm good. We're two games to one up and looking good in this one too."

As Deirdre collected a few more glasses from the area she flashed Dave another smile as she brushed past him, ensuring her breasts brushed his chest as she did so. She trotted off back behind the bar positive in her own mind that Pete Greensleave must now be seething with jealousy and would soon be texting her begging for a meeting. Dave Preston looked over anxiously at his best mate who was totally disinterested and concentrating on the game, before turning and watching the retreating posterior of Deirdre Dillage in shameless admiration, shifting nervously to try and hide the sudden bulge of an erection in his trousers. Due to his World class ugliness Dave had never had first-hand knowledge of carnal pleasure, apart from one trip to Amsterdam for Pete Greensleave's stag weekend several years before when he had paid for a half hour session with a prostitute called Olga who had performed oral sex on him. Dave had deemed the financial outlay well worthwhile and all of the other stag attendees never had the heart to tell him that Olga was actually a fella. Deirdre appeared to be giving him encouragement but as a friend of Pete's he was anxious about hurting his feelings and needed to make sure Pete was happy for him to pursue the landlady.

Most of the Dog & Gun's regulars had been interested onlookers in this game of sexual cat and mouse for several weeks now. Seeing as Ted Grangworthy, who was Pete's father-in-law of course, had left for the evening they could have a more open discussion on the subject. Local garage owner Jimmy Duggan was first to break the silence.

"Seems as if Pete's playing hard to get these days?"

"Mmm," mumbled Ralph Chubb in agreement. "I thought I hadn't heard the usual corn field cat o' whaling this Summer now you come to mention it."

This prompted Bill Grudge to lean in on the table and quietly retell the story to anyone who wanted to hear it again, of how he had woken up in the corner of a field when he was supposed to be on duty one afternoon to find Pete and Deirdre having noisy sex up against his combine harvester.

"Sat up from my slumber like a flick knife I did!" he recalled. "You should have heard 'em. Never seen or heard anything like it before or since and believe me I've seen some weird things during thirty odd years in the force. They were only fifty yards or so away from me and she was screaming like she were being murdered. He was going at it like there were no tomorrow, the pair of 'em sweating away, oblivious to the World they both was."

Bill was on a roll now, "I was right on the edge of the ploughed bit where Pete had already been with his enormous harvester, so I assume if Deirdre hadn't appeared to lure Pete's attentions away from his ploughing I'd have been mincemeat, so in a strange way I have Deirdre Dillage to thank for still being here today and I will always be grateful for that. Last time I slept on the job I can tell you. Anyways, there I am wondering how I can get away without being seen and all of a sudden Pete lurches, Deirdre screams even louder and they both fall to the ground where they stay for several minutes silent as church mouses. Eventually Pete gets off her and swings round to pull his trousers up. As far away as I was I can tell you his manhood nearly took my chuffin' eye out!"

Jimmy, Ralph and one or two others who were listening started laughing uncontrollably, even though most of them had heard the same story several times before. Bill was not finished.

"Anyways, there I am, hiding in the unploughed wheat or corn or whatever crop it were, and I'm in a right dilemma see. How can I get over the hedge, retrieve my police bicycle and pedal away without being seen? Luckily for me Pete's boss appeared across the field in his Landrover. He tells Deirdre to quickly hide in the cab of the combine, which she does with some struggle I might add, her bare backside glaring me in the face as she did so, and Pete walks over the field in the other direction from where I am to talk to his gaffer. So I takes the opportunity to make my escape and they were none the wiser about it to this very day. " Bill sat back in his seat to a small smattering of applause, prompting Bob Dillage to come over.

"What are you old reprobates all guffawing at then?" he asked.

Harry had returned to the group by this time, having misheard a few patchy sentences of Bill's story. "Who's Pete shagging now then?" he said loudly and rather untactfully causing Jimmy Duggan to kick him under the table. Unfortunately, Bob Dillage now sensed a fresh bit of gossip he had not been a party to before and pulled a stool alongside the group in order to sit amongst them.

"Come on then you old buggers, spill the beans!" he demanded.

Bill, Ralph and Harry all looked at each other in horror, not knowing what to say for the best. Luckily Jimmy Duggan was on hand to step in, adept as he was at last minute explanations when questioned on the size of some of his repair bills by many of his indignant customers.

"You're not gonna believe this Bob, but he's only been screwing the wife of one of his workmates. Right old battle axe she is as well by all accounts. Be sure you don't say owt to Ted Grangeworthy now will you Bob?" he ordered assuredly. Bob got up from the stool tapping his nose as if they had all entered into a pact and went back behind the bar satiated in his unremitting thirst for scandal.

"Fucking hell, nice one Jimmy," gasped Harry who had virtually held his breath since almost letting the cat out of the bag.

"Yes, well done Jimmy," agreed Bill Grudge.

"Seconded," said Ralph Chubb.

"So who is this other woman he's bloody nailing then?" asked Harry with a look of confusion.

Deirdre Dillage had spent the last five minutes quizzing Mrs. Dibble about her trip to her cousin's. "Where in Shropshire is it then Mrs. D? Only I know Shropshire quite well as our daughter lives in Shrewsbury and we've been all over the county in our time."

Mrs. Dibble appeared a little flustered at this request and inexplicably delayed an answer whilst she drained the last drop of her dry sherry. "Another one in there please Deirdre."

When Deirdre had returned to Mrs. Dibble with her drink, she noticed that her usual calm and collected appearance had returned to her aged yet attractive features.

Mrs. Dibble took a sip of the fresh sherry, licking the sweet liquid from her lips before explaining, "The thing is I wasn't actually in Shropshire. I don't like telling people of my exact whereabouts when I go away. I do like to keep my private life private if you don't mind Mrs. Dillage."

"Oh no darlin' that's perfectly fine," replied. "Us girls got to have some secrets eh?"

Mrs. Dibble nodded as if in agreement then turned her head away from the landlady towards the ongoing darts match, thus signifying in no uncertain terms that their conversation was now well and truly over. It was an awkward moment, for not only did Mrs. Dibble have absolutely no interest in darts but also because Deirdre Dillage felt as if she had been snubbed somehow, especially as Mrs. Dibble had now struck up a conversation with Reverend Arsley.

"You look troubled about something vicar," enquired Mrs. Dibble.

"Do I?" answered the nervous clergyman. "Oh dear. Well one does tend to have the worries of the World on one's shoulders in the religious game I dare say. All the parishioners' woes to listen to and advise upon and so forth."

Arsley, who often enjoyed a late night tipple in the Dog & Gun after evening worship, was struggling to contain his teeth more than usual it seemed. The reverend had just been informed by Bill Grudge that he had passed the church earlier and a gentleman was enquiring as to the vicar's whereabouts, and this had made him nervy for some reason. He was going to call it a night but decided to join Mrs. Dibble in a round of sherries instead, but they were both struggling to attract the attention of the publican husband and wife who were in deep conversation at the bottom of the stairs to their living quarters which was a few yards back from the bar and through an archway. Bob Dillage had just waylaid his wife on her way upstairs to patch up her make-up.

"Hey-up you'll never guess what bit o'juicy goss I've just heard?" he said tantalisingly.

Deirdre was immediately intrigued. "Go on then, let's hear it."

"That Pete Greensleave is only screwing the wife of one of his work pals, dirty beggar," he continued. "Right slapper she is they reckon. Apparently he has a bit of a freaky fetish for ugly old women," he chortled, and left Deirdre to return to the bar, unaware of the deep colour rising in her face.

Deirdre looked out into the bar at the back of Pete Greensleave's head as he took his turn chalking the scores of the darts match which was still in progress, a mixture of emotions welling up inside her, none of them good ones. She mumbled under her breath, "You're going to regret making a fool out of me you cocky little bastard", before stomping off upstairs to try and compose herself.

Back in the bar John Simmons had appeared, like Mrs. Dibble fresh from a holiday. A lifelong batchelor, his private life had been subject to some scrutiny in previous years, several villagers still being convinced that he was a homosexual, and so his holiday destinations always came under close analysis by the gossip mongers. Nobody had any foundation for such conjecture and indeed John Simmons had never given any indication of such sexual leanings but at the same time he had never denied it either when bar room banter had suggested as such. Ever generous shopkeeper Chubb offered to buy John a drink, but it was merely a ploy to engage him in conversation about his holiday in the hope of finding out for sure what they all suspected.

"Good holiday was it John? Where did you get to?"

John Simmons was wise to the antics of the regulars and liked to play along wherever possible and said rather naughtily, "Oh just a few days in Brighton visiting a friend, then we both headed up to London to do a bit of sightseeing." As a consequence, several rib cages were nudged and drinks spilled during the seconds following this disclosure. Needless to say John had been nowhere near Brighton or London.

Jimmy Duggan leant in towards Ralph Chubb and said in a low voice, "He's definitely not dancing on our side of the ballroom that one."

John Simmons was a bit of a puzzle. He dressed quite the dandy most days, in clothes that certainly did not assist those protesting that he was not gay. Some would have called him quite fashionable, but really his dress sense just cried out for a woman's touch. Before stepping out, most married men are called back to change one item of clothing at least with the sentence "You're not going out dressed in that combination!" John Simmons was a lifelong bachelor and did not have that luxury.

"Thanks for watering the garden Bill," John said to Grudge quietly so that Harry could not hear them.

"My pleasure John," said Bill Grudge. "I must say you have some super looking veg. A master stroke of yours to grow your show veg in your garden this year. My wife wouldn't allow me to do that, says it makes the garden look like an allotment!"

"One of the advantages of a batchelor life dear man," John continued, "I can do what I please, when I please." And with an afterthought he naughtily added, "And with whom I please!"

Simmons now noticed Mrs. Dibble at the bar, still in conversation with the vicar. "Hello there Mrs. D," he shouted flamboyantly, "Good holiday?" he asked, winking as he did so.

Mrs. Dibble turned around, annoyed that her discussion with Reverend Arsley had been quite so rudely interrupted. "Yes thank you John," she spat, and turned back to Arsley to continue her discourse.

"Oooer," John laughed, "looks like I've ruffled her feathers!"

Ralph Chubb had returned from the bar with John's drink. "I've noticed you do like to wind her up don't you? What do you know about her that we don't?"

"Oh nothing really," John said. "But I reckon she was a right vixen when she was younger don't you think? Her husband died long before she came to live here. I reckon she killed him with her sexual demands."

"Good grief," spluttered Bill Grudge. "Where on Earth do you get these wild thoughts from? What did you used to lecture on at that university exactly?"

"Psychology," John answered.

"You sure it wasn't psychopathy?" suggested Ralph Chubb.

The darts match had now finished, the Dog & Gun emerging victorious, and as was usual a supper was always provided by the hosting establishment. Deirdre had suddenly complained of a raging headache and retired to bed so Bob Dillage had enlisted the services of Jane Tallboys to help him fetch out the trays of faggots, chips and mushy peas for the hungry players.

"You'd best get plenty down you tonight Pete," Bob advised, "all that farm work must give you a healthy appetite eh lad?" and he winked as he left them to it, causing Pete Greensleave to become very nervous about what Bob actually meant by his strange remarks.

"Fucking hell," he whispered to Dave Preston. "He's on to me. But I've not been near Deirdre in weeks. Bollocks!"

"Well done boys," Jane congratulated suddenly whilst she placed herself in front of Pete and Dave in order that they could gain ample admiration of her generous cleavage. "By my reckoning that puts us second with one match to go and that's against the league leaders, the Gay Gordon's in Tithampton.

"Mmm, we won't win that one Jane," Dave remarked. "They always beat us. Summat about that pub that always puts us right off."

"Well we got our secret weapon this year haven't we?" Jane proposed, smiling at Pete Greensleave who had joined the team that season for the first time and had turned out to be their best player by a mile. "Your arrow seems to hit the right spot every time so I've been told," she said naughtily.

Pete realised that Jane was flirting with him and slyly manoeuvred himself between her and Dave Preston so that he could talk to her one to one. "Well, it's nice of you to notice Jane. Have you been watching my action then?"

Jane giggled. "No I'm afraid I haven't, it's just what I've been told. I hope to get an opportunity to see you in action before too long though Pete. Perhaps you could teach me how to hold it to best effect?"

Harry Ecklethwaite was in good form, telling anyone who wanted to listen, and several who did not, that his vegetables were probably the best he had ever grown. "Aye, if I was unbeatable before then nobody has a chance this year. I feel sorry for those twats that come over from Tithampton way each year trying to beat me, never mind the other growers in the village. Has the Gazette been in touch recently Grudge?"

"Yes Harry, we have had close contact with them," Bill answered. "They'll be turning up about mid-afternoon on the day and I'll find out what they want to take photos of."

"Well aint that fucking obvious Grudge?" Harry scolded. "They'll want to photograph the show champion. And that'll be me of course."

"I wouldn't be so sure this year Harry," Ralph Chubb suddenly declared. "I've heard of a few growers far and wide who are saying they've got some good stuff to challenge you with. You get to hear lots of things in that shop you know."

"Pah!" Harry sniffed nonchalantly. "They're just having you on. Heard it all before."

Outwardly Harry was all confident bluster, but inside he was starting to doubt how good his own produce really was, and whether Chubb's words had a shred of truth and which growers he might be referring to. In this of all years he simply could not afford to lose his crown. Most years the Gazette carried a few sentences about the show and Harry's name only got a quick mention in the lists of winners, usually misspelt, but this year they were going full page.

"Just supposing that nonsense was true," he resumed, "which growers have you heard about then Chubb?"

"Ha! You're worried!" Ralph scorned triumphantly.

"Am I fuuuuck," Harry protested, turning away with his pint, "don't give a flying fart."

As the night drew to a close, the villagers engaged in much more speculation, drank much more alcohol, and generally jockeyed for a position of importance in each other's lives, but most important of all they each stored up information that may be of use to them in future days, weeks, months or years. Not often in life would you see so much energy being used to go down so many blind alleys and get absolutely nowhere as a result.

THIRTEEN

Curiosity killed the cat

As the day of Jim Lightfoot's return from holiday approached Mary mulled over the possible contents of the letters she had seen in his bedroom drawer. Each day since the discovery it had been gnawing away at her like an itch that she could not quite reach, but she carried out her duties in the garden and resisted all temptation to return to Jim's bedroom for the purpose of reading the missives. Were they love letters from an ex-girlfriend she wondered, for she was sure the writing was undoubtedly that of a female hand. Might they enlighten her somehow about the reasons for Jim's reticence in their awkward relationship, or worse still reveal that he was still nursing a broken heart over someone else and that consequently Mary could never replace that person in his affections? She even conceived of the idea that Jim was currently holidaying with this mystery woman, and that he was perhaps stringing them both along, having his cake and eating it. Although as cakes went, Mary knew all too cruelly that hers had not had a slice taken out of it as yet.

Eventually the day of Jim's return had arrived and Mary knew that if she wanted to know what was in the letters then she would have to act immediately or maybe she would never know. He was due to step foot through the door in the early evening assuming his flight was on time, and Mary had made an early start on the watering as she wanted to make sure everything was tidy for his return, and give herself plenty of time to read the letters if her curiosity got the better of her, as indeed she probably knew it would. Sure enough, by early afternoon Mary once again found herself pushing open the door to Jim's bedroom.

She hovered momentarily over the notepad where Dick Tallboys had mischievously drawn the love heart around Jim's and Mary's names, fingering the ink and sighing.

"This is so wrong," she whispered barely audibly, "but you've got me so confused Jim there are things I need to know."

She slid the drawer open and saw the two letters once again, as well as the small photo album which she decided to look at first. Opening the cover she saw that there was an inscription on the inside in the same handwriting as on one of the envelopes, Mary having now decided that the other one was in a different hand.

To my darling James.

A few mementos of happy days spent in London.

I will always love you

M x

The photos were unmistakeably all of Jim, and apparently taken when he was just a teenage boy on a sightseeing trip around the capital. Mary instantly recognised the Tower of London, Westminster Bridge and St. Paul's Cathedral, all the photos having Jim in the foreground looking somewhat bored and embarrassed, even gawky. At the end of the album was a photo of Jim with a woman, taken inside what appeared to be a theatre. She looked happy, a very attractive and smart looking lady in her late thirties perhaps, and she had her right arm around Jim who looked completely the opposite, most definitely unhappy. Mary assumed this was Jim's mother and having satisfied her curiosity carefully placed the album back in the exact same position she had found it. She decided she would not open the letter that was written in the same handwriting as she had found in the album, content that this would be a letter from his mother. Mary had somehow convinced herself that it would be wrong to read that one.

She picked up the other letter. As with the other one the postmark was barely legible and offered no clues as to its origin. She could not be sure but she somehow sensed it was a man's writing, and upon opening it, reticently at first, she found this indeed to be the case.

Dear boy,

Got back from the States last weekend and found your mother in a rare old pickle. She told me what had transpired and let me tell you I won't tolerate such behaviour again. Her nerves were shot to pieces. If you can't be civil then we think perhaps it's best if we cancel any idea of you coming with me on the next trip. Think carefully about your life going forward from here young man. You only get one shot at it.

Your loving father.

The tone of the letter shocked Mary. "I wonder what that was all about? And why would he keep it? Poor Jim!" she mused.

She stood reading the letter another couple of times before returning it exactly where she had found it, not quite sure what she had discovered if anything. Could his father's abruptness explain Jim's lack of feeling toward her she wondered? Were his parents even still alive? So many questions and so many unanswered she thought. Next she opened the diary but was dismayed to find nothing but notes on when to sow certain vegetables, when to feed and so on. Jim would be back in the next few hours so she scanned the bedroom one more time and hoped that she would be returning to the room as an invited guest before too long. Sighing, she left the room and closed the door gently behind her, but before descending the stairs she thought she would try the front bedroom again. She was surprised to find that, unlike her first attempt a few days before, this time the door opened easily.

"Weird!" she said and entered, to find a carpeted room, smartly decorated but with not a single piece of furniture or ornamentation to be seen anywhere. In one corner was a built-in cupboard which Mary approached and opened to reveal a few blankets, towels and overcoats. Having satisfied herself that there really was nothing of interest in the room Mary turned her attention to the door that had somehow defied her attempts to open it only a few days previously. It was certainly opening and closing with singular ease now so she could not understand why she was unable to prise it open before. There was no lock on the inside and the paintwork on the door surround and the door itself was sound. The only thing Mary noticed that was a bit puzzling was a small 'V' shaped notch, or indentation on the frame of the aluminium door handle where some damage had occurred, for it was made all the more noticeable by the complete lack of any other defects to be seen anywhere else in room.

Mary took one last look around and left the room, closing it behind her before descending the stairs and grabbing her jacket from the bottom newel post.

"Right then Jim, I've done my best and hopefully you'll be rewarding me for my efforts before too long. I'll be back just before you arrive so I can get the kettle on and I'll have you a nice slice of cake ready."

With that she opened the front door and closed it behind her, flicking her hair from side to side as she skipped down the street and back home again.

Back inside Peony Cottage the spirit of Dick Tallboys' was watching her from the lounge window this time.

"I hope you get properly rewarded as well lass. You deserve it. Harry isn't going to know what's hit him on Show day. But it's a damned good job I hid those other albums and letters from Jim's bedroom or else you wouldn't be skipping away so cheerfully now, you nosy little minx!

FOURTEEN

Marrow escape

Whilst Jim had been away Harry had been very busy indeed on the sabotage front. As we have seen, he had already made sure that John Simmons runner beans had suffered from black aphid and his caulis had been eaten by caterpillars, or at least he had done nothing to prevent them from suffering by acting as most good neighbours would probably (and hopefully) have done. He had also travelled to several allotments in the area after dark to check on how some of his rivals' vegetables were progressing. On most he found nothing to worry him too much but on a large site near to Tithampton from whence a couple of growers often ventured to compete at Allaways Show each year, Harry noticed some nicely shaped large onions growing away in a padlocked greenhouse. With a bolt cropper he had soon broken into the greenhouse, and with a large hessian sack managed to pilfer a dozen of the largest and best onions over his shoulder which he threw from his car window into the hedgerows one by one on his journey back.

"Where have you been?" asked Mary one evening after Harry had walked in from one such clandestine damage-fest, a few nights before Jim's return. Truth was, apart from this one occasion Mary had not noticed her father's nocturnal comings and goings as she had been retiring to her room early each night. Conversely, he had not complained about her leaving the house every morning to tend to Jim's garden because he had often been asleep in his shed recovering from his nightly bouts of vegetable vandalism, and was not even aware she was spending hours away from the house looking after a potential deadly enemy. Their 'ships' more or less passed each other unnoticed the whole fortnight of Jim's vacation, and since Bill Grudge had told Harry about his watering services not being required up at Peony Cottage Harry was contented that no competition was going to be forthcoming from that particular corner of the village.

"Out!" came Harry's terse and not unusual retort.

"Ask a silly question I suppose. I'm off up to bed. Night dad."

"Night lass. Oh, hang on a minute. That poncy pillock from Peony Cottage isn't back in the village yet is he do you know? Only he hasn't been in the pub for days."

"I believe he's still on holiday dad. Why do you ask?"

"Oh no reason. Just being neighbourly. There's a lot of them bloody gypos roaming about the area and things are getting pinched or being damaged. If you look in the Gazette there's some reports of big onions being stolen from an allotment near Tithampton. Terrible shame. I wouldn't want any of Lightfoot's veg to meet the same end. We need every entry we can to make sure the Show's a big success this year, what with it being the one 'oondredth and all that."

"Well I don't think Jim was going to enter anything into this year's show dad. He's not long got his garden cleared from the mess Dick Tallboy's left behind."

"Oh? That's a shame. Maybe next year then? I'll have to take him under my wing and give him some more advice. We need some new blood at the show."

"If you say so dad," said Mary, a wry smile breaking out across her lips, "goodnight now."

As she climbed the stairs and shut her bedroom door behind her, Harry felt reassured that what Bill Grudge had told him about Jim's garden was in fact true, and that his daughter and Jim were still not seeing eye to eye since the day trip when to all intents and purposes Jim had seemed to be coming under the vice-like grasp of Jane Tallboys. Harry was just about to retire to bed himself, for his nocturnal escapades were starting to make his body ache having had to scale so many gates, fences and walls over the last few evenings, when there was a sharp knock at the front door. Harry opened it quickly to be confronted by the sight of a rather large policeman on his doorstep and a squad car with blue flashing lights announcing its presence to the whole street causing several curtains nearby to start twitching.

"Oh. Hello. Errr. What is it officer?" Harry asked. Looking up and down the street as he did so.

The policeman waited a few moments, no doubt weighing up the gentleman stood before him, before answering. "Sorry to trouble you sir, but have you been anywhere in the vicinity of the Croft Road out of Tithampton this evening?"

Harry did not quite know what to say for the best, but decided on this occasion that the truth might be a good option. "Yes I 'ave as a matter of fact officer. Been to visit a friend in the town, in the Red Lion near the church actually if you must know. Came along that road about, oooooh, must be thirty minutes ago. What seems to be the problem?"

"Well now, we've had a few reports of some theft and damage from a couple of allotments over that way and we have CCTV footage of a car matching your description in the vicinity. I don't suppose you saw anything suspicious did you?"

Harry was momentarily flustered but composed himself adequately. "No I'm afraid I didn't officer."

The policeman checked his notebook. "A strange route to take to get back here if you don't mind me saying so sir? Those allotments are on the north side of the town, and you would have needed to come south back to the village. How do you explain that?"

Harry dithered again. "Now look here, I don't like the tone of your questioning young man. I'm a law-abiding citizen and I don't go about desecrating people's vegetables."

"Just answer the question please sir," replied the policeman authoritatively. "And I don't believe I mentioned anything about any vegetables being 'desecrated' as you so quaintly put it."

"Well no, that's quite right, you didn't. But if you'll excuse me the Gazette's full of stories of vandalism to folks' prized vegetables so I just assumed it was more of the same when you mentioned allotments. I absentmindedly took a wrong turn in the town centre and ended up doing an unexpected detour that's all," countered Harry rather more assuredly on this occasion, which seemed to placate the policeman somewhat.

However, it was only a momentary reprieve. The boy in blue had not come all this way to investigate the incidents to be turned away so easily.

"Do you mind if I have a look in your car sir?" asked the man in uniform.

Harry now decided he would try going on the offensive. "As a matter of fact I fucking do, you can't come here interrogating old men in the middle of the night without good reason. Just because I happened to be driving along that road doesn't mean I had anything to do wi'it all. I bet a dozen crimes of different sorts have been committed along my route this evening. Did I fucking do all of 'em then?"

"There's no need to swear Mr. Ecklethwaite," said the policeman forcefully.

"How the fuck do you know my name?" Harry asked bluntly.

"A quick check on the computer is all it takes these days sir! Now, your car if it's not too much trouble? If you've got nothing to hide then you have nothing to worry about have you? I could always return with a search warrant but it won't just be your car if I do!"

"You can look in my car no problem but I'm telling you this, when you find nothing I want a written apology from your commanding officer or this'll go straight to the Gazette," said Harry as he fumbled in his jacket pocket for his car keys, before leading the policeman towards his battered old Peugeot estate car parked in the street in front of the house. "Bloody disgrace this is. Nowt but victimisation."

Harry unlocked the car whilst the policeman inspected the exterior with a torch, before he opened the rear door and peered inside. It was a disgrace, even for Harry.

"Phwoooooah!" gasped the policeman stepping back in recoil. "What the hell have you had in there?"

"Oh behave you big girl's blouse. Just a few sacks of farmyard manure and dried blood from t'abbatoir," replied Harry chuckling at the policeman's lack of stomach. "Go on then, get yer 'ead in and do a proper search then."

However, the policeman just shone his torch inside Harry's vehicle from a distance and decided against it. "No thank you sir, that'll be fine for now."

Then he shone his torch on Harry's far side wheel arch, before kneeling down beside it to touch a substance that appeared to be dripping from it, then giving it a sniff under his nose, "This smells suspiciously like mashed onions don't you think? How do you explain that sir?"

Harry replied confidently, "I'm not surprised. I ran over several that seemed to have been dumped in the road, bout halfway between here and Tithampton. You want to get back there and scoop a few up cos I'll be willing to bet they'll have the culprit's fingerprints all over 'em officer!"

The policeman looked confused and excited all at the same time. "Righto sir, thanks for the information. I'm sorry if we troubled you but a fair few people have been seriously inconvenienced and extremely upset over this vandalism, so we have to look into all possible avenues you understand."

"Oh not at all officer. We have our own village show in a few weeks. I've had my veg tampered with in the past so I know how demoralising it can be, believe me." Harry was now starting to relax as the policeman put away his notebook and torch, giving him the impression he was off the hook all of a sudden. "If you need any further assistance please don't hesitate to pop back officer."

"Oh I won't Mr. Ecklethwaite. If you remember anything else, or see and hear of anything in the next few days that might help with our enquiries then give the station a call. We're determined to catch this piece of low-life scum," said the policeman with just a slight hint in his intonation that he was still far from convinced about Harry's innocence.

A few moments of silence now followed as Harry let the policeman's words sink in. "Well yes, quite right. We don't need that sort do we?" Now don't forget those onions on the B9189. Fingerprints!"

"And CCTV," the policeman was quick to counter, a knowing smile plastered across his face as if to say "gotcha!" The policeman took great pleasure in elaborating. "Some of the sites affected installed CCTV cameras after a bout of vandalism this time last year so whoever is responsible will no doubt have left us a lovely clear mugshot. Good night sir."

The two men shook hands and Harry watched as the policeman walked back to his car, slamming the door behind him. The blue flashing lights went off suddenly and then the policeman could be seen talking into his radio device as he no doubt filed a preliminary report back to his station. After a minute or so he pulled away and drove towards the end of the road, turning left at the junction in the direction of Tithampton, Harry waving nonchalantly for the benefit of three or four curtain-twitching rubber-neckers who were still persisting from various addresses nearby.

Harry waited a few minutes for the sound of the car engine to die down completely, before rummaging about in the back of his car. Under an old hessian sack he found a balaclava hat which he popped into his jacket pocket and a pair of rubber gloves which he put on before pulling up a flap in the trunk of the car where a spare tyre would normally be stowed. Harry lifted up a couple of huge onions from the otherwise empty compartment, closed the car door and walked back up to the house before throwing the two vegetables into a dustbin by the front door.

"Missed those fuckers didn't you Clouseau?"

FIFTEEN

Return

At the appointed hour Mary slipped out of her house unseen so as not to rouse her father's suspicions and returned to Peony Cottage. Under her arm was a wicker basket in which she had placed a fruit cake she had baked, covered by a tea towel for it was still quite warm. She popped the kettle on so that it could be quickly reheated as soon as Jim stepped through the door and sat at the kitchen table and read through a few seed and garden sundries catalogues that had been delivered in Jim's absence. He had also received a few letters and Mary noticed that one of them was written in the same female hand as the one she had seen upstairs and which was also in the old photo album. It was post marked London.

She did not have long to wait. A bare fifteen minutes had passed when she heard a car draw up outside, and rushing to the front window she saw it was indeed the taxi conveying Jim from the airport. Whilst Jim dragged his luggage from the car boot and paid the driver Mary had enough time to make two cups of coffee and cut a slice of cake for him. She reached the door to open it just as he was about to put his own key in the lock.

"My, hello brown boy," she remarked, a huge smile beaming across her happy face.

Jim was tanned. Very well-tanned indeed. He heaved his luggage to just inside the door and bent down towards Mary and kissed her on the cheek.

"Well this is a nice surprise having you here to greet me home," he said. "How has the garden been?" With that he brushed past Mary and made straight for the back door, opening it and standing just off the back step and scanning the garden. "Wow! It looks fantastic. You have done well Mary. No problems I hope?"

Mary was still standing in the hallway slightly disappointed that the kiss to the cheek had not progressed to something more akin to lovers, but the praise Jim had then lavished upon her soon had her heart melting away yet again.

"Oh, no, not really. Once I got the hang of it I soon rattled through all the chores you left me. It was nothing," she answered.

"Nonsense," Jim replied adamantly. "This all looks marvellous, it really does Mary."

With that Jim left the door step and started to walk around the garden carefully inspecting every crop for any sign of pest damage or disease. He could find none. After a few minutes Mary became impatient.

"Jim! I've made you a coffee and cut you a slice of cake. Come and sit down for ten minutes. The garden will still be here when you've finished," she ordered.

Jim felt suitably admonished. "Yes, sorry Mary. Oh wow that does look good," he said as he sat down at the table. "So now, what gossip do you have? Anything happened in the village whilst I've been away?"

Mary sighed, for she really wanted to know all about Jim's trip and what he had got up to, but she humoured him for now.

"Not much I don't think Jim. Molly's plans for leaving Pete on Show day are gathering pace. Deirdre Dillage has been trying hard to attract Pete's attention by all accounts but he appears to have well and truly kicked her into touch. Too little too late. Jimmy Duggan's mechanic has finished with Jane Tallboys because she was flirting with one of his mates in the pub although Jane insists she finished with him because he always stank of engine oil. Bill Grudge was all of a panic the other day because the vicar still hasn't located the gazebos. Oh and the police were up at Cock Hall last week after an intruder was spotted in the grounds by Ralph Chubb when he delivered the groceries. They didn't catch anyone but Lady Belton is a bit ruffled by all accounts. I think that's about it?"

"Pretty mundane then Mary?" Jim suggested.

"All very boring really," she continued. "Apart from the police investigating a string of vandalism attacks on allotment sites in the area. The Gazette's there if you want to read about it later."

"Really. Let's have a look at that!" said Jim, immediately picking the local rag up in order to read all about it.

There was a long silence as Jim read the article from start to finish. No names were cited but there was mention of the police trailing a vehicle to the village of Allaways and questioning a man. The reporter seemed to wallow in the story, using quite flamboyant language. Indeed the headline of the piece set the tone.

'Prize veg targeted by jealous rival in show season sabotage spree shocker- by Daz Bilkin'

One paragraph in particular stood out as far as Jim was concerned, and not just for the atrocious spelling and grammar.

'In the cource of my investigaition's I spoke to sevral local grower's and the name of one man kept on cropping up as a potential culpret. For legle reason's I am unable to name the allegded person but he does have a reputasion for this sort of despicabel behaviour. Rest assured dear reader's that I will be following up on the story as the horticultural show season gets underwhey.'

"How bizarre," said Jim. "The most difficult word is the only one spelt correctly! I assume we both know who is being implicated?"

"Dad denies everything of course," Mary said. "He was insisting in the Dog & Gun that some of his local rivals from Tithampton have it in for him and have sent the police in his direction out of spite. He's telling anyone willing to listen that they have absolutely no proof of anything involving him! That reporter has been to the show several times over the years. He's very ambitious and sees himself as potential Fleet Street material but in truth there's only him, a couple of other old journalists and a photographer at the Gazette. He's a bit of a joke around here to be honest."

Jim appeared to be reading the article again so Mary cleared up the coffee cups and took them to the sink. "So are you going to tell me all about your trip or not?" she asked at length, her back turned away from him.

"Mm? Oh yes of course," replied Jim, sensing a degree of irritation in Mary's tone. "Tell you what though, let me freshen up then we'll go for something to eat over at the pub. My treat for doing such a great job with the garden. I'll tell you all about it then? What do you say?"

Mary was delighted. "That sounds lovely Jim. You're on!"

"Excellent. I'll ring Bob Dillage and reserve a table. Ok, so if you pop home and change I'll grab a quick bath then I'll call for you en-route. Eight o'clock sound about right?"

Mary nodded disconsolately, eventually forcing an acceptance from her lips. To Mary it sounded like a dismissal however. She was good enough to look after his garden whilst he was away, but not to stick around whilst he freshened up, or even to share his bath. Had he even missed her she wondered? He obviously had not noticed that she had already smartened herself up to welcome him back anyway, and in fact she did not have any clothes much better at home in which to change into. Jim kissed her on her cheek yet again before climbing the stairs to run a bath.

"I've got lots to tell you Mary," he said on the way up. "Oh and I've got a little present for you, but you'll have to wait until I've unpacked. I'm famished. Looking forward to the meal." He winked at her as he neared the top of the stairs before disappearing from view.

Mary's mood lightened considerably upon receiving the news of the gift, and she heard the bath taps being turned and water start to splash onto the ceramic. She wondered whether to wait until he was in the bath and then present herself at the bathroom door naked, but she soon thought better of it. She told herself that he would have had a very long trip and energetic sex was understandably not high on his list of priorities, before shouting up to him, "I'll be waiting at the end of the road just before eight then Jim. You need to be careful dad doesn't get wind of all your veg in light of the stories in the Gazette don't forget!"

"Ha! Indeed," came Jim's response from upstairs, completely unaware of the threat contained within Mary's sentence, albeit meant as a joke for now.

As Jim melted into the hot bath he heard the front door slam shut as Mary left the house. "Bliss!" he said as he closed his eyes and relaxed, for he had been looking forward to a hot bath since leaving Abu Dhabi airport earlier that morning. He had almost drifted off to sleep when he became aware of a presence in the bathroom. Without opening his eyes he said dismissively, "Have you missed me Dick?"

Dick Tallboys stood at the doorway looking at Jim's naked body, and in particular his penis which suddenly appeared in the middle of the bath as the bubbles departed the area momentarily.

"Pissing useless you are lad."

Jim opened his eyes and sat up as if about to speak but Dick had his hand up to stop him.

"That soft cock of yours should be pumping in and out of Mary Ecklethwaite at this very moment, and yet here you are fannying around in a bubble bath."

"I beg your pardon?" replied a visibly shocked Jim, but Dick was on a mission.

"You got away with it by the skin of your teeth these past two weeks. You sent her off unfulfilled before the holiday, and yet she looked after your veg better than any wife could have been expected to do. Played an absolute blinder the kid has. I've not seen veg looking that good in this garden since I was in my prime twenty years ago. And what does she get in return when you get back? A second rate dinner in the Dog & Gun, a pat on the back and no doubt some tacky ornament from a kasbah."

"It's a very expensive bracelet actually," Jim protested.

"You could bring her some gold, frankincense and fucking myrhh for all that lass cares Jim, tell her all night that she means the World to you, but all she really wants to feel and hear is the sound of your balls banging against her arse."

Jim rolled his eyes and huffed his cheeks out as if bored at this persistent line of questioning. "How wonderfully descriptive. But we have an understanding and I'm not the sort of person who uses sex to gain favours. And I'm certain Mary is not the type of girl who would accept them without proper friendship as a foundation. Now if you'll excuse me, can you bugger off and let me finish my bath?"

"Aye alright. But you're wrong about her. She has deep feelings for you Sunshine, and the way her father has been acting the past couple of weeks you need to make sure you don't upset her between now and Show day."

"I shall endeavour to reward her properly for her efforts, you just leave it with me," said Jim, sliding back into the bath and closing his eyes.

"Whatever," replied Dick, disdain apparent in his voice as he descended the stairs, before shouting back, "Oh and by the way. She's been snooping around in your bedroom!"

Jim's eyes opened immediately, the shock of what he had just heard causing him to lose equilibrium in the bath tub, water cascading over the side as he slid around trying to regain his balance. With control reclaimed, Jim sat up in the bath on his arms behind him and contemplated this last piece of news. Perhaps Dick was right. He would need to tread very carefully over the next few weeks he thought to himself.

SIXTEEN

<u>Jim thanks Mary....</u>

Just before eight o'clock Jim left his house and headed in the direction of Mary's. In the two or three minutes it took him to walk the distance Jim had made a few decisions and determined to carry them out without much further ado. Mary was waiting at the top of her road for him as promised, and as was usual. Jim spoke first.

"Hi Mary. You look stunning. Are you hungry?"

Before Mary could reply Jim had planted a kiss full square onto Mary's lips, embracing her with such unaccustomed gusto that she was taken completely by surprise.

"Mmm. Very hungry. Do you feel better now you've had a nice hot bath?"

"Much better thank you," enthused Jim, "and I had a proper stroll around the garden before I came out. I can't believe how well you've done. I really do owe you a huge amount so I don't want you holding back tonight, you order whatever you fancy okay?"

Whatever she fancied? Mary thought about this as they strolled along towards the Dog & Gun, her arm linked into his with Jim's hand on top of hers giving her an extra feeling of tenderness towards him. What she really fancied had been lying in the bath in Peony Cottage half an hour ago, but spending a couple of hours in the company of the same over a nice meal and a few drinks would be decent enough compensation for now. And with the mood that Jim appeared to be in there was no telling how the night might end she was thinking. Mary was feeling as happy as she could remember for a long, long time as she skipped along beside the man she was starting to fall desperately in love with.

The pub was exceedingly quiet, which Bob Dillage was quick to explain was due to the holiday season still affecting business, many of the villagers having gone away. A recently published set of reports on a travel website giving the Dog & Gun one star out of five and heralding the landlord as the most inadequate, ignorant and rude proprietor since Basil

Fawlty probably had not helped either, a bus load of travellers being quick to post a series of scathing messages after a stop-off from a seaside daytrip had found Bob in a very reluctant mood to work any harder than usual to provide them all with victuals.

Jim ushered Mary to their usual table in the hidden corner of the lounge away from prying eyes, and as usual, much to the annoyance of the landlord. Taking her chair and making sure she was comfortable Jim approached the bar to get a menu and some drinks.

"Good holiday Jimbo?" the publican asked.

"Yes, excellent thank you Bobbo. Good to be back though." Jim replied.

"Bet you've missed seeing those lovely big jugs of hers though eh?" Dillage suggested, nodding his head in the direction of Mary as he poured their drinks.

"You're all obsessed with sex in this village aren't you Bob? You obviously can't be getting any old boy," hissed Jim as he perused the menu, turning his back on him as he did so. "Bring those over when they're poured Bob. Many thanks."

The landlord had taken Jim on and lost out yet again, and he stared at Jim's back in hatred. "Cunt!" he said to himself, his evening having now taken a turn for the worse that he would struggle to get back on track for the rest of the night.

"Here you go Mary," said Jim offering her a menu. "So then, Molly is all poised is she?"

"Yes," she replied, "I might meet up with her soon for a girly few hours so I'll know more then. Her mind is set so there's no going back. Pete's brother went round last week for one of the children's birthday party. I popped in briefly myself. He's a bit of a looker I must say, very smart and has done very well for himself so she'll be well cared for. He seemed very attentive to Mary and Pete never noticed at all."

"What about her?" Jim asked, nodding in the direction of Deirdre Dillage who could be heard in the bar area, her distinctive screeching voice pervading the pub's ambience.

"Oh she'll get her comeuppance one day. Now, enough of village gossip, I want to hear all about your trip," asked Mary, adding forcefully, "from start to finish!"

Jim paused as Bob Dillage delivered the drinks to their table. "You lovebirds ready to order your meals yet?"

"A few more minutes I think Bob," replied Jim. "I'll give you a nudge when we're ready."

"I bet you fucking will," mumbled the further annoyed landlord to himself whilst walking away.

"Well then, my trip," continued Jim. "There was a bit of work involved. A couple of projects I'd left behind before they were completed needed paperwork signing off. Just a bit of inspection, checking all the loadings, liaising with the architects, that sort of thing so I was tied up for about three days. As soon as the Sheik heard I was in town he insisted I visit him socially so that took up another day. You simply don't turn the Sheik down. And then I spent the rest of the holiday with my old colleagues and their families and did a bit of sightseeing that I didn't get chance to do when I was working there."

"You must have got some time to relax as you're nice and brown," Mary suggested.

"Oh I've never been one for lying around sunbathing. You just tend to get caught by the sun anyway walking around in forty degree heat."

Mary waited for more information to be divulged, but soon realised a little awkwardly that Jim appeared to have finished his story. Jim clicked his fingers in Bob's direction, who in turn came back to their table with a little sarcastic curtsy that Jim did not notice but Mary did.

"You first Mary. What are you having?" said Jim

"I'll have the soup to start please Bob, followed by the fillet steak, medium-rare."

Bob duly noted Mary's choice in his notepad. "And for your Lordship?"

Jim did not bat an eyelid at the landlord's latest and futile attempt to rile him. "I'll have the mushrooms to start and pork scallops for mains please Bob. And a bottle of decent champagne if you have any?"

Jim handed the menus back without looking at Bob. A ploy he had learned over the years was that once you had delivered a put down never make eye contact with your opponent, but give attention to something or someone else immediately and leave them to fester. Jim smiled at Mary. Bob Dillage was indeed festering. Mary felt awkward.

As Bob left them alone, no doubt to make the chef's life a misery for a few minutes, Mary remarked "He'll explode at you one of these days you know."

"No doubt he will, but if he does he'll have lost well and truly," replied Jim, continuing, "He should know his place. Why do village landlords somehow think they're the most important person in the village? They only serve a few drinks to paying customers after all."

"Mm, get you Mr. L!" laughed Mary. "I can see why you were so in demand in the desert. I bet you didn't take any messing?"

"I was always a diplomat. You have to be. But every now and again you would often come across a character who tried to make your working life awkward. Dillage is nothing compared to some of the workers I faced up to over the years. Enough of them though. How have you been the past two weeks? You look lovely as always."

Jim's sudden compliment caught Mary by surprise and in mid-sip of her drink.

"Oh, why thank you," she half spluttered. "Well I feel good. Much better now I've got you back of course."

"I have a present for you Mary," Jim said before pulling a small felt bag from his jacket pocket, soon revealed by an eager Mary to be the bracelet that Jim had told Dick Tallboys about.

"Oh it's lovely Jim," beamed Mary. "Thank you so much but you shouldn't have.

"Nonsense," Jim protested. "I don't think a National Vegetable Society champion grower could have looked after my veg any better than you have. It's the very least I owe you. I hope you like it."

"I love it Jim," said Mary, and she leaned across the table and kissed him on the lips, lingering just long enough that Bob Dillage saw them as he bought them their starters.

"Aye, aye, someone's happy!" he teased.

"Well let's hope your food doesn't spoil the mood then?" said Jim quick as a flash, causing Dillage to mutter under his breath yet again as he left them to their food.

Mary giggled at Jim's manner with the landlord, and put the bracelet on before she started eating. "A perfect fit. Just like us!" she said, holding her arm out to admire her new adornment.

Jim smiled a little nervously, for a subject had now been bought to the fore that he knew he would have to broach at some point during the night, albeit a little earlier than he had envisaged. He cleared his throat and started to speak.

"I do like you Mary, I hope you know that? But I'm the sort of fellow who likes to do things properly, and something tells me that you're the sort of girl who expects decent behaviour from a man. I'm not wrong am I?"

"Err, well no, that's quite right," mumbled Mary a little unsure about what Jim was talking about.

"Well that's excellent then," said Jim somewhat triumphantly. "It seems we have an understanding. I can't abide some of the folk around here making certain assumptions about our friendship. We both know what we are and what we want don't we?"

"We certainly do Jim," added Mary assertively, although in her head she was wondering whether their relationship had not somehow just gone back to square one.

"How is your soup Mary?"

"Hot and tasty, just like you!" she replied.

They both laughed and passed the rest of the night enjoying each other's company. Jim felt reassured that he had clarified his situation clearly and precisely and in a manner that Dick Tallboys would approve of, whilst Mary soon forgot his verbal drivel and expected to be in Jim's bed come next morning having spent a very pleasant night being pleasured in every conceivable way and from most of the physically achievable angles. That was, at least, right up until the walk home when Jim stopped at the top of her road, kissed her on her cheek and bid her good night!

SEVENTEEN

D-day minus 7

There was only a week to go before the Show and Jim was now fully occupied, leaving him little time to spend with Mary. Many vegetables intended for the show bench come to grief in the week before a show if they are not looked after properly and Jim was up at the crack of dawn each morning making sure everything was ticking along and no creepy crawlies suddenly appeared to do their worst, or diseases descended from the sky to render his babies ruined.

Mary called round most days but soon got fed up watching Jim fussing over his garden and left him to it. She could not even persuade him to sit down and share a coffee with her. Her father was just as bad if not worse than Jim. One morning she awoke to hear him shouting in the garden and upon looking out of her bedroom window saw him chasing a couple of wood pigeons that were struggling to take off. They had gorged themselves on Harry's cauliflowers so much that they were flapping their wings desperately. A couple of bricks aimed in their direction soon had them taking flight, but Harry then held his head in his hands as one of the bricks landed full square on a bed of beetroot and took several of them clean out of the ground.

After being frustrated again by a lack of attention from Jim she was sat at his kitchen table watching him working outside when she texted Molly Greensleave and asked if she had time for a chat? Whilst she observed Jim crouching down over a bed of radishes Mary's phone beeped.

'Sounds super kiddo. Kids at nursery. See you in 5. Moll'

"Jim, I'm off to see Molly," she shouted out of the open window, grabbing her things as she did so.

"Okay no problem. See you tomorrow?" he replied.

"Yeah no doubt. Love you, bye"

Jim did not reply to Mary's parting words much to her annoyance. She even shocked herself that the 'L' word came out of her mouth anyway, but it had just seemed a natural thing to say at the time. As she walked to

Molly's she was hugely upset with herself at having said it. Molly was already on the doorstep waiting for her as she arrived at her garden gate.

"Hiya chucky, not seen you for few weeks. But then you've had other things to occupy you so I've been hearing," Molly cackled.

Molly Greensleave was a village lass through and through, a qualified hair-stylist who earned a few pounds once Pete was home from work cutting and shaping the hair of many of the village ladies. She looked and sounded honest and earthy. She had mousy brown hair, a slightly freckly face on otherwise perfect milky-white skin and despite the ravages of two difficult child births had maintained the same slim figure that had first attracted Pete to her. She skipped around her kitchen making Mary a cup of tea, all the while making conversation. Mary was keen to know how her elopement plans were coming along.

"All arranged Mary," Molly confirmed. "Mike will come to the show as usual and whilst Pete is busy we'll get the kids and luggage all loaded then I'll tell Pete. I need to do it now whilst the kids are still little or else I'll never do it."

"And Pete has no idea what's about to hit him?" asked Mary.

"None that I know to Mary. I saw his slaggy mistress in the shop the other morning. The way she swans around the place after what she's done to me is galling to say the least. Part of me wants to storm into the pub and play merry hell but I'm better than that. She's done me a favour really cos me and Pete have never really loved each other. We just sort of came together and got married out of desperation I suppose. There wasn't really much choice in the village was there girl?"

Mary's heart heaved at this last point. If Pete had been more of a man and they had both stood up to her father then she would possibly have been married to Pete and not Molly, for in her way she had loved Pete at the time. He was an outsider to the village, moving there with his parents when he was eighteen and a couple of years older than they were. His brother had already started out on his successful career and Molly did not meet him until their wedding day eight years ago. They did not have their children until well into their thirties, more of an afterthought really and in order to appease Molly's dad Ted Grangeworthy who desperately wanted grandchildren. To that day Molly still knew nothing of Mary's and Pete's earlier romance.

"Well good luck to you Molly. I know you've had a miserable time in recent years, but I'll really miss you," Mary said with sadness in her eyes, struggling to fight back the tears that were welling up inside them.

"Hey now come on you, don't cry," Molly pleaded. "It's all starting to turn out well for you too isn't it?"

"You think so?" sobbed Mary.

"Well you tell me. That Mr. Lightfoot seems a right catch. You are going steady aren't you? That's what everyone in the village seems to think anyways."

"Well I think so," said Mary, "but it all gets a bit weird at times."

"What do you mean Mary," asked Molly.

"Well, several times now we've been alone, and.....you know.....there's me expecting things to be taken to the next level.....and......(sob)....nothing ever happens?"

Molly laughed. "You mean you want to be shagged senseless?"

Mary coughed at Molly's bluntness, and then laughed herself. "I suppose I do. I don't want to dry up now do I? I'm not getting any younger am I Molly?"

Mary proceeded to detail several recent instances of Jim Lightfoot's seeming sexual reticence, and related Jim's awkward words from the pub a few nights previously. At the end of it Molly sounded triumphant.

"Aha! He's a keeper Mary, don't you see? He wants to court you properly. He's not out for a cheap shag like most of the men round 'ere. Sex to him is precious. He wants to get to know you first, to cherish you, then it will happen and it will be wonderful."

"Do you really think so Molly?" Mary asked.

"Yes I bloody do," Molly replied, "Your problem is you think life's like one of those trendy novels you keep reading, the ones that keep going in flashbacks so you don't know if you're coming or going, but you get snippets of information about the past. Real life ain't like that. And the way

I see it you have two choices. You either grasp the nettle and tell 'im you want to be screwed, but that might scare him off. And if you can't do that then I have something that might make the waiting a little more bearable."

Molly ran upstairs and after a few moments returned with a plastic carrier bag. "Here. Try this bad boy. Still boxed, never been used. Bought it once when I couldn't bear Pete touching me but never got around to trying it."

Molly handed Mary the carrier bag. Inside was the largest, nobbliest, pinkest vibrator sex toy that Mary had ever seen. The two women laughed like cackling fish wives, Mary wafting the pink wand around like a light sabre.

"At least you've only got a few days to wait for a bit of fun Molly," Mary suddenly suggested. "How long has it been since you and Pete....you know?"

Molly looked puzzled. "Why, last night of course you silly sausage."

Mary's jaw dropped open but no words came out. Molly continued.

"Don't look so shocked girlfriend. Pete may be a monumental bastard but he's also damned good at sex so I've not been denying myself in that department! Don't see why I should. No point in wasting it is there? His brother's equally well-endowed but isn't as skilful. Yet! I'll soon have him up to speed though. And if he can't satisfy me proper like, then I'll just nip back to Pete from time to time for a quickie."

"MOLLY!" squealed Mary. "You are awful!"

As the two women laughed loudly and carried on their man talk, they didn't notice a small red sports car flashing past the kitchen window. Deirdre Dillage had swiftly left the pub two minutes previously having told her husband that she was on her way to the wholesalers, leaving Bob no time to inform her he had already been the afternoon before.

"Confounded woman!" he called after her to no avail as her dinky soft top sped out of the inn's courtyard, scattering pea gravel over the bonnet of his large silver Mercedes.

Deirdre was going nowhere near the wholesalers of course. She would eventually pick up the text that Bob was currently sending her and tell him she had got all the way to Tithampton before she read it, giving him grief for not telling her sooner so that she did not have a wasted journey, for she knew full well that Bob had already been the day before. Instead she intended to ambush Pete Greensleave somewhere and find out once and for all what game he thought he was playing. She also wanted to discover the name of the woman he was now seeing and find out what she had that Deidre did not.

Ever since the Show committee meeting when Pete had surprised everyone by saying he would not be helping on the outside bar this year Deirdre had been growing ever more frantic about their diminishing relationship. For several years she had merely needed to send him a text demanding a meeting, usually in some dusty storage shed on his boss's land somewhere that Pete had access to, and Deirdre would have been sufficiently fulfilled and satisfied for a few days. But Pete had not replied to any of her texts since that night and he had always made sure he was in company at the pub so that she was unable to get him on his own. If he would not go to her then she had decided she would go to him. After cruising the country roads around the large farm estate on which Pete worked for half an hour or so, she eventually caught sight of him working alone in the far corner of a field, his head buried in a particularly troublesome tractor engine. He was engrossed in his work and did not notice her as she parked up in a layby and walked along the edge of the field and crept up behind him, putting her arms around his torso before fondling his groin area through his overalls.

"Hello lover. How's my favourite body part?"

Pete stood upright in terror, banging his head on the engine flap of the tractor.

"Fucking hell Deirdre," he screamed, rubbing his head with an oily rag. "Don't do that, it's dangerous when you're working on machinery."

"Ooooh, get you Mr. Nastyknickers," Deirdre protested in mock fashion. "Okay I'm sorry, but no harm done is there? Come on now, you've been avoiding me for weeks and I need my fix. Grounds dry so come on."

Without warning Deirdre lay down beside the tractor and pulled up her skirt, revealing that she wore no underwear and that her previously bushy undercarriage had been completely shaved for the occasion.

"Thought you'd like that," she said noticing the surprise on Pete's face, "gave Pussy a niiiiice trim for you."

"Get up Deirdre," Pete ordered. "I'm not doing that anymore. I love Molly and I'm trying to make a go of things with her again. I'm sorry."

"You're sorry?" Deirdre screeched. "You're fucking sorry? Who the fuck is she? I know you're having someone else. The gossip's all around the pub."

Pete was genuinely clueless about Deirdre's accusation, the one which Jimmy Duggan had made up quickly in order to divert her inquisitive husband.

"I don't know what you're talking about Deirdre. There is only Molly. You and me were a mistake, one I'm not gonna make no more. So please, get up and just leave."

"But I love you darling," Deirdre pleaded unexpectedly, causing Pete to look around from the engine he had started to work on again. "I need you. Please don't finish us. I only need your cock once a week. Twice tops. I won't make any trouble for you darling, I promise."

Pete took a deep breath. He had been dreading this moment ever since the meeting in the village hall. "It's not going to happen anymore Deirdre so please don't make this any 'arder."

"You agricultural piece of shit," Deirdre spat as she got to her feet. "You're going to fucking regret this. I'll tell Molly. In fact I'm going to drive round to your house this instant."

Pete sighed lengthily. "You must do what you must do Deirdre. But if you do then I dare say Bob will kick you out and you'll be homeless. Whatever. I'll still want nothing more to do with you so just get on with it if you must. You'll just be ruining several lives unnecessarily."

He turned away from her again and continued working on the engine as Deirdre stood rooted to the spot, not knowing what her next move might be. She had banked everything on Pete giving in to her threat to tell Molly, and when he did not cave in as expected she had nowhere else to manoeuvre. He had indeed grown some balls at last. And he was absolutely right. To tell Molly would risk everything for her as well. She could not risk Bob finding out and casting her out, for she enjoyed her lavish lifestyle, although she was blissfully unaware that virtually the whole village knew of their affair. Most had heard it. A select and unlucky few had even been unfortunate enough to witness it.

Deirdre huffed and stomped off back along the field edge to her car, embarrassed at having exposed herself so physically and emotionally to Pete. She was angry and determined to gain some level of revenge against him somehow. For now though she was at a disadvantage and needed to compose her feelings and so she sat in her car for several moments as her rage subsided. She caught a glimpse of herself in the mirror. It was as if all of a sudden the Laws of Nature had crept up on her and completely overtaken her. She realised she was old. Pete had grown repulsed by her perhaps? For a while she thought that she could not blame him, and that she could easily settle back into domestic comfort and be a good wife to Bob again. That was until she glanced back into the corner of the field and saw Pete chatting cheerfully over the fence to Jane Tallboys who had just happened to cycle past.

"You arrogant little fucker," Deirdre spat.

Back in the village Mary had left Molly's, cheerfully carrying the electronic phallus that potentially offered some alternative to her ongoing frustration in a carrier bag. She felt better for having gone to visit her oldest friend, and her feelings for Jim had certainly been put into some sort of perspective as a result. He was a good man she thought, one that she would do well to wait for, which is indeed what she intended to do.

As she reached her own garden gate just a few yards away, Deirdre's vehicle came spinning around the corner like a rally car. Instinctively Mary waved but the landlady had a focussed face like thunder and did not notice her. As she sped away Mary gave a wry smile as she observed her back disappearing from view.

"You'd best get all that straw out of your hair and cardigan before Bob sees it," she laughed.

EIGHTEEN

The Tithampton Terror

"Bilkin!" screamed the Tithampton County Gazette's editor, Mike Jeffers, a grizzled old hack who should have retired years ago, "in 'ere now."

Daryl Bilkin, or Da, or even Daz as he preferred to be called, hurried in from his desk through the fug of smoke in Mike Jeffers' office for he was no advocate of the workplace smoking ban and had continued to light up defiantly, despite the regular protestations of his workforce.

"Yes boss?" Bilkin asked.

"You got anywhere yet on that veg theft story?" Jeffers never even looked up from that week's issue that he was carefully proof reading, no doubt missing as usual the multitude of spelling and grammar errors that Bilkin and his colleagues were prone to.

"It's the big show in Allaways this weekend gaffer so I'll be seeking out more facts then," Bilkin informed him.

"Facts?" shouted Jeffers, his face still buried in a large magnifying glass supported on a stand, "since when 'ave we been worried about facts? Get down to Moor Lane allotments and interview some of those sods what had stuff nicked this week. And find out a name. They must suspect someone."

"What do you want me to do if they give me a name then guv?" asked an increasingly bemused Bilkin.

"For fuck's sake, call yersen a journalist? Get to the guy's 'ouse or 'lotment and make a nuisance of yersel! Do some digging, and make 'em crack. This story's got legs I'm sure o'it. Now fuck off."

Daryl Bilkin stopped off at his desk on his way out to collect his notebook and a couple of pens, quickly firing off an email to his wife saying he would be home late. As he did so he glanced at a sun faded certificate in a frame which was hanging on the wall in front of his desk, presented to him during an awards night at a previous employer, a newspaper in Birmingham some fifteen years before, when he was named best up and coming journalist for a report he had done on a local street gang. As Daryl

Bilkin was driving the couple of miles from the Gazette's ramshackle offices to the aforementioned allotments he wondered how on Earth he had fallen so low. He had ambitions to be a top reporter on a National daily, covering important stories, interviewing major political figures and gaining important awards for services to cutting edge journalism. But here he was in some backwater town writing lightweight stories about disappearing vegetables. He had aimed for much more than this since leaving college twenty years before, but unfortunately for Daryl Bilkin, successive editors on the various publications he had worked on never quite had the heart to tell him he was useless at writing, and even worse at spelling, grammar and constructing a remotely interesting sentence. In fact, the aforementioned award had been comprehensively rewritten by his then editor who had taken a shine to him, to the extent that the finished article bore no resemblance to his original story. His latest editor would have told him in no uncertain terms about his many shortcomings if his own eyesight had not been failing, and anyway Jeffers just wanted to order him around and get him covering all the crap jobs that no-one else wanted to do.

In Daryl Bilkin's many pieces on life around the town over the last few years, he had often given himself the nickname of 'The Tithampton Terrier', as if he was hell-bent on sniffing out the latest scandal and bringing it to the attention of the public. In the pubs, homes and businesses of the town and surrounding villages however, he was known rather as the 'Tithampton Terror' for his habit of spelling people's names completely wrong, for using grammar that was so bad on occasions it made no sense whatsoever and for getting his facts so entirely wide of the mark the paper was forever having to publish apologies in the following week's edition. Daryl actually always intended to tell the truth, and always had his head in his pocket book whenever he was interviewing anyone. The problem was that he was so incompetent he either did not write down what he heard or else he wrote down what he thought he had heard and deemed that good enough.

Arriving at Moor Lane Allotments in Tithampton, Bilkin parked up on the grass verge outside the complex and jumped over the waist height metal gates that were locked, only allotment holders having a key in order to be able to drive through. Bilkin immediately noted how easy it thus was to gain access for felonious purposes, and how the vegetable thief would not have had much of a barrier to stop him in his evil tracks. He had not walked ten paces along the track when a voice boomed out from somewhere across the expanse of allotments.

"STOP RIGHT WHERE YOU ARE YOUNG MAN!"

Bilkin stood dead still and nervously scanned the grounds for the origin of the voice. After a few moments a man appeared about fifty yards in front of him on the lane and started to walk towards him, a garden fork poised menacingly in his hands. As he approached him, Bilkin could see that the man, although quite large in stature, was probably well into his eighties and quite unsteady on his legs.

"Who are you and what d'you want?" ordered the old man.

"Good afternoon sir, my names Bilkin, Daryl Bilkin, and I'm a reporter for the local Gazette. I was wondering if there's anyone I might be able to talk to about these vegetable thefts you've suffered recently? As you may know, Croft Road allotments had similar spate of thefts a few nights ago. You may have seen my report in last week's edition?"

Daryl waited nervously as the old man surveyed him suspiciously. "Then ye'd best come this way young'un," answered the elder. "There are armchairs in the trading shed."

Bilkin followed the old man obediently a hundred yards down the track where they turned left and walked another hundred yards or so to a ramshackle wooden building. Inside several men and women were sat around tables chattering away over tea and biscuits, but the talking stopped abruptly as soon as their fellow plot holder walked in with the stranger.

"This be that reporter from t'Gazette who's vowed to solve the mystery of the vegetable thief," Bilkin's escort announced.

"There aint no mystery though is there Harold?" piped up a voice from the group of people. "Everyone in't county knows who it is."

Daryl studied the man making the accusations for several moments. He was perhaps in his late sixties, his thinning black hair brylcreemed into the faintest excuse of a rock and roll quiff, his round face peering through his thick rimmed glasses giving him the air of a rotund comedy caricature from the television. Daryl's prolonged gaze eventually forced the man to introduce himself.

"I'm Tom, site chairman. You've met Harold already our longest serving resident." Tom beckoned Daryl to a chair. "What can we do for you then?"

"Well now, it's an unusual story, and one I'd like to get to the bottom of." Bilkin could almost feel the warm arm of congratulations from his editor in the pub that night over a pint, something they were both quite partial to after a long day chasing stories and getting them wrong. "You say you know who the culprit is? I'd be very interested to know who that was."

"Well it's Ecklethwaite at Allaways isn't it," stated Tom suddenly, "he's a crook. Been doing it for decades he has. Always manages to avoid detection though. Dunno how he does it for he's hardly the build of a cat burglar."

"And you have proof of this?" Bilkin asked. It was the same name that residents at Croft Road allotments had offered him the week before.

"No proof. But we know it's him," one of the group retorted. Everyone in the county has suffered over the years but he never has. Says he's just vigilant."

"I see," Daryl continued, his heart sinking, "I'm afraid without proof I can't go around naming him. What have the police done about it?"

"You can't name him but we can," Tom the Chairman spluttered. "And we have done, many times. To his face an'all. Never seems to bother him though. And as for the police, don't make me laugh, those useless buggers are no help nor use to us. They just see it as a joke. We took to taking turns staying on the site overnight one year but, well, none of us are getting any younger and it's a big site. Those that didn't fall asleep on the job got the 'eeby-jeebies and sat like quivering wrecks in the hut all night without venturing out."

"Have you not got any security cameras at all?" Bilkin asked helpfully.

"Oh we got cameras all right," Tom explained. "And we've got footage of the fellow in the act. But he goes to great lengths to ensure his face can't be seen, wearing black clothes and a balaclava, and he wears gloves so he don't leave no fingerprints. It's so obviously Ecklethwaite, you can tell it by his gait, but the police reckon the evidence is....what's the word...in'unmissible?

"Yes, that's the word," Bilkin confirmed authoritatively, all the while scribbling away furiously in his notebook. "Look you've all been very helpful. I think I'm going to pay this chap a visit, see if I can't get him to crack, or at least make him see the error of his ways."

"Pah!" retorted Harold, the old man who had escorted Bilkin to the shed. "I've known that old rogue for over forty years. Some of the roughest sorts in the county have threatened him over the years and he aint stopped. What makes you think you can succeed where they failed?"

"Never underestimate the power of the pen!" was all Bilkin would say.

***

Twenty five minutes after leaving Moor Lane allotments Bilkin was parked outside Harry Ecklethwaite's house. As was his usual method, he sat for ten minutes or so surveying the area and watching for any local comings and goings to get a feel for the neighbourhood, a trick he had acquired over the years and which he felt was a must do requirement for the best cutting edge journalism. He saw Mary leave the house and wander up the street for she was meeting Jim at the end of the road for their nightly routine of a walk to the pub. Bilkin's eyes lit up when he saw her. She was attractive, very attractive, and looked confident. From his research he knew Ecklethwaite had a daughter but had not expected her to look like that. He watched her walk away from him with particular interest in her shapely rear view which he felt suited the blue dress she was wearing perfectly.

Harry Ecklethwaite himself then appeared on the doorstep, his neck craning upwards over the hedges, but he did not notice Bilkin in his car. Harry was trying to see if Mary was meeting Jim Lightfoot, for he had heard conflicting evidence and reports in the last few days that Mary and Jim were a couple, and he did not know what to believe. At that moment Bill Grudge wandered down the street on the opposite side of the road, saw Harry and waved over at him cheerfully. Harry smiled and waved back out of habit, and quickly retreated inside as he did not particularly want to become involved in a conversation with him, but not before George had also shuffled by and managed to raise his trilby hat to him reverently.

Bilkin remained in his car watching with interest. Far from being the miserable outcast in the picture he had painted in his mind, Harry Ecklethwaite appeared to be a well-liked figure. At that moment there was a tap on his car door window and he looked up to see a very attractive blond haired girl looking down at him, and she had a black Alsation on a lead. Bilkin wound down his window.

"Excuse the intrusion, but we have a neighbourhood watch system around here and I've noticed you've been there for quite a while, so can I help you?" asked Jane Tallboys, struggling to hold her dog which was straining on the leash trying to jump up at the car's occupant.

"No, errrr, yes, errrr, no thank you. I'm just popping in to see Mr. Ecklthwaite but I was a little early so I was merely waiting a while," Bilkin lied. "I'm a reporter from The Gazette."

Jane appeared to be reassured. "Is it to do with the Show at the weekend?"

"That's right," confirmed Bilkin. "Do you know Mr. Ecklethwaite then? What's he like?"

"Oh Harry's a wonderful human being. One of the absolute best," Jane replied as she was walking away.

Bilkin got out of his car now that he felt Jane's hound was at a safe distance. "Thanks for your help," he called after her. He had completely failed to notice the overwhelming dose of sarcasm in Jane's voice.

***

"Yes, yes, come in lad. Take a seat. Would you like a cup of tea? A slice of cake? Freshly made by my lovely daughter less than an hour ago."

Bilkin was totally taken aback by Harry Ecklethwaite's welcome. It was a far cry from what he had been expecting when he knocked on the door and explained he was from The Gazette. Perhaps everyone was wrong about him for all he had witnessed and heard so far was respect and praise for the man.

"Tea would be lovely, thank you."

"Well now, this is nice," said Harry in his grandest sounding voice as he flicked the switch of the kettle. "Our little show being in The Gazette will put this wonderful village on the map I dare say. I've been involved for a long time as you've no doubt heard. We all work very hard to make a success of it and we're hoping the one hundredth will surpass all previous shows."

Bilkin observed Harry as he made the tea. He was not at all scruffy as he had been lead to believe, in fact he was very smart in a pressed white shirt and dark trousers, a loosened tie around his neck and the jacket from the suit over the back of one of the chairs. He was clean shaven, his hair combed and slicked back neatly. Surely there was no way this dapper gentleman could possibly be responsible for clambering over fences in the dead of night to sabotage a few vegetables he was thinking to himself.

"Now then young man, what can I do for you?" Harry asked Bilkin as he slid his tea and cake across the table to him.

Bilkin had been nonplussed by Harry's hospitality and instead of interrogating him on his possible involvement in the recent spate of vegetable thefts, found himself interviewing him on his commitment to the Show, what it meant to him and his recent history as undefeated champion of many years standing. He found himself being captivated by this local character, and marvelled at some of the vegetables in Harry's garden during a tour of it after they had finished their drinks. Harry got out his old photo albums and showed the reporter snap after snap of his many triumphs, Harry holding aloft the Cock Cup, or next to one of his large marrows. By the time he left, Bilkin was looking forward to covering the Show at the weekend and, when Harry offered to give him some guidance, even thought he might try growing a few vegetables himself next year.

***

"So your dad's been to a funeral today then Mary?" asked Jim Lightfoot as they settled into their usual seats in the Dog & Gun.

"That's right," said Mary, "I don't know why though, it was a chap he never liked, from Sopping-on-Cock. Someone who used to enter some nice vegetables at the Show. He came back ridiculously happy knowing he was definitely dead and therefore wouldn't be entering anything on

Saturday and potentially taking points off him. He's incorrigible. I must say he did look very smart in his suit though."

NINETEEN

Anticipation

It was the Thursday evening before the show and Bill Grudge was nervously pacing the entrance lobby to the village hall awaiting the appearance of all his show helpers. He had asked them to be there for 7.30pm prompt, so that they could all run through the timetable for the day's activities and iron out any last minute glitches, and with only five minutes to go nobody had yet showed up so he was starting to get very nervous.

Over at the Ecklethwaites' house Harry was doing a last minute check of his garden, the show schedule in his hand, pacing up and down ticking each of the class numbers he intended to enter. He was feeling smug, confident that he would emerge triumphant yet again due to a combination of his own high quality produce and the fact that he had gone to great pains to destroy the best that any of his closest rivals might be able to throw at him.

"Right then Harry," he said to himself, "all looking good my old son. Just need to get all this lot lifted and prepared then loaded up tomorrow evening for an early rise Saturday morning. Job's a good'un. As always!"

With that Harry crept around a large and rambling marrow plant that had completely swamped a whole corner of the garden. Lifting up some foliage he peered underneath at a large marrow fruit lying on a wooden pallet, still attached to the plant and covered in blankets to keep it warm at night in order to extract every last possible ounce of weight out of it.

"Sleep well my baby. You'll be in the Gazette come Monday," he said gently patting the knobbly, dark-green monster like it was a sleeping child.

In the upstairs front bedroom Mary sat up from her bed gasping and bathed in sweat.

"Oh my word," she said as she pulled something from under her skirt, holding it up to examine it closely. It was the pink vibrator that Molly had given her the day before. "You beauty. Who needs a man when a woman has you to help her out? And you don't talk non-stop about vegetables either do you? My God, thank you Molly!"

She glanced at the alarm clock by her bed and stood up quickly, grabbing a pair of knickers from the floor and pirouetting awkwardly as she tried to put them on, her legs still wobbling from the magnitude of the orgasm she had just given herself.

"Best get a move on. Bill will be waiting for everyone," she thought to herself although sorely tempted to lie back down and give her pink persuader another workout. In the end she smiled, bit her lip, closed her eyes and collapsed back onto the bed. "Another five minutes won't make any difference."

At the village hall people had started to arrive at last, much to Bill Grudge's immense relief, Jim Lightfoot and Jane Tallboys among them. Jim searched the group of people for Mary's familiar face but soon realised she was not there, and Jane Tallboys had already spotted her chance to make another move on him. Fresh from performing oral sex on Pete Greensleave just after Deirdre had seen them chatting she had already decided to move on to her next conquest having concluded, with some considerable regret, that she would not be having full sex with him due to the outrageous size of his penis. Whilst curvaceous and busty, Jane was nevertheless quite small in height and she was afraid of serious internal damage if Pete's mammoth member penetrated her.

Pete Greensleave had also arrived and was trying to get Jane's attention. As yet he had no idea the snatched blow job was all he was ever going to get out of her, but once again his brains had well and truly dumped themselves in his genitals. If there was any doubt Molly was not about to make the right decision his actions of recent days would have made her mind up for good if she ever found out, and in the fullness of time she no doubt would have done had she stayed with him.

"Are you all ready for a dunking or two on Saturday then Jim?" Jane asked. "Weather forecast is good so it'll be bathing cozzies for us two. I tried mine on earlier. Look." Jane pulled out her mobile phone to show Jim a photo she had taken of herself in the mirror that afternoon. "What do you think?"

Jim kept his cool. "That should go down very well with the punters Jane. Pete, here have a look at this!"

Before Jane could respond Jim had grabbed the phone off her and was showing Pete the photo of a scantily clad Jane Tallboys, much to her horror.

"Beautiful, don't you think Jim?" Pete said admiringly, which went some way to calming Jane's temper somewhat. However, this was not a question Jim wanted to answer particularly, for fear of giving Jane any encouragement whatsoever, so he collected his thoughts before answering, but the best he could muster was;

"Yes indeed, if only I was thirty years younger."

"Oh Jim, you silly sausage. Don't you go putting yourself down like that. I'm quite partial to the older man actually if you ever feel like reliving your youth!" she said, running a finger up his chest and tickling him seductively under his chin, totally ignoring Pete Greensleave who heard everything.

Pete looked downtrodden as he caught Jim's eye who just looked severely embarrassed. Luckily for Jim, Bill Grudge chose that moment to clap his hands and call for order, sending all the attendees scurrying for chairs. Jim managed to grab an end seat next to Mrs. Dibble, thus escaping Jane's clutches for now.

"Thanks for coming ladies and gentleman. I think most of the important people are here, but I'll just hang on a few more minutes for any late comers," Bill announced to a few groans from people who wanted to get it over with so they could go to the pub or back home for the evening's television.

As the sound of conversation started up again, Jim leaned in to Mrs. Dibble. "Are you well?"

"Very well thank you Jim," Mrs. Dibble replied. "I'm really looking forward to the Show. It should be the best one yet."

Jim thought to himself how Mrs. Dibble was very much the heartbeat and backbone of the village, typically British, somewhat reserved but stoical and very much WI. "I hope you're right Mrs. Dibble. It will be my first and it's the sort of thing I moved back to Britain for."

Mrs. Dibble was holding a writing pad and a pen in her lap and at that moment the pen became detached from the pad and fell to the floor. "Oh dash it," she cursed and leaned downwards to retrieve it. As she did so her blouse momentarily rode up from her trouser belt slightly, and Jim was highly surprised to catch a fleeting sight of a tattoo on her lower back. It looked like a cat or something similar in the quick flash that Jim was afforded, and he could just about discern the letters S-U-Z before she recovered the offending pen and sat upright again.

Jim mused for several moments at this highly unexpected turn of events and wondered whether to raise the subject with her. He was not against tattooing personally, but the sweet and sedate Mrs. Dibble was the last person he expected to have one. In the end he decided against mentioning it, assuming it may have been a pet cat she must have once had. As Bill Grudge stood up again Jim turned to glance at the door in the hope Mary was one of the aforementioned latecomers, but he only succeeded in catching the eye of Jane Tallboys sat four rows behind him and who now smiled and waved at him seductively.

The next hour went on interminably for most of the attending members as Bill Grudge went into great detail about the impending Saturday's arrangements. Most of them had been doing the Show for many years, and knew exactly what they had to do, where they had to be and when, but it never stopped the officious Grudge double checking that everyone was working from the same task sheet. The biggest problem was that the vicar had still not located the gazebos he had been asked to look for at the last meeting in June, so Bill and Ted Grangeworthy agreed to accompany him back to the church after the meeting to try and locate them. The lack of these critical pieces of equipment was making Bill very irritable indeed.

"Lord preserve us vicar, they must be there somewhere," he had lamented as soon as Reverend Arsley had owned up. Other than that there were no other problems and the meeting was dismissed just before 8.45pm, although Bill was still barking orders at everyone as they vacated the hall.

As he stepped outside Jim pondered whether to pop across to the Dog & Gun or get back to Peony Cottage for an early night. He would have a long day tomorrow so the second option won the day. Before he had set foot for home, Jane Tallboys appeared beside him and linked arms. "Goin' my way handsome?"

"Err, yes I guess so," was all Jim could offer in return and before he knew it Jane was dragging him off.

Behind them Ted Grangeworthy was watching them walk away and noticed Pete Greensleave doing the same. "Doesn't seem fair does it Pete. That bloke's fighting 'em off these days eh?" Ted was still unaware of Pete's philandering ways and also his daughter's plans to leave Pete in a couple of days' time.

Pete was just about to reply when he noticed Deirdre Dillage was about to leave the building, and not wishing to be engaged in another argument with her quickly headed off home himself, head bowed at how stupid he had been yet again.

Jane clung on to Jim's arm with increasing vigour as they strolled along, to the point that Jim was starting to wonder how on Earth he might possibly extricate himself from her. She lived in a slightly different direction to him and this would necessitate a short detour to walk her home if he was to do the noble thing, which he really felt he should. But on the other hand he had seen Jane walking on her own after dark before so why should he start escorting her now? As he was pondering his options the unmistakeably buxom figure of Mary came walking towards them.

"Hi guys," she said cheerfully, still flush with the excitement of several climaxes, oblivious to the fact that Jane Tallboys appeared to be staking a claim to her man, or the imploring looks of Jim who was hoping she might suggest a nightcap in the pub, anything that would mean he could escape Jane's vice-like clutches. "Did I miss much? I got a bit bogged down in something and couldn't get away."

"Not a lot Mary," Jane replied. "This nice fella was just walking me home, weren't you Jim?"

"Jolly good," said Mary cheerfully, "well I may as well go back home then if there's nothing I need to know. I was going to find Bill and apologise for missing the meeting but what do you need to know about running a bric-a-brac stall after all hey?

And with that she kissed both Jim and Jane on the cheek and bid them good night. Just for once Jim had hoped that she might get a fit of jealousy and link into Jim's other arm, but instead she turned tail and headed back home. The allure of Perky, the name she had given to her new best inanimate friend, was proving too enticing. Jim stood motionless with his new pet limpet, wondering whether to call Mary back and suggest a nightcap at Peony Cottage, but figured that would be just giving himself double trouble.

Jane could not believe her luck. After the annual day trip she had felt Jim and Mary's relationship was coming to an end but then she had watched Mary coming and going to Peony Cottage every day during Jim's recent holiday and realised she was not about to give up on him too easily.

"My, looks like you've been deserted Jim," she said suggestively.

Jim was panic-stricken and didn't know what to say, so Jane took the initiative.

"Fancy coming back to mine for a nightcap?"

Jim knew that to set one foot inside Jane's flat would be dangerous, and that he needed an excuse quickly. He had no doubt that she wanted to have sex with him, and that in all probability it would be quite magnificent if her local reputation was anything to go by, but Jim was old and wise enough to realise it would cause more trouble for him in the long term. It was still quite early so he could not really play the fatigue card. He really was in quite a pickle, but just as he was about to dribble out a pathetic acquiescence the voice of Ralph Chubb came to his rescue.

"Hallo Jim. Wonder if I might grab a few minutes of your time?" the shopkeeper called from across the road. He was carrying a large sack that appeared to be bulging with items.

"Oh, yes no problem Ralph," replied Jim, relief coursing through his veins. "Sorry Jane, I'd best see what he wants. I'll see you at the show. Night."

Jane watched the back of Jim walking away from her and across the road with a mixture of amazement and sympathy. "Bless him," she thought to herself. "He's shy." It made her doubly determined to succeed at a later date however and she started to walk home, swinging her bag in her hand. "I'll have you before too long Mr. Lightfoot."

Jim meanwhile felt like kissing Ralph Chubb. "What can I do for you my dear man?" he asked the shopkeeper.

"Got a load of stuff here for you that you may find useful on Saturday," Ralph offered.

Jim took the bag from him. Inside were various lengths of black cloth, pieces of wooden board, dishes and bags of something Jim was unable to discern. "What is it all?" Jim asked.

"Look Jim," Ralph continued. "I know you've got some good stuff for the Show, don't ask me how I know, but I do. Have you considered how you're going to display it all?

"Well, I assume you just plonk it on the benches in the appropriate section don't you?" Jim answered quizzically.

Ralph shook his head. "No, no, no Jim, trust me you'll need to display it on various boards, rings, trays of sand all carefully made and fit for purpose, like the ones in this bag here. It's what Harry will be doing."

"Ah. Heck!" said Jim worriedly. "I hadn't really given it any thought, but now you come to mention it I do remember my granddad doing similar things when he used to show his veg many years ago. I'd best get into my shed tomorrow and get producing then. Can I borrow all of these as a guide then please Ralph?" he asked pointing to the items in the sack."I'll let you have them back."

"I can do better than that Jim. I've been trying for years to beat that old bugger and never come close. I know you can do it and I would like you to have these," said Ralph offering Jim the sack of paraphernalia.

"Wow, if you're sure. That would be great," said Jim.

Ralph was not finished though. "And how are you gonna transport all your stuff to the village green? You don't own a car do you Jim?"

"Well no I don't, I was going to put it in my wheelbarrow and make four or five trips," Jim stated.

"NOOO!" Ralph shouted. "They'll get damaged. You can borrow my car for the task. Much safer."

"I really don't know what to say Ralph."

Ralph Chubb's features narrowed and became serious looking. "Don't say anything. Just make sure you beat that bastard. You can buy me a drink when you do."

TWENTY

Bingo night

It was the evening before Show day. The village green had been transformed from a bare expanse of verdant sward to a veritable arcade of marquees, fairground attractions, vintage cars and various stalls. At the eleventh hour the vicar had managed to locate the gazebos in time for a quick clean before they were thrown together and filled with bric-a-brac, hook-a-duck, splat-a-rat or whatever else they could come up with to try and entice the paying public to part with their hard-earned pennies. Most of the hard work having been completed, many of the villagers had now retired home to prepare their prized vegetables, to bake cakes, label jams or simply to recuperate and recharge their batteries ready for a long day tomorrow.

Some had retired to the Dog & Gun, for Friday night before Show day was always bingo night in the pub, as the Show organisers like Bill Grudge, John Simmons and several others relaxed after a hard day lugging trestles and hauling guy ropes. For many years Lady Belton herself had partaken of a book of bingo tickets or two, shouting 'House' with surprising force when her numbers came up one year. This year was no exception as Harrison helped her into a seat next to Mrs. Dibble and Jane Tallboys, before ordering her a small sherry at the bar.

As the pub filled up with customers prior to the first game at 9pm prompt, Bill Grudge could not help himself but talk final arrangements once more with John Simmons and Ted Grangeworthy.

"It's all gone too well so far gents. Something's bound to go wrong tomorrow."

"Behave," John Simmons responded. "Everything's in place and everyone knows their duties. Even the weather forecast looks good. Quite warm and no rain either. It's going to be a good day I can feel it."

"I hope you're right," Grudge worried.

"There's only ever going to be one problem, and it's the perennial one," Ted suggested seriously, "and that is how much Harry Ecklethwaite protests. It's like a storm on the horizon. You know it's coming, you can see it, almost feel it and taste it, but you don't quite know when it'll reach you and how bad it's going to be."

"I reckon this could be the year his head gasket blows," Ralph Chubb proposed audaciously.

"What on Earth do you mean by that?" Bill queried.

"Oh nothing. Just a feeling I've got," Ralph said, and offered no more on the subject. He was still feeling very smug about Jim Lightfoot's prospects and quietly congratulated himself on not having given the game away to Harry on multiple occasions. He had dearly wanted to rub his nose in it during Harry's daily visits to his shop, but had to bite his lip and allow him to gloat as always. Hopefully, he would soon be having twelve months with the shoe very much on the other foot if all went according to plan.

Dave Preston was now going through his sound checks on his microphone.

"One, two, three. Can everyone hear me?"

"Y-E-E-E-S", came a chorus of voices.

"Okay then, five minutes to the start of the first game so get your drinks in, once I've started I won't be finishing for a long, long time," and with that Dave winked knowingly at Deirdre who walked past him at that moment.

Ted Grangeworthy caught Dave Preston's eye and mouthed 'Careful!' at him, for the committee were still nervous about his potential for rude bingo calls, especially with a few beers inside him.

Bob Dillage came over to Bill's and John's table to collect glasses, observing as he did so, "When I looked out over the green just now I noticed the light was on in the horticultural marquee chaps."

"Yes that's fine," said John Simmons. "A few growers, mainly committee members and helpers, asked if they could put some exhibits in tonight to save them time tomorrow. I'll go and switch it off when I leave here."

"Well I hope there aren't any cakes out tonight," Bob Dillage declared. "I heard tell of a fox getting into a marquee out Tithampton way a few years back. Carnage there was next morning. Bet ol'Reynard couldn't believe his luck that night. Free fruit cakes, eggs and bread. Although his teeth wouldn't last long if he bit into one of my Deirdre's Victoria sponges. You could repair a dry stone wall with one of those fucking things."

They all laughed but resolved to check the ties on the marquee door flap as soon as they finished their games of bingo. Dave Preston was now ready with the first game of bingo and called for order.

"Okay folks here we go with the first number. Eyes down. Two fat bitches, eighty eight."

Ted Grangeworthy broke the end of his pencil and glared in the direction of Dave Preston but could not attract his attention, and looked over in the direction of Lady Belton nervously instead. However, he calmed down a bit as Dave announced the next few numbers.

"Dancing Queen, seventeen."

"Quack, quack, twenty two."

"Rise and shine, twenty nine."

"My age, thirty two."

This bought a few hoots of derision from several of Dave's workmates. "Yeah right, about fifteen years ago!" one of them guffawed.

"Barely legal, sweet sixteen."

"Yyyyyaaaaayyyyyy," roared the farming voices, which visibly empowered Dave Preston.

"A meal for two with a Brazilian view, sixty nine."

"I'll flaming well have him later," Ted sneered.

"Don't stress about it," John Simmons calmed, "No harm done it would seem," he said nodding in the direction of Lady Belton.

Bill, Ted and John anxiously looked over at Lady Belton who seemed oblivious to Dave's double entendres and breathed a sigh of relief.

Elsewhere in the county growers were working long into the evening preparing their prized vegetables for entry into the big Show tomorrow. Allaways Show was a prestigious one in the area, even bigger than the one a week later which would be held in the much larger Tithampton itself. Growers of perfect show vegetables are an amusing bunch to those on the outside of the hobby, and are not averse to washing their potatoes in milk to bring out a gleaming skin finish, rubbing talcum powder into their onions to assist ripening to a golden straw colour, or immersing their beetroot overnight in a bucket of salty water to enhance the purple colouring of the washed root. These tricks and many more besides were being practised by a dozen or so growers within the village boundaries and several from outside it, all dreaming of coming back to their exhibit after judging to find a coveted 'red ticket' next to it.

Harry Ecklethwaite had just about finished for the day and was loading the last of his many vegetables, fruit and flowers into his car. Over the years he had made several sturdy boxes to the correct dimensions in which his various crops were now safely nestled, meaning they could not get damaged on the short journey up the road to the Show tomorrow morning. The last of his vegetables to be loaded were his large cabbages which he just about managed to fit into the gap between the boxes and the roof of the boot. A long rack with several compartments was on the back seat, each compartment being an old plastic tube with a sealed bottom. These were filled with water and each one contained a dahlia bloom, a cane attached to each stalk to prevent it from snapping. His marrow was in the front seat, safely secured with the seat belt to stop it falling forward if he had to break suddenly. He was as excited as a small child on Christmas Eve for this was the second best day of his year, and tomorrow would be the best. He had some good vegetables and could not see past himself being Show champion yet again.

Just before ten o'clock he was done, and locked the car door for the night. At that moment George came idling by on the other side of the road after visiting the pub for the bingo.

"Ay up George," shouted Harry over the street, "don't you forget to come and visit my marvellous vegetables tomorrow. Best I've ever grown."

George nodded and raised his hat, causing Harry to laugh and wave goodnight. He closed the door behind him and went upstairs and ran a bath for his first proper wash in many months, then shaved in it. Mary would discover the residual scum of Harry's rank body mixed with the thousands of cut whiskers lining the bath as a grey tide mark the next morning and throw her hands up in despair before cleaning it off so she could bathe herself. He also drenched himself in aftershave so that he was ready for the photographer and did not have to waste time washing in the morning before leaving for the show.

Harry never drank the night before a show, preferring to keep a clear head come morning when he would need to be on the top of his game. He was not getting any younger and each year it took that little bit of extra effort to get the veg up, prepared and loaded. He threw a tatty dressing gown on and went downstairs to lock up. He was feeling tired and knew he would not need much rocking to get to sleep. Mary had already retired for the night so Harry turned on the television to get the last of the news, and decided to have a quick shot of whisky, purely as a celebration he assured himself.

On the arm of his favourite chair was the Cock Cup that Mary had polished for him earlier that day, so Harry picked it up and studied it its gleaming surface. This was what it was all about he thought to himself. A large, antique silver trophy engraved with the names of many former villagers who had long since departed their mortal coils. It was a little battered in places and had several layers added to the base when the engravers ran out of room and new spaces had to be found. Harry proudly ran his finger over the many places his own name and that of his father had been etched, echoes of many past victories playing out in his mind.

Holding his whisky aloft he proclaimed, "To the undefeated Harry Ecklethwaite, an Allaways legend. Ain't no one within fifty miles good enough to beat you."

Jim Lightfoot had just returned home to Peony Cottage, a picture of serene calmness. He popped the kettle on and put a couple of slices of bread into the toaster, before tidying up a work top full of dirty pots including a large cake mixing bowl, many knives, bits of foliage and flower petals. It had indeed been the busy day he had envisaged but he was now done for the night.

"How has it gone?" Dick Tallboys asked, suddenly appearing in the hallway behind him.

"Good I think," Jim replied. "Everything looks good so I reckon I'll give Harry a run for his money."

"Super," squealed the ghost, "I only wish I could be there to see his face and not tied to this place for all eternity."

"So you're always going to be knocking around this house then?" Jim asked somewhat taken by surprise.

"I assume so," Dick replied. "Why, does that bother ye?"

"I guess not. You're not bad for a ghost I suppose, although you do look a tad paler than you normally do!" Jim laughed.

"Even us ghosts can get excited you know! Well I reckon you'll be needing me more than ever next season," Dick continued, "after tomorrow Ecklethwaite is really going to have it in for you so you'll need to be careful he doesn't go doing to your garden what he's been doing to many others in recent weeks. You have read the Gazette haven't you?"

"Yes I have," replied Jim, "a pity they all don't have their own guard ghost like me!"

"Aye true," laughed Dick, "but he'll also have you in his sights for courting his daughter, that's if you ever get your act together and give her what she wants."

"Not that subject again," groaned Jim, still rattled by his close encounter with Dick Tallboy's amorous niece the night before. "This whole village must be on intravenous Viagra. I thought I was coming here for a quiet life and yet I appear to be surrounded by sex craved country folk who are noisy with it to boot."

Dick Tallboys smiled broadly. "You only know a fraction of it lad. Best of luck tomorrow. Get back here and let me know how it's gone as soon as you're able."

TWENTY ONE

Show Day arrives

A British village show held amongst the aroma of newly cut grass under canvas is a truly unique affair to be witnessed nowhere else in the World. It is often the one time of the year when the whole community comes together, where lifelong friendships are forged and love affairs sometimes begin, a time of happiness or perhaps remembrance and reflection. Set against a backdrop of a brass band playing, maybe a World War Two Spitfire roaring overhead or a steam engine hissing, a typical British Summer's afternoon will see hundreds of people strolling amongst the many attractions with ice creams in their hand or else rushing for cover as a sudden deluge descends. Invariably there are flower and vegetable competitions where the best local growers will exhibit their prized onions, carrots, pumpkins and chrysanthemums. The local ladies also come together to compete against each other with their cakes, and jams, or their knitting and flower arrangements. There are often painting and photography classes to tempt the local artists and pretentious Lord Snowdon's who will photo-shop their snaps to within an inch of their lives so that they bear absolutely no resemblance to the image they originally captured nor indeed a photograph as most normal people would recognise it. Children will roll up with an assortment of animals made from vegetables, the judge for this class, usually the local vicar or visiting mayor often taking ages over his deliberations before deciding on a one-two-three, sometimes bottling a decision entirely and giving each and every child a 'highly commended' and a chocolate bar.

Most of this is intended to be in the name of fun and indeed the majority of participants enter into it with the same spirit but often rivalries can span decades and encompass varying degrees of bitterness between the protagonists. The nastiest of these rivalries usually revolve around the horticultural classes and it is not uncommon for official complaints to be made after judging by the grower who came second. Sabotage is also something growers have to watch out for, as Dick Tallboys had discovered many years before. It is not uncommon at shows for exhibits to be tampered with behind the owner's back. For instance, cucumbers must be shown with the flowers still intact but these very often mysteriously get detached and are never seen again after the grower has left them on the staging bench, thus resulting in him being marked down by the judges. Other tricks include onions having finger nails furtively sunk into them to ruin the skin, or vases of flowers emptied of water so that the flowers have wilted by the time they are judged. A judge also has to be on the look-out for dirty tricks carried out by the growers themselves to enhance their own produce, with pumpkins and marrows often being internally syringed with water to make them weigh more, carrots may have orange furniture polish expertly applied to a crack or a hole and in the longest runner bean class exhibitors will splice two beans together by fixing it to a wooden batten using tape to conveniently hide the join.

Allaways-on-Cock's annual show was no stranger to such shenanigans. Like most similar shows the growers, bakers, painters and florists have to display their exhibits by a certain time when the marquee will be vacated by everyone except the esteemed judges and their accompanying stewards. This was Harry Ecklethwaite's stamping ground, his raison d'etre, his beginning and his end. He always got to the marquee a few minutes before it opened for entries at 8am on show day so that he could start reverently placing his sixty or so exhibits in the many classes, thus giving him plenty of time to get the task done before the judges turned up in a few hours. He also liked to give himself plenty of time to weigh up the opposition as and when it appeared, delaying them in conversation if needs be so that they became flustered and made mistakes in their own staging. Four or five growers, sometimes more, from the wider environs of Allaways would come to compete against Harry and Dick when he was alive, but in all of its one hundred plus years the cup for most points had never been won by anyone outside the village. Harry's reputation spread far and wide and many had tried to usurp him but to no avail, Harry often using underhand methods, some of them described above to ensure such a thing could never happen.

On the occasion of this, the one hundredth show, Harry woke unusually late having stupidly gone from a quick nightcap to four or five large glasses of whisky, his banging head making him more irritable than usual. He liked to get prime position right next to the opening flap of the marquee so he had less distance to walk compared to his competitors. When he eventually got there several cars were already in front of him meaning he had many more yards to walk during the course of the morning. As a result he was already in a morose mood and knew he would have to get a move on to be finished in time before the judges turned up and the whistle went signalling everyone had to vacate the marquee.

Consequently, he had no time to assess the competition, no time to try and intimidate his rivals and no time to cause the Show Managers Bill Grudge and John Simmons any undue headaches about rules and regulations, what spacing was allowed for his marrows and onions, or complaints about anyone else's vegetables not being legal. He also had even less time to be aware of the many exhibits already staged across the multitude of classes that had been covered over with damp cloths and newspapers to exclude light and thus keep them as fresh as possible. These were all Jim Lightfoot's exhibits.

Jim had gone the night before and staged his vegetables having learned from Mary of Harry's usual timetable. It is one thing to tamper with something that is in full view but altogether a different kettle of fish if you cannot actually see it and exhibitors tend not to interfere with something that is covered, even cheats like Harry, a fact Jim knew full well from helping out his grandfather all those years ago. None of this mattered to Harry at that moment in time because he was blissfully confident that nobody in the village or from the wider area would be able to challenge him and stop him from taking his rightful column inches in next week's Gazette.

Jim Lightfoot turned up about an hour after Harry with a basket of decidedly second rate vegetables and proceeded to enter them into five or six classes he had purposely missed the night before. These were decoys and Jim made doubly sure that Harry clapped his eyes on them, along with an unmistakeable smirk of disdain.

"By eck lad", mocked Harry, "them's all a bit flea-bitten. Still, top marks for trying and well done for having a go, you'll get a wooden spoon if nowt else."

"Why thank you Harry", said Jim, "hopefully I'll learn enough from you in the coming years to make me better and perhaps earn a few prizes one day?"

"Whatever you say sunshine. Don't be fooled though, I'm just pretending that I care!" retorted Harry with a venomous delivery that caused everyone within ear shot to look up and either roll their eyes or stand open-mouthed at such rudeness.

Jim was unflustered however, and just smiled. By this time Mary had turned up with a few cakes to enter in the domestic classes. When her mother was alive and Harry's rivalry with Dick Tallboys was at its zenith

Harry had been known to get his wife to bake a cake which he had then entered in his own name in order to gain him a few extra points. Mary had always simply refused to do this, much to his disgust, and had won most points herself in the domestic section several times.

"Dad!" she cried, "just for once can we not simply enjoy the day and respect all other competition?"

Harry looked quite shocked at this sudden and hitherto unknown public admonishment from his usually placid daughter. "A'reet lass, it's only a bit o'banter. No harm done is there eh Jim?"

"No offence taken," offered Jim Lightfoot, "if you can't take it you shouldn't give it. As you will find out later when I beat you to most points Harry."

"Hah", that's a good'un," guffawed Harry loudly, and off he trotted to finalise the placing of his last few exhibits including his giant marrow which he always bought from the car at the last possible moment to great fanfare, usually an embarrassing mock trumpet salute from his own lips, leaving him twenty minutes spare to get his entries booked in with the officials. As he queued to do this there were several other growers in front of him who had also now finished placing their own fruit and vegetables, including Jim Lightfoot.

A seated John Simmons at the front desk looked up and greeted him. "Ah, good morning Jim, how many entries have you got?"

"Sixty eight," replied Jim Lightfoot, "an entry in every fruit and veg class plus a half dozen or so in the dahlia and cut flower classes."

A hush descended on the immediate vicinity followed by an audible gasp from everyone assembled within it. Harry stood for a moment in confusion, not quite sure whether he had heard correctly, until the whispers and nudges of those around him confirmed it. A couple of chaps from several miles away and who had been coming for many years trying to beat Harry turned round and one of them said "Did you hear that Harry? Sixty eight entries. How many have you got in?"

"Sixty nine," replied Harry Ecklethwaite, "burr it dun matter how many entries you got if they're all crap," he further added haughtily.

As John Simmons and Bill Grudge gave Jim Lightfoot a roll of sixty eight numbered sticky labels to mark his exhibits, Jim turned and winked cheekily towards the end of the queue where Harry was still patiently waiting. He then proceeded to go around the marquee taking the covers off all those vegetables he had staged the night before, applying a sticky label to each one. As the queue gradually receded Harry could do nothing but watch Jim reveal a succession of high quality vegetables that were as good as his own and in many cases even better. Finally Harry got to the front of the queue.

"Sixty nine entries and a point of order Mr. Chairman," he said as he confronted Bill Grudge.

"What is it Harry?" asked Bill, resigned to the inevitable complaint that had thus far not been forthcoming due to Harry's lateness of arrival.

"Some of Lightfoot's exhibits weren't staged this morning so he's damn well cheated. You can't go giving folk extra time. It aint fair on the rest of us. I demand he's disqualified."

"Well then Harry," said Bill, handing over Harry's sixty nine labels, "you haven't read the rules very well have you? At the AGM we agreed to allow staging on the Friday evening before the show as some of the committee members were so busy on show day they didn't have time to enter anything themselves. You were there when the vote was taken but as I recall you were too busy telling George how you were going to object to the motion to delete the heaviest marrow class. Now if I were you I'd get a move on and get those labels stuck on because the judge has just turned up and by my watch you have exactly seven minutes left. Any entries without a numbered label will be automatically disqualified don't forget!"

This was a pointed barb at the many times in the past that Harry had got similar such unlabelled exhibits of other competitors disqualified, the assumption being that Harry had actually removed the labels himself although of course it could never be proven. Harry looked outside and sure enough the National Vegetable Society judge's car was manoeuvring into a parking space. Harry's face was red raw with rage by now but he had no time to waste and busily got about the marquee sticking labels on each of his sixty nine entries, which he managed to do with a minute or so to spare, his large marrow being the last one to which he proudly affixed his one remaining label. After doing so he felt a sense of achievement and despite the undoubted quality of Jim's produce was still confident he would emerge triumphant. As he admired his own marrow, in actual fact the only one entered in that class, he allowed himself a loud and hearty congratulation.

"Well Ecklethwaite, there's still nobody to touch thee when it comes to big marrers," turning just in time to see Jim Lightfoot approaching him with a single sticky label in his hand and a confused look on his face. "Wassup withee lad, can ye not count then?"

"Obviously not Harry, it's most strange," said Jim, scratching his head in seeming confusion. "Ooooh hang on a goddam minute," and with that he got on his knees and pulled out from under the benching a large wooden pallet on which was resting a marrow the size of which had not been seen in Allaways-on-Cock since Dick Tallboys was in his horticultural prime. "Mr.Chairman, could you possibly give me a hand?"

Bill Grudge suddenly appeared from behind an open-mouthed Harry Ecklethwaite and proceeded to help Jim Lightfoot lift it onto the table, for it was undoubtedly a two man job. Jim applied his last sticky label with a theatrical flourish just as John Simmons piped out, "Time's up ladies and gentlemen, please vacate the marquee as the judges are about to start their deliberations. Everyone out please."

Harry stood like a statue for several moments, his bottom jaw so low that dribble was starting to collect around the edge of it. "Whaaaaat the fuck? Who's fucking grown that for you Lightfoot? Mr. Chairman I have to object."

"HARRY!" shouted John Simmons, his teacher training coming to the fore, "Out. NOW!"

"B,b, but....," stammered Harry, pointing at Jim Lightfoot's enormous vegetable which was dwarfing his own offering.

"OUT!" screamed John Simmons again, with which Harry eventually and reluctantly exited the marquee, out into a bright, clear, blue-sky afternoon as the various judges filed past him to do their duties.

"Summat's not right," Harry protested as he was leaving. "I'm not having this I tell ye. There's some cheating been going on somehow. Make sure them judges know what they're fucking doing, d'ye hear me?"

It was all now to no avail. Harry stood on the grass of the village green helpless as the door flap of the marquee was closed and tied from the inside. Turning round Harry noticed Jim Lightfoot next to his car in deep conversation with a couple of exhibitors from outside the village and stormed over to them. "Yer a cheatin bastard Lightfoot. You aren't grown them veg so where have ye gotten 'em from?"

Jim held himself in dignified check, "Actually I have grown each and every one of them Harry, and if you'd like you can follow me to my garden now where you will see many other vegetables just as good that are still growing away healthily. I actually had an even bigger marrow but couldn't get it in the car. I was just discussing them with Tom here who's on the Tithampton committee as I may enter their show next weekend."

The Tom in question, was of course the chairman of Moor Lane allotments with the fading quiff and who was interviewed by Daryl Bilkin earlier in the week. He had been waiting for this day for as long as he could remember, for he was one of the regular visitors from outside the village who had often found themselves on the receiving end of Harry's underhand tactics. "Don't judge everyone else by your own standards Ecklethwaite."

"Eh?" queried Harry, "what the fuck are you on about now?"

"You know damn well," Tom countered. "You've been cheating your way to most points for as long as anyone can remember, and I don't suppose you had 'owt to do with my onions going missing from the polytunnel on my allotment did you?" Turning to Jim and offering his handshake Tom continued, "Well done lad, it'll be a close run thing but I reckon you might just do it and fair play to you."

"I'll fucking have you up for slander if you repeat that claim again!" spluttered Harry

"Do what you like," huffed Tom, "but we're all fed up with you Ecklethwaite. Well and truly. We tried to tell the police the figure we caught on CCTV was you but they reckoned there wasn't enough evidence. But we all knew it was you and you'll not be pulling stunts like that again in future."

With that everyone got into their cars and drove them the few hundred yards to the local car park. This was in order to allow other attractions time to set up around village green as the whole area would then be pedestrians only for the duration of the show. Harry was left standing alone, utterly shocked, open-mouthed yet again, as if surveying the desolation of his broken dreams.

TWENTY TWO

The results are in

Word of Jim's daring challenge to Harry had spread far and wide in a matter of less than an hour, so much so that a sizeable crowd had gathered outside the marquee awaiting the opening of the tent. The major protagonists were among the throng of villagers and outsiders alike, straining to see through the cracks between the marquee's canvas panels and the opaque UPVC windows for any clues as to the direction of this year's silverware. Mrs Dibble was first to emerge from her duties as steward to the judge in the domestic classes. She skirted round the crowd, pausing briefly to chat to Jim Lightfoot, tapping him on the shoulder before going off to get set up on the bric-a-brac stall. As a result of Mrs. Dibble's appearance many folk now assumed the marquee would soon be open to viewing.

Eventually John Simmons emerged causing several folk at the front to step forward but John held up a hand to halt their progress.

"Sorry ladies and gentlemen. Due to a record amount of entries in the horticultural sections this year the vegetable judge in particular is going to take longer than usual I'm afraid," he announced.

"Bugger off John," came the unmistakeable guttural drone of Harry Ecklethwaite, "it shouldn't take 'em that long to work out my stuff's best for fuck's sake."

"Maybe it aint the best this year Harry?" sang out one of the local farm lads bravely behind him, safe in the relative anonymity of the crowd. Harry turned to try and identify the source of this irreverence, his face filling with purple bile.

"Actually," piped up John Simmons after a brief burst of raucous chanting, some of it quite rude for a supposedly genteel event, "it's going to be a really close run thing this year. Harry and Jim Lightfoot are currently neck and neck with about six of the veg classes still to be judged. Oh hang on....,"

Simmons had noticed Bill Grudge beckoning him back into the tent. The crowd fell silent as John entered the marquee and observed him in deep conversation with the Chairman. After only a couple of minutes that seemed like an hour to Harry and Jim, John emerged into the sunlight again.

"After the globe beetroot and runner beans have been judged Jim is now one point ahead of Harry!"

With this announcement came a loud cheer from the assembled throng, several straw hats were thrown into the air as Jim was lost in a sea of arms desperate to pat him on the back. Harry stooped to engage George in conversation, his arms flailing and his fingers wagging animatedly. In due course the noise stopped and everyone settled down once again for further news as if awaiting the appointment of a new pope from within the canvas cathedral. John Simmons' every appearance was greeted with several folk somehow elevating themselves above the crowd to put their index fingers to their lips to give a fervent "Shhhhh!"

"Courgettes!" exclaimed John Simmons amateur theatrically on his next foray out into the gathering, "Jim third, Harry first, (an audible groan from the crowd at this point) which means that Harry leads by a point."

"Ha. Normal order resumed!" gloated Harry Ecklethwaite arms aloft as if he had just scored the winning goal in the cup final, but his bubble was soon burst at John Simmons' next report.

"Result from the tomato class, Harry second, Jim first. It's neck and neck with two remaining results to come. The judge is just weighing the heavy marrows, then it's onions as grown. This is going down to the wire folks."

Several villagers were now embracing one another. Others were rooted to the spot and did not doubt they would remember these moments for the rest of their lives, moments akin to knowing where you were when President Kennedy was assassinated as far as this little village's affairs were concerned. At this last revelation Harry's heart sank knowing full well as he did that Jim's marrow had utterly dwarfed his own and he would be ahead by a point going to the last class. He knew his onions were good, the best he had grown for a few years and in fact they were the ones that he had bullied Pete Greensleave into giving to him after the weedkiller episode, but he had not observed what Jim Lightfoot's were like due to his haste at the end to get everything labelled. People were chattering away weighing up the different options amongst themselves, knowing there was three points for a win, two for second and one for a third. Sure enough

John Simmons surfaced to confirm Harry's worst fear about the marrow class.

"Jim first and Harry second. I believe that's the first time in sixteen years that Harry hasn't grown the village's heaviest marrow. In fact, it's an Allaways Show all-time record of seventy two pounds eight ounces so well done Jim. Upshot is that Jim is a point ahead going into the final class."

Another voice piped up from the crowd, "Jim's marrow dwarfed Harry's. A mere one point difference is a travesty!"

This prompted Harry to turn round angrily once more in search of the voice's identity, but he was shocked to observe a sea of happy faces all chattering away and looking at him in anticipation of his impending dethronement.

All this while Jim had stood on the right hand edge of the crowd, mostly in pleasant conversation with several locals including Mary who as ever hung on his every word and motion. As each twist and turn was announced he joined the others in oohing and ahhing, laughing along as if the ultimate result did not matter one single jot. But it certainly did. Inside Jim was desperate to emerge triumphant, to go back to Peony Cottage with the coveted Cock Cup and shout out to Dick Tallboys' ghost that he had beaten his nemesis and to raise a glass in his honour. Harry's actions in the past twenty years had been pretty despicable and it was about time the village had a new champion to put him in his place.

Mary's emotions were a little more complicated. She desperately wanted Jim to win but feared what effect such an outcome might have on her father. He had pretty much ignored her and not spoken to her that much since first learning of her romantic attachment to Jim, save the odd grunt at meal times, but he was her father after all and for all his failings she still loved him. However something deep inside her told her that he needed taking down a peg or two, that there were more important things in life than who could grow the biggest marrow.

The waiting seemed to go on forever. People strained their eyes through the semi-clear windows of the marquee to see if John Simmons was any closer to coming and putting them all out of their agonising curiosity. The judge could just about be discerned in the far corner of the marquee where the last of the vegetable classes was being adjudicated.

Surely he could not take much longer to come to a decision people were thinking?

At length Harry could take no more and started shouting through the door flap. "Come on for fuck's sake. How much longer you all going to be? The Gazette'll be here shortly and wanting to take my photo."

In truth the Show proper had actually been declared open by Lady Belton in the far corner of the village green some half hour before which just added to the numbers of people waiting with baited breath for the horticultural marquee to open. Mrs. Dibble had to step in and assist her in the job that Bill Grudge usually did, because Bill was still in the horticultural tent nervously checking his watch and double checking the results to make sure the points had been totalled correctly. He knew full well that Harry would double check every single result, jotting it down in his little notebook to make sure it was correct. The National Vegetable Society judge was nothing if not thorough in his deliberations. He was an experienced man who had been judging at Allaways for only the past four years, which actually made him the longest serving judge in recent history because many previous judges had become so fed up with Harry Ecklethwaite questioning their ability afterwards that they had always refused to come back. After the last judge had said he would never return the committee had frantically scoured the area for another, eventually having to pay extra for one to come all the way from Derby some seventy miles away. Luckily for them, this one would have turned up to open an envelope if you paid him enough.

"How do you think your onions will fare Jim?" asked Mary.

"Who knows?" replied Jim, "but your father seems awfully nervous doesn't he?"

"He can see his whole World crumbling around him." Mary seemed a little upset at her last statement. No matter how naughty a child is and how other parents might perceive them to be a little devil when it's your own loved one you can usually forgive them anything. Her father was in many ways like a little child. He had simple tastes and had never learned how to appreciate things from another person's perspective.

"Nothing lasts forever Mary. Things will always come out in the end, just you wait and see," said Jim cryptically.

Mary looked puzzled but had no time to dwell on this as John Simmons appeared. To the crowd's consternation he proceeded to tie back the door flap of the marquee first rather than divulge the all-important information they were all on tenterhooks to hear.

"C'mon John," shouted one as others laughed at this deliberate lengthening of the suspense.

At length John Simmons finished securing the door flap and stood upright in front of the sea of expectant faces.

"Ladies and gentlemen, the result of the onions as grown. Harry Ecklethwaite second, Jim Lightfoot....."

There followed a long pause as John surveyed everyone in front of him, the silence only broken by the odd distant cry of a child on the dodgems on the far side of the green. Eventually someone called out. "For crying out loud this aint the bloody X-Factor John!"

Recognising he had probably pushed things as far as they would go John continued, "Jim Lightfoot was unplaced."

Pandemonium now broke out, or as close to pandemonium as one could expect to see in a small English village on a sunny day in September, mainly in the vicinity of Harry Ecklethwaite one might add. Elsewhere in the throng there was a general feeling of deflation and anti-climax. This latest result meant Harry had picked up the two points he needed to leapfrog Jim Lightfoot in the horticultural section. And as the horticultural section constituted the biggest section of the show by far it followed more often than not, that the horticultural champion also won the Cock Cup for most points on most occasions during the Show's one hundred years of existence.

Harry launched into a tirade, the release valve on his pent up nervousness finally blown, "And *STILL*, the undisputed, undefeated village show champion for the twelfth year running," before pointing over at Jim Lightfoot "Who are ya? Who are ya?"

This was all too much for rockabilly Tom from Tithampton who looked particularly crestfallen, "You miserable, ignorant, ungracious twat Ecklethwaite. When you're dead there's a lot of folk round here who will happily dance on your grave."

"Excellent," retorted Harry, "cos I'm leaving clear instructions that I be buried in fucking quicksand. Now where's that fine young man from the Gazette? You can fuck off now Jim, he'll only want to talk to the winners."

As the throng swept into the marquee with Harry and his entourage of supporters to the fore, basically George and a couple of the farm lads, Jim and Mary held back. She had worn her favourite summer dress for the day hoping to impress Jim, a simple, figure hugging number with a floral pattern, quite low cut to make the most of her generous cleavage. Mary noted that Jim still seemed relaxed and happy. As people passed by them several patted Jim on the back and commiserated with him.

"How strange," said Jim thoughtfully, "Mary, the Cock Cup IS for most points in the whole show is it not?"

"Indeed it is Jim, why do you ask?" Mary replied.

"Just wondering. Right I'd best be off to the dunking machine. I think Jane's already done a half hour stint so I'll go and relieve her. See you later Mary." And off he went totally oblivious to Mary's inclined cheek upon which she had expected a kiss to be planted.

TWENTY THREE

Best laid plans

Allaways-on-Cock annual show was always a well-supported affair. Hundreds of people from the surrounding villages and towns descended on the large village green to drink in the atmosphere of well-being that the event invariably created. The one hundredth such show was turning out to be no exception and a warm, sunny day had certainly helped. This was most welcome to Jane Tallboys and Jim Lightfoot as they got submerged dozens of times each during the course of the afternoon. On warm days the settings on the machine were always tampered with to ensure dunkings came more often than on cold afternoons. Today, Ted Grangeworthy who was manning the attraction at the front had trouble keeping up with the enthusiasm of everyone wanting to have a throw, often pleading for an orderly queue or begging for no pushing or shoving.

In the days before the Show Jane had determined to seduce Jim Lightfoot to try and repair the sense of lost honour that still rattled around in her head. She had purchased a new skimpy bathing costume that left very little to the imagination and indeed had the farmhand boys from miles around throwing money at the attraction in order to get Jane thrown off as often as possible. They were all hoping her skimpy top would come off sooner or later and give them more than they had paid for. With each submersion a raucous cheer went up which turned to a mock groan of disappointment each time she emerged with dignity and modesty intact.

When it was Jim's turn to take the stool the farm lads all booed and went elsewhere on the showground, although there was still a steady turnover of revenue from the attraction as several of the village wives who had taken a shine to Jim's cheeky smile and toned body chanced their arm on a few throws themselves. Around the middle of the afternoon the attraction had a half hour break and they both found themselves in the small enclosed tent next to the pool with several towels around them to keep them warm, Jim having just finished a stint and finding Jane alone well wrapped in a large beach towel. Jane had already seen her chance.

"You have a mighty muscular body for your age Jim I must say. I dare say you work out a bit?" with which she walked over to him and started running her hand up and down his arms in mock admiration. As she did so she allowed the large towel she was wrapped in to slip from her grasp, which thus started sliding from her body in seeming slow motion to reveal that she was totally naked underneath it.

Jim sat in silence, mildly amused but not shocked for he had suspected Jane might try a stunt like this. Her chilled nipples almost took his eye out as she swung her breasts across his gaze and parted her legs in an unashamed invite to go further than just looking, water droplets glistening on her trimmed Brazilian. Jim calmly stood up, took her shoulders to position her against the central support pole of the tent causing Jane to close her eyes in anticipation of being screwed frantically up against it. She threw her head back and moaned in anticipation at what was about to happen, the naughtiness of it heightened by the thrilled voices drifting into the tent from outside. But instead Jim merely picked the towel up from the grass floor and wrapped it back around Jane. As she opened her eyes again he was walking away from her back to his chair.

"Now then Jane, we can't have you getting hypothermia now can we? I'll do the next shift as I need to be in the horticultural marquee for prize giving at 4.30."

A shocked Jane was just about to launch into him, to call him all manner of names for daring to deny her, for embarrassing her in such a way when there was a hearty "yoohoooo" from a female voice which preceded Mary's appearance in the tent a few moments later.

"Hi guys," said Mary cheerily, "you're both doing very well I must say. Ted says you've earned a record amount already. You look very sexy Jane. That bikini is an absolute masterstroke." Mary raised herself up on tiptoe to kiss Jim on the lips, "and you don't look so bad yourself you gorgeous hunk of manhood. Don't forget prize giving at 4.30 in the horticultural tent darling. Dad is being an absolute nuisance in there and wanting to know why the reporter from the Gazette hasn't asked to talk to him yet but Bill Grudge says he'll have to wait until prize giving and that they're still totalling the points up. But Dad's added everything up himself several times just to double check he's a point ahead of you though so he can't see what the delay is." Mary sighed, "Never mind, I think you did amazingly well and I'm sure you'll beat him next year. It'll make my life a bit easier seeing as I have to live with him I suppose?"

Mary definitely gave this last sentence a question mark at the end in her intonation, which did not go unnoticed by Jim or Jane. Jim followed

Mary out to take his place on the dunking stool, aware that he had left Jane silently seething behind him.

Mary had one more bit of gossip for Jim to digest, "Oh, by the way, Bill Grudge and John Simmons have had a terrible falling out in the marquee at the front desk. I really don't know what's happened to cause such upset, but the outcome is that John Simmons has immediately resigned from the committee and left the marquee in a right huff. It was all a bit embarrassing really. I was on a break from the bric-a-brac and walked right into the middle of it. There were several members of the public within earshot."

Jim climbed the steps to the dunking stool amid a cascade of good natured booing from those hoping to see Jane in her bikini again. As Jim sat in his elevated position he was able to scan the whole of the village green. There were still hundreds of people milling about. On the bric-a-brac stall Jim saw Mary chatting away excitedly to the many children and pensioners who stopped to look, several people pausing to give her a hug for Jim had discovered that Mary was well liked and admired in the village in spite of, or maybe because of, her father. At the entrance to the horticultural marquee Harry was gesticulating wildly with his arms and explaining why his vegetables were the best to anyone unfortunate enough catch his eye, cigarette smoke being blown in their faces whether they liked it or not. Old George had seemingly been attached to Harry by a short piece of cord all afternoon and was busy nodding away in agreement with everything Harry said. Just inside the doorway Jim could discern Bill Grudge in deep conversation with a couple of gentlemen, one of whom had large camera over his shoulder and another who was scribbling into a notepad. Jim discerned that they could only be the much anticipated journalist and photographer from the Gazette. And over in the far corner of the green, away from most of the crowds, Pete Greensleave appeared to be pleading with his wife Molly who was stood next to a large and rather smart Jaguar car. Another man was loading suitcases into the boot of the car, Molly and Pete's two young children having already been strapped into the rear seats. At length Molly got into the passenger side leaving the unknown gentleman pointing his fingers at Pete before getting into the car and driving away. Pete was left at the side of the road looking crestfallen. Some yards away Jim noticed Dierdre Dillage who was serving under the beer gazebo looking over in Pete's direction, a large and quite vindictive looking smirk plastered across her smug face. Every now and again Dave Preston sidled past her, feigning a lack of room in the gangway behind the trestles on which the beer pumps were mounted in order to rub his genitals up against her posterior. For her part Deirdre appeared to be enjoying it, although in actuality of course she was only trying to make Pete jealous.

The villagers must have been getting tired, or else they were saving their most accurate shots for Jane because Jim managed to go a whole half hour without getting wet. As Jane brushed past him at the changeover she hissed a quite venomous "Twat," towards his face and stomped up the steps to the stool mounting platform. Jim smiled and was able to change into his casual clothes very quickly now that he did not have to dry himself off first.

As he was walking across to the horticultural marquee he heard a 'thwump', then a splash, followed by a loud cheer meaning that Jane had succumbed to a dunking already. This was soon followed by an even bigger cheer which signified to Jim, although he did not bother turning around to confirm it, that Jane had not fastened her bikini top securely enough after trying to entice him earlier and it was now presumably floating across the pool of gunge. Jane was no doubt washing the green gunk from her eyes as yet unawares that her two best features were making several illiterate farm boys and quite a few other male villagers, whose wives were not there to drag them away, very happy indeed.

Jim paused several times on the way to the marquee as several people made him loiter in order to say how sorry they were that he had not beaten Harry. Ralph Chubb was one.

"Don't get too downhearted lad. Closest that terrible old rogue has been pushed since Dick Tallboys were alive. I do hope you aren't going to give up. I'd love to see him get his just desserts before I kick the bucket. In fact most of the village would like to see it."

"Well Ralph I hope I can do that much sooner than you think. Come on now, the prize giving is about to start. Even if you don't like someone you should be generous in defeat and offer your congratulations hey?"

And with that they ambled along together and joined the crowd of people inside the tent who had assembled for the presentation of the trophies, which had all been polished by previous recipients and were now glittering away on a raised platform. Bill Grudge had already started his address as Jim and Ralph entered.

"..........with great thanks to all who have joined us today to make this, the one hundredth annual show, such a success yet again. I must thank a few people....."

At this point Jim became aware of Harry Ecklethwaite towards the front and who now turned round to the line of people behind him and said, "Fucking hell will someone stop him poncing on and on."

Unluckily for Harry, Mrs Dibble was in this line of people and was in no mood for his ignorance and boorishness.

"Shush Mr Ecklethwaite, show some respect for once, there are women and children present." She ordered. Harry was duly chastened and sheepishly turned to face the front once more.

............"so could you all join me in thanking Lady Belton for her continued patronage.........." (clapping)

Jim was nudged in the ribs by Tom from Tithampton who had now appeared next to him, "Don't know why I put myself through this every year Jim," he said. "It's always painful seeing that awful man get the accolades after all he's done and said, but you have to show some decorum don't you?"

Jim was mildly amused at the dejection his defeat appeared to have caused to Ralph, Tom and a few others. "He'll get his just desserts sooner or later Tom don't you worry. How did you do old chap?" Jim asked.

"Mainly seconds and thirds. Just making up the numbers against you and that rotten swine really. No-one expected such a close challenger out of the blue this year. We'll have to get our heads together next year. See if I can't divert my growing to take prizes away from him in classes he's strong on and stay away from the classes you're good at," suggested Tom.

................"and finally, the time has come when we must present these wonderful trophies to those who have been lucky enough, or skilful enough to win them here in the marquee today"............

"Halleluyah!" cheered Harry, who was then given a sharp dig in the ribs from Mrs. Dibble's bony arm.

After several minutes of presentations to various schoolchildren for their winning paintings, flower necklaces and vegetable animals followed by the adult photography and paintings and then the WI sponsored flower arranging cups, Bill Grudge announced that for reasons that would soon be divulged the cups for the horticultural section would now be presented. Jim noted that Harry glanced sideways at nodding George with a confused look on his face. Tom was soon whispering in Jim's ear an explanation for Harry's puzzlement.

"Strange. For as long as I can remember the domestic section is usually next. Horticultural section is always last and the Cock Cup the last cup of all to be announced," expounded Tom.

There were various minor trophies up for grabs before the major trophy winner was to be announced, including best dish of potatoes out of the many different classes for spuds, best dish of onions and so on. Not for the first time in recent years John Simmons won the salver for the best overall exhibit in the vegetable section, a fine set of long beetroot that he had grown at home out of Harry's line of fire and most definitely under his radar. Harry had already made a mental note of Simmons' subterfuge and would be on the lookout for him next season. However, due to his argument with Bill Grudge a couple of hours earlier John Simmons was not in attendance to collect the trophy, but Bill Grudge still gave him a very glowing reference and then waited patiently in the hope that John would emerge from the crowd somewhere.

"I believe this is the ninth time in the last fifteen years that John has won best vegetable exhibit," he praised, waiting patiently and hopefully for John to step forward.

"Look at that intolerable man's face," Tom from Tithampton said to Jim, referring to Harry. "Ecklethwaite very rarely wins best veg. Jack of all trades but master of none he is. Dick Tallboys used to win it most years but Harry dismissed it as a minor trophy for also-rans. When Dick was regularly winning the Cock Cup Harry actually won the best veg salver a couple of times. It suddenly became a very important trophy for the next twelve months. Look how arrogantly he dismisses it."

Jim made a note to study what he needed to do to win the salver in future years. He would find out later that winners of the Cock Cup rarely won best veg because they spread themselves so thin over so many classes in an effort to get most points. A few of the domestic cups were presented next, including one to Bill Grudge's own wife for most points in the section and one to Ted Grangworthy for the 'men only' rock cakes, a class that was always hotly contested. At length there were only two trophies remaining, including the one which was most sought after, and Bill Grudge now had complete silence.

"Ladies and Gentlemen we've had a right royal battle for most points this year and normally the grower who gains most points in the veg, fruit and flower classes is the one who wins the Cock Cup for most points overall in the whole show, which is of course our most prestigious award."

"That'll be me for the twelfth year running and twentieth in all then!" called Harry, arms aloft as he turned to make sure everyone in the marquee had no doubt who was the village's champion grower.

After some muttering, booing and hissing, which had Harry urgently surveying the crowd for the perpetrators of such disregard once again, Bill Grudge appealed for quiet and continued. "As I say, in most years the winner of the horticultural section usually wins the Cock Cup. However, this year one grower also has the added distinction of winning the cup for the most meritorious exhibit in the domestic classes and because of that, added to his points from the horticultural section, I am delighted to announce that this year's winner of the Cock Cup is first time exhibitor at the show, Jim Lightfoot."

An uncanny silence now descended on the marquee as people struggled to come to terms with what had just been announced, but before long a few cheers from the back had rippled through the crowd so that by the time Jim had struggled through them to the front the noise had become cacophonous. When he got there he discovered Harry attempting to wrench Bill Grudge's clipboard from his grasp.

"Not so fucking fast Lightfoot, this twat's added everything up wrongly," coughed Harry.

Bill roughly yanked his clipboard back from Harry, "Enough Harry! You've been beaten fair and square. Don't make a fool of yourself any more than usual."

Bill then ushered Jim up on to the temporary staging where Lady Belton handed over the all-important Cock Cup to him as well as a rather splendid cut glass trophy for the best exhibit in the domestic classes. Jim shook Lady Belton's hand and turned to the crowd with a huge smile across his face, lifting the Cock Cup into the air as if he was lifting the trophy at the Cup Final, shaking it in defiance in Harry Ecklethwaite's direction.

Bill called for order. "Just in case you're all wondering Ladies and Gents, the best exhibit in domestic this year was the carrot cake that Jim baked in class thirty four. First time a man has ever won best domestic I believe, and added to his points for veg, fruit and flowers means he pipped our regular champion Harry Ecklethwaite by a mere two points overall," explained Bill in the vain hope that by mentioning Harry in passing and in glowing terms might shut him up.

Jim continued to hold aloft the Cock Cup, the cheering showing no sign of abating. Rockabilly Tom from Tithampton was hugging Ralph Chubb as if they had both won themselves. As Jim returned to the throng with his spoils he saw Mary waving at him frantically. It was the first time he had seen anything of her since she left him at the dunking pool. Having finally struggled through the sea of people all wishing him well done and slapping him on the back Mary finally managed to make herself heard, "Jim, before you say anything, please let me explain."

"What's wrong Mary?" said a concerned Jim.

"Look, I'm really, really sorry, but when the last of the veg was judged and just after we spoke outside I came in here and noticed that Bill had left his spreadsheet unattended. It was when he and John were having that terrible barney. Well anyways, I know I shouldn't have but I tippexed my name out and put yours on instead."

"Mary," said Jim, "what on Earth are you chattering on about?"

Mary continued "I baked a carrot cake and entered it in class thirty four and put your name on Bill's form instead of my own. Don't you see Jim? You only won because I cheated on your behalf in spite of the fact that I've refused to do just that every time Dad has asked me all these years."

"Well then this is most strange," said Jim. "Come with me," and taking Mary by the hand he lead her to the cake class in question. "Which one is your cake then Mary?"

"Well it's this one of cour.....Oh!" Mary was stopped dead in her tracks at the site of her cake on the unmistakeable plate she had displayed it on several hours before, covered with her mother's antique fly screen. Next to it was a prize ticket, on which the words Jim Lightfoot had been written by Reverend Arsley in his best italic handwriting. Most first prize cards the length and breadth of the country are red. This one was blue. Mary's cake in Jim's name had come second. "I, d-don't understand," stammered Mary.

Jim ushered Mary a couple of feet further along. There, mounted on a wooden pedestal that was reserved for the show's 'premier cake' was another carrot cake, a small slice neatly taken out of it where the WI judge had sampled it. Jim's name also adorned the prize ticket, but this was a bright red one. Unlike a lot of similar shows, Allaways allowed someone to make more than one entry in a class, but only the highest scoring one was allowing to count towards the overall points tally. Harry had also utilised this method in the past, putting several entries in his strongest categories to ensure his competitors did not pick up a second or third prize.

"You see Mary," explained Jim, "I also baked a cake. When Mrs. Dibble emerged from the tent earlier she came round to offer me her congratulations as she'd been stewarding when the judge from the WI had proclaimed mine first prize and she'd gone to find out from Bill's spreadsheet who had baked it. She did say something later on to me along the lines of your other cake wasn't too bad either which I couldn't quite understand, but I just assumed she was confused because I hadn't baked any other cakes."

"Oh thank goodness," gasped Mary. "That means mine made absolutely no difference then?

"So it would seem," replied Jim. "But thanks for doing what you did. It was a sweet thought. I'm not sure I could have stayed quiet if it had affected things however!" he laughed.

Mary continued, whilst examining the cut glass trophy, "Well then this puts a different gloss on things doesn't it! As you can see I have my name on here five times myself. You have some catching up to do. Where did you learn to bake such a good cake then?"

"My grandmother actually," replied Jim. "She gave me the recipe many years ago and I've always kept it close to my heart. I've never written it down either. It's almost as if she's guiding me along every time I bake it. Although I can't bake anything else to save my life to be perfectly honest Mary!"

They both cackled like excited children as they exited the marquee, Mary linking into Jim's arm, carrying a trophy apiece. The photographer from the Gazette had beckoned Jim outside to take his photograph. Daryl Bilkin also appeared in order to take a few notes on his great achievement. Meanwhile Harry Ecklethwaite had only just begun his barrage of objections on the outcome that had just been publicised, and which would probably last an entire year until the next show.

"I demand to see your spreadsheet Grudge. You never could fucking add up properly and you've made a mistake again today. Remember that time twenty years ago when you got mine and Bob Appelby's points mixed up? You had me second then until I pointed out your error and had to make a public apology. Well you've obviously done summat fucking similar again this time!"

"Harry," groaned Bill, "you're not having the spreadsheet. I've checked and double checked because I know what you're like. For your information I hadn't cocked up the points all those years ago. Bob Appelby came to me and graciously owned up to a mistake by one of the stewards who had put his name on a prize card instead of John Simmons. You think I actually enjoy having you rant at me every year? Jim has beaten you fair and square so just accept it. It's not the worst thing that could have happened is it surely?

"It's the principle of the thing," Harry riposted, "I don't mind getting beat, never have done, you know that Bill. But when a mistake's been made it needs putting right. That fucking judge doesn't have the first fucking clue. You know we all call him that dithering dick from Derby? Look at the parsnips. How can he put Jim's thin ones first and my huge ones third?

"Because Jim's are straight and spotlessly clean and yours are forked and full of fly damage I suspect Harry," Bill countered confidently.

"Well what about that Scottish chap from the other side of Tithampton? One of his parsnips is almost black and he's come second. That can't be right surely?

"Granted that doesn't look good Harry," agreed Grudge, "but I can assure you when it was judged they were pristine. Looks like he's rubbed 'em too much during cleaning and the bruising's only just come out but it doesn't alter the result. Now I'm not going to stand here pandering to you all afternoon like in previous years so if you'll excuse me……"

Harry was not to be denied. "Not so fucking fast Grudge. Are you sure Lightfoot baked that fucking cake? Seems very convenient to me does that."

"Well Harry, if we challenge him on that point it would mean we have to challenge you for all those years you entered a cake to help boost your points tally now wouldn't it? We have to take him at his word, just as we took you at your word on so many previous occasions as I recall?" Bill was readier than he ever had been with answers to Harry's objections.

Harry was starting to get desperate, for he could see Daryl from the Gazette outside the marquee interviewing Jim, when it was surely he who should be there telling them all about his twelfth successive triumph. What's more his only daughter was also out there looking up at him in awe. "Bill I demand you get that fucking judge back in here and ask him to go round with me explaining every one of his decisions."

Bill had had enough and said, calmly at first. "Harry. Be in no doubt. That isn't going to happen. The judge took way too long as it is because of his experiences in the past with you challenging his every decision. Now will you kindly FUCK OFF!"

Harry was as shocked as he had ever been in his life. He had been told to fuck off many times in the past, but never by Bill Grudge. Bill had in fact never spoken to anyone else in his life like that before, his policeman training meaning that he was always calm and collected under pressure. As Bill walked away Harry remained motionless and rooted to the spot, the last stragglers of the afternoon sidestepping him to have one last look at the vegetables before the Show closed at five o'clock. At length he shouted after Bill, causing several onlookers to turn around, "You're a bunch of useless twats do ye'hear? You're all going to pay dearly for this!"

Things were probably never going to be the same in Allaways ever again.

TWENTY FOUR

Aftermath

Life always returned to relative normality pretty quickly after show day in Allaways. Marquees were taken off hire, and trestles, gazebos and stalls were safely packed away in various villager's sheds and garages for another year. Everyone who was involved, which was most of the village, had their specific tasks assigned to them and set about them as soon as the Show was declared closed by Lady Belton. Running the Show was thirsty work and most wanted everything tied up and put to bed for another year so that a few celebratory drinks could be quaffed. By nine o'clock the village green was finally clear and most of the organisers and stalwarts had retired to the Dog & Gun for a well-earned nightcap or ten. Bill Grudge had managed to wedge John Simmons into a corner of the bar.

"I'm sorry if I got a bit upset with you earlier John but I didn't think it was right you going out and announcing the results like that when it all hadn't been officially verified. When I was made aware of Jim's cake a short time later I knew there was going to be an almighty kerfuffle at presentation time so I'm afraid I lost it. Please accept my apologies."

"No apology required Bill," said John magnanimously. "I was in the wrong old boy. I just got carried away with the occasion. I realise now I should have waited for the official result at presentation time and it won't happen again I can promise you. I wish I'd been there to see Harry's face rather than stomping off."

"Aye, well, it has certainly been a momentous day that's for sure." Bill stated. "And I reckon it's been the best show ever, and we're certain to break all records with the proceeds. Same time next year old chap?"

"Consider it a date," John answered. They shook hands and all was well again within the horticultural society.

In the opposite corner of the building Pete Greensleave was well on his way down his eighth pint since tea time, as well as a couple of shots of whisky. He had been inconsolable since Molly had sped from the village in his brother's car. Bingo calling farm labourer Dave Preston was doing his best to cheer him up, but with his usual propensity for saying completely the wrong thing at the wrong time he was making a piss poor job of it.

"She'll be back Pete. Give her a few days to think things through then go after her. I don't suppose you'll mind if I have a crack at Deirdre myself then mate?"

"You're fucking welcome to the old hag," slurred Pete. "I should never have got involved with her. My Molly's gone forever. That bastard of a brother of mine's been planning this moment since the day we married. The fucking, fucking, fucker."

After a few moments of sympathetic head shaking, tut-tutting and superficial reflection Dave suddenly asked, "So is Deirdre shaven down below or has she got a growling badger?"

Mrs. Dibble was sat demurely on a bar stool with a glass of sherry telling a very interested Bob Dillage all about the drama of the day. "It will be interesting to see if Mr. Ecklethwaite dare show his face in here tonight after his disgraceful behaviour today."

Bob pressed further, "I do wish I weren't tied to this place. Show day is our busiest of the year as you can imagine. I'd loved to have seen that. Mind you, knowing that Jim Lightfoot, we might have got rid of one smug bugger but we've created another for sure. I bet he was all over Mary weren't he Mrs.D? She came in here briefly this afternoon and that dress she were wearing looked like it were sprayed on. Lightfoot'll be nailing more than one Ecklethwaite today I reckon."

"Really Bob," scalded Mrs. Dibble, "there's nothing wrong with two young people enjoying themselves, there's no need to be so crude. Jim has been nothing but a gentleman since he's been in the village and today has been no exception."

Jane Tallboys meanwhile was chatting to the landlord's wife at the opposite end of the bar. "Last time I volunteer for that dunking machine I can tell you Deirdre. Some of those farm lads are too bloody accurate. And when my top came off I could have died. Luckily Ted Grangeworthy was on hand to throw a towel around me before anyone could get their camera phone clicking away, otherwise I'd be plastered all over the internet by now."

"Oh you poor daaaarling," Deirdre commiserated. "And you say Jim Lightfoot made a pass at you?"

"Yes he did, dirty old bastard. Pulled my towel off me and pushed me against the tent post. I dread to think what he'd have done next if Mary hadn't come in at that moment for let me tell you he was already in a very advanced state of arousal."

Ralph Chubb was in an excellent mood, for like many others he had been waiting for this day for a very long time, and was sat with Ted Grangeworthy taking great delight going over every last detail of Harry Ecklethwaite's overthrow.

"I tell you Ted he didn't know what had hit him. I was in the tent when Jim pulled that marrow out from under the table and you should have seen Harry's face. He just stood there speechless."

"I wish I'd been there this afternoon as well," Ted replied, "I was winding things up at the dunking tank and I'll never forget hearing that roar coming from the horticultural marquee when Bill Grudge announced Jim as the winner this afternoon. I tell you Ralph, I dropped everything and ran over to the tent. Yes. Ran! At my age! Just to experience a major event in the life of the village."

All such conversations came to an abrupt halt as the door swung open and Jim and Mary walked in together. A ripple of applause spread throughout the inn, building up to quite a crescendo before eventually dying down. Storekeeper Ralph Chubb was first to welcome the new village champion.

"Let me buy you a drink Jim. Some of your veg today was really top notch," he said, continuing with an outright lie, "we had no idea you were up at Peony Cottage producing all those exhibits. You have been busy." This was of course not strictly true as Ralph Chubb had been back up to Cock Side bell tower several times over the summer with his binoculars to double check how Jim's produce was progressing, so he had always had an inkling that a new champion was in the pipeline.

"Oh it was nothing really," protested Jim.

"Nonsense," interjected Bill Grudge, "you've been a credit since you came to the village and no-one has had a bad word to say about you since day one."

This was of course not strictly true either, as Jim had been viewed with considerable suspicion from day one by most of the regular pub dwellers, but on that day he had well and truly broken down the barriers and become one of them it appeared.

"And he can bake a mean cake too," piped up Mary.

Mrs. Dibble was quick to concur. "Yes indeed. The lady judge from the WI was in absolute raptures about your carrot cake Mr. Lightfoot. It's a good job you know your way round a kitchen otherwise we'd all have to suffer another year of Mr. Ecklethwaite's boasting. Sorry Mary."

"That's ok Mrs. Dibble," Mary soothed, "even I have grown tired of his single minded selfishness."

Mary had popped home straight after the show to check her father was alright, but he was still ranting on about how a huge injustice had occurred in the village that day, and how he was not going to let them all get away with it. She had decided to leave him to stew and gone for a walk along the river whilst she phoned Molly Greensleave from her mobile phone to check she was fine. She certainly was. Mary had noted how happy Molly sounded, and there was going to be no second thoughts on her part, she had no doubt about that.

"You grab that Jim Lightfoot whilst you can Mary," Molly had said on the phone. "I can tell he's a good'un."

This had prompted Mary to cut short her walk and pop into Peony Cottage instead of going back home. Jim had seemed as happy as she had ever seen him in the few short months she had known him and was already talking of his plans for next year's show. They cut a slice each out of Jim's champion carrot cake and sat on the patio with a glass of wine, chatting away well into the evening until it had got dark. They also had some of Mary's carrot cake that she had mischievously entered in Jim's name and laughed as they compared the two.

"I was robbed!" Mary had joked.

"Then I robbed myself according to the prize cards!" was Jim's comeback

Eventually Jim had suggested a trip to the pub when he noticed the goose bumps appearing on Mary's arms, for the night air had taken a sharp fall in temperature and she was still in the flowery dress she had worn all day for his delectation. She was hoping, as she had done all Summer, that he would suggest they retire to bed for the night, but a walk into the Dog & Gun on his arm as a couple was a good second best she thought. However, as soon as they had stepped foot in there she started to think it was not such a great place to be as Jim was taken over in conversation by everyone else wanting a piece of him.

For the next hour or so Jim was passed from person to person, each of them thrusting a drink into his hand and devouring his every word. Jim was an accomplished raconteur and could engage anyone on any subject, and he revelled in his new found fame. The bonhomie within the pub that night was as warm, convivial and lively as anyone could ever remember as everyone relaxed after the months of hard work preparing for the Show. But outside the Dog & Gun one man stood for a long time looking in through the windows at the carousers within, silently seething at constantly hearing his name being mocked.

After Mary had left to go on her walk Harry had got into his car and driven out of the village with no particular destination in mind. At length he had come onto the car park on High Ridge overlooking the Cock valley and had sat for over an hour, numb with the sense of loss, just staring out over the horizon until the sun had finally departed the day. He realised he had nothing else to look forward to that year, that his reason for being had been taken away from him by an outsider to the village.

He determined to drive back to the village and visit Jim Lightfoot and ask him outright if he had cheated, to plead with him to come clean to Bill Grudge and admit he had not baked that cake after all, or that he had not grown that monster marrow, threatening him if he did not, although he had no idea what he could yet threaten him with. Walking up to Jim's house though he had heard voices coming from the garden and soon determined that one of them belonged to his daughter. They both sounded very cosy and comfortable in each other's company, so much so that Harry feared he might be losing more than just his position as village champion to Jim Lightfoot that day.

Harry had made himself scarce as they both emerged from the garden gate and walked to the pub, Mary's arm linked into Jim's. He had followed them quietly a hundred or so paces behind, and then witnessed the cheer that greeted Jim's appearance through the door and the ensuing enthusiastic chatter, and all the jokes at his expense. He even heard Mary's response to Mrs. Dibble which pierced his heart like a poisoned dart. In previous years he might have stormed into the Dog & Gun and blazed a trail of blasphemous cursing, sparring with anyone stupid enough to denigrate him. But Harry instinctively knew that Jim Lightfoot was different. He felt he had probably met his match intellectually and physically and he would need to tread a different path in order to vanquish him. He also held his daughter's heart in his hands and Harry knew that banning her from seeing him had not worked, so he did not want to push her any closer to him. He had seen and heard more than enough for now and retreated.

Last orders were called in the pub but Bob Dillage knew a good thing when he was onto one. People were happy and spending too much money for him to let them leave. "Shut that door Deirdre, this is a lock in." A huge cheer went up at this announcement. "But do me a favour ladies and gents, if that snooping fucking police sergeant from Tithampton comes by then we're just having a private party and no money has changed hands. Ten per cent off all drinks okay?"

Bill Grudge was first at the bar. He might have been a policeman himself once upon a time but he had been in more lock-ins than there were hairs in his ample bushy beard. He was closely followed by several others all glad of the opportunity to carry on drinking and discussing the not insubstantial gossip of such a momentous day. Only Mary was disappointed. She had designs on getting a tipsy Jim back to Peony Cottage and into his bed at last. She was nervous about going home tonight, fearing the mood her father might be in and was hoping there might be at least a temporary sanctuary at Jim's. She was more than a little piqued that he had not already offered her a refuge seeing as how it was his fault she was going to be faced with such awkward living arrangements from now on, certainly for the next year at least.

She had not spoken to Jim for well over an hour, flitting between Mrs. Dibble and Ted Grangworthy but had ultimately settled next to Pete Greensleave who was still drinking steadily. "You need to pull yourself together Pete. You've only got yourself to blame, carrying on with Deirdre behind Molly's back like that."

"I know, I know. I'm so stupid. Oh Mary what am I gonna do? Molly was like I've never seen her before. Her mind was made up I could see it in her eyes. She's paid all the bills and left instructions on what needs paying when, how the central heating works and so on. And that swine of a brother just stood there with a smug look on his face. I can't look after myself Mary d'ya hear? I don't know how the washing machine works, I can't cook to save my life and I'll be the laughing stock of the village."

Mary could not quite bring herself to tell him he had been the village laughing stock for several years. "It sounds as if she's left everything in order for you then Pete so you should at least be thankful for that."

"I should have stood up to your dad all those years ago Mary," he slurred, "We'd be happy together now if I had I feel sure o'that. You were truly awesome in bed Mary, your body was the most beautiful I've ever seen."

Mary was momentarily shaken by this sudden departure from the previous subject matter, but after composing herself and quickly looking around to make sure nobody else had heard Pete's compliment she afforded herself a brief moment of inward satisfaction at this surprise revelation. For an even briefer moment her memory wandered back to snatched afternoons in her bedroom before her father came home, in the fields on sunny days, in the Bell Tower or in the back of Pete's old van when the weather was less fair. For several months she and Pete had certainly made the most of their teenage vitality. "Now now Pete, that's just drink talking. You need to get yourself off home and get some sleep. Things will be clearer in the morning."

"Come with me Mary, I don't want to be alone tonight. You can sleep in my bed and I'll stay on the couch I promise!" pleaded Pete.

"I'll forget you said that," countered Mary. "Molly is my best friend remember, and I've just been speaking to Ted and he doesn't know his daughter's left you yet does he?" But she couldn't deny the stir of lust she now felt deep within her, one she had hoped would be satisfied before too long by the man who was still encircled by several of her fellow villagers and would no doubt be deep in conversation with for a long while yet. She looked around the bar for assistance and caught Jane Tallboys' eye as she was getting her coat on in readiness to leave.

"Come on Pete. I'll help you home. Jane, can you give me a hand with him to make sure he gets back safely?" asked Mary of her arch rival for Jim's sex.

"No problem my dear," replied Jane, secretly happy that Mary was obviously not going to get bedded by Jim Lightfoot that night at least. Bob Dillage appeared and unbolted the door to allow them to leave.

After some stumbling Mary and Jane managed to extricate Pete from his evening's bolthole and after saying their goodnights, including a rather annoyingly perfunctory one from Jim at the far end of the pub, the three of them headed out into the night. A steady drizzle of rain made Mary exclaim in shock as soon as it hit her skin, for she was still only wearing the lightweight dress she had worn all day and which she had hoped would end the night on Jim's bedroom floor rather than steadily getting drenched and clinging to her frozen and unfulfilled body. They supported Pete between them and staggered for several hundred yards towards Pete's house.

"Who on Earth has a bonfire going at this ungodly hour," said Jane suddenly.

Mary stopped in her tracks causing Pete and Jane to lurch forward unbalanced. "That's no bonfire," she said. "It looks like a house is on fire and it's coming from……oh no!"

She immediately let go of Pete and as Jane could not hold him up on her own he fell face first onto the grass verge. "Jane, have you got a mobile?"

"Yes I have why?" replied Jane.

"Ring the fire brigade immediately and tell them Peony Cottage is on fire. I'm going back to the pub to warn Jim."

TWENTY FIVE

Embers

The rest of the night passed in a blur for every resident of the village, for few of them were actually able to sleep. By the time the fire brigade arrived from Tithampton, Peony Cottage was well and truly ablaze. As dawn broke a scene of complete devastation greeted them all, and in particular Jim Lightfoot, for his home was now little more than a smouldering shell of charred timber and masonry.

At first everyone had looked mystified at a bedraggled Mary as she lurched into the pub not ten minutes after she had left it. Dave Preston and a couple of his pals had nudged each other like children, transfixed as they were by the sight of Mary's nipples poking through the soaked linen of her dress, as well as the enticing lacy outline of her underwear. Eventually she had recovered her breath and blurted out that Peony Cottage was on fire causing everyone to fall silent. Jim ran from the pub closely followed by everyone else, a motley collection of people of all ages and varying mobilities making their drunken way through the village towards Jim Lightfoot's house.

They could all do nothing once they got there except wait for the fire brigade, for the flames were already forty foot high or more. Jim stood with his hands on his head, whilst Mary put a comforting arm around him and they just waited, neither of them uttering a word. As daylight came the chief fire officer allowed them to leave the rest of the crowd and at least enter his garden although he could not yet enter what was left of his home, for a scene of crime investigator was just about to start his inspection.

Jim's new polytunnel was now a grotesque mess of molten plastic, such was the ferocity of the flames some fifty feet away. His vegetables were covered in ash and ruined for the next show at Tithampton. An expensive ornamental Japanese Maple in a large pot by the back door had burned to a crisp. But there was one small piece of good news. Beside the bench Jim and Mary had sat on the night before over wine and carrot cake the two trophies Jim had won were safe and sound on the patio floor where he had neglectfully left them, although the garden furniture itself was blackened beyond repair. Jim picked the two trophies up and walked back towards the crowd of villagers, Bill Grudge, John Simmons and Jane Tallboys amongst them.

"Looks like these have come through unscathed," he announced, holding them aloft.

"That's a sign!" offered Bill Grudge dramatically. "A phoenix from the flames."

"Absolutely," continued Jim. "The show must go on! Bricks and mortar can be repaired but these beauties are a part of the village fabric. Pub?"

Bob Dillage chimed up above the ripple of cheers, "Yes folks, half priced breakfasts follow me."

Before they could all march away however, the Detective Police Sergeant from Tithampton, a rather officious and unpopular man by the name of Phillip Feltham held both hands up to halt their progress.

"Not so fast I'm afraid. We'll need to interview each and every one of you before you do anything else to ascertain what might have occurred here last night. I want you all to make your way to the village hall where a team of my officers is waiting to talk to you all. Quick as you can please."

A rather uncomfortable couple of hours now ensued for Bob Dillage. He had suffered a few run-ins with Feltham when he had been a mere uniformed officer and pretty much every statement from every person who had to be interviewed mentioned separately that they had been in the pub until gone two o'clock in the morning. Whilst this provided them all with a fairly indestructible alibi it was merely stockpiling a whole heap of potential trouble for the landlord. He just prayed that they had all remembered to say it was a private party at which no money had changed hands. An unlikely prospect given the amount of alcohol imbibed and the excitement that had passed in the meantime.

As well as the same alibi being submitted time after time, Feltham's team soon got their heads together and realised that one name kept cropping up as a possible suspect for an arson attack, if indeed deliberate incendiarism turned out to be the cause. Mary was one of the last to be interviewed, Feltham deciding to carry out the cross-examination himself in light of information he had now been made aware of.

"So then Miss. Ecklethwaite. You've been having an affair with the owner of Peony Cottage?"

"Not that it's any of your business Sergeant, but we have been good friends recently, nothing more." Mary said forcefully. She sighed, for she was not lying and wished that she could.

"Detective Sergeant," he corrected her indignantly. "Hmm. And what does your father think of that? He's not too happy about it from what we've been told," countered Feltham.

Mary smirked. "I know where you're going with this one but he wouldn't have done a thing like this. He's intolerable at times, but he's not an arsonist."

"Well that's interesting you say that," countered Feltham quickly, referring to his note book, "but I have it on good authority that he set fire to a garden shed at that very address once upon a time. What do you say to that?"

Mary's jaw dropped. For she had to concede her father had once flicked a lit cigarette towards Dick Tallboy's garden shed during a particularly heated argument about the ideal shape of an onion many years ago. Unbeknown to Harry Ecklethwaite at the time Dick had stored a gallon of paraffin in the shed and the whole thing had gone up in seconds. The police had been called but Harry had only been cautioned, because Dick had not wanted to press charges thinking it might make Harry thankful and stop his incessant and unnecessary war of vegetables. In fact it had only served to make him angrier and more resentful towards Dick.

"Oh really sergeant, that was an unfortunate accident." She argued, feeling the weight of evidence piling up against her nonetheless.

The Detective Sergeant continued in triumphant tone, especially as Mary seemed intent on refusing to use his proper title. "Miss Ecklethwaite, where is your father now? In spite of all the commotion last night no-one has seen him since yesterday afternoon. For such a large and loud man he's been surprisingly invisible."

"I'm sure he must still be in bed sleeping off his disappointment at losing his trophy," replied an agitated Mary.

"Fair enough," Feltham now had the bit between his teeth, "then let's go round to your house and raise the man shall we?"

Mary was escorted from the village hall between two policemen to a waiting car, casting an anxious glance at Jim as she passed by him outside. The village was now awash with rumour, pretty much all of it having centred upon the possibility that Harry had launched a revenge attack on Jim Lightfoot's house for daring to usurp him. Several people had mentioned in their statements, quite correctly, that Harry had threatened to get even with Jim, whilst some had even dared to venture, quite wrongly, that he had said he wanted him dead.

As Jim watched the car carrying Mary away Bill Grudge appeared next to him and said, "Now then Jim, would you like to stay with us? We have a spare room now the youngest has finally moved out and you'd be very welcome until you get sorted. Stay as long as you wish."

A thoughtful Jim was still watching the police car as it disappeared round the corner towards the Ecklethwaites' house. "Thanks for the offer Bill. It's very kind of you but I have somewhere to stay."

TWENTY SIX

<u>Where is the man?</u>

Mary's hand shook nervously as she struggled to fit the door key into the lock. Upon entering her house it seemed unchanged from the way she had left it the night before, for as yet she did not know that her father had left moments after her the previous evening.

"Dad?" she shouted up the stairs after a quick look around the ground floor.

Feltham nodded to the two other officers who immediately raced upstairs. After several minutes, during which time the Sergeant and Mary eyed each other uneasily the two policemen descended, both shaking their heads.

"Right then Miss Ecklethwaite. I'd be obliged if you could stay here and call me on this number if your father returns," instructed Feltham handing Mary a card, "Good day."

And with that the three men left, slamming her front door behind them leaving Mary all alone. The last few hours had been such a whirlwind of activity Mary did not know what to think, what to do next, or who to call if anyone. Jim did not own a mobile phone so he was out of the question, but she hoped he might call round soon enough, although she thought he might be keeping his distance understandably, and he had never stepped foot in her house before anyway for obvious reasons. She could phone Molly she thought, but after all her years of misery she did not want to spoil her moment of fun on what was effectively her first full day of happiness for a long time.

Mary was now left feeling quite alone, very scared about what people might be thinking about her father, and also increasingly worried about where on Earth he might be at that moment in time. Whilst all these thoughts swirled around in her head she stood in her kitchen rooted to the spot, looking out of the back window at their garden, which was very untidy due to the whirl of activity that had preceded her father's exit for the Show the day before. Harry was not the tidiest of gardeners anyway and always complained he could not find anything when he needed it. Cabbage leaves, plant pots and tools were strewn everywhere. It was a far cry from Jim's tidy manor she thought. A sudden and loud rap at the door shook her from her contemplations. Mary opened it in high anticipation only to find a very bedraggled looking Pete Greensleave.

Pete had spent several hours on the damp grass verge where Mary and Jane had left him the night before, eventually coming round enough to stagger off home where he had fallen asleep on the sofa. Mary suddenly remembered leaving Pete in Jane's care last night and had a pang of guilt. "Oh hi Pete. Errr, did you get home last night okay?" she asked, screwing her face up in embarrassment as she did so.

"Yes thanks Mary. Well when I say yes, I woke up in the house but have no idea how I got there. Anyway I was just wondering if your Dad is about? I woke up and saw the police cars bombing about and.....well, just can I have a word with Harry please?"

"I'm afraid you can't Pete, he hasn't been seen since yesterday afternoon. In truth the police cars are all probably looking for him. Why do you need to speak to him?" said Mary suspiciously.

At Mary's revelation that the police were looking for Harry, Pete suddenly looked much more relaxed.

"Oh nothing really Mary, it can wait. Take care now."

With that Pete skipped up the garden path and back down the street where he lived a few doors down leaving Mary even more puzzled. Despite calling after him he refused to come back and explain. If Mary had actually phoned Molly Greensleave she would have learned that Pete's brother's car had been vandalised overnight. Of course Pete was the culprit having driven over to Tithampton before embarking on his mammoth drinking binge in the Dog & Gun, but on the way back into the village he had seen Harry parked up at the ridge car park, although Harry had not seen him. When he had woken up and seen all the police activity Pete had assumed they were looking for him and wanted to check if Harry had noticed him driving back to the village, and if he could use him as an alibi.

Mary was thus even more unsettled. Did Pete know something of her father's whereabouts perhaps? She felt helpless and despite Detective Sergeant Feltham asking her to stay put she was hopeless at sitting around waiting for something to happen, so she showered, changed and went back out into the village to look for her father.

The first person she met was Ted Grangeworthy, out walking his dog although in truth the dog had travelled the length and breadth of the village several times that morning, for Ted was just after some gossip. Mary's first thought was for Molly.

"Have you heard from Molly since yesterday afternoon Ted?" she asked.

"No I haven't Mary. Not seen her since the Show. Why do you ask?" replied Ted.

Mary speedily realised he still might not yet know about his daughter's recent elopement with Pete's brother and thought it best not to worry him unnecessarily, although she did find it odd that he had probably been scouring the village looking for scandal as yet blissfully unaware some of the juiciest tittle-tattle involved his own kith and kin.

At length she found herself outside the village hall where the police had set up an impromptu incident room, so she skirted round the building quickly in order to avoid Phillip Feltham and headed up to the Dog & Gun, crossing the village green en-route where the first person she came across was John Simmons. He did not waste any time on niceties.

"He's gone way too far this time Mary. It's only a village veg show for crying out loud!"

"Now hang on just one minute," snapped Mary, "None of us know what caused the fire and it may well be just an accident. Has lekky Dave been interviewed do you know? I wouldn't trust his wiring and neither would you!"

"I feel for you Mary, I really do," said John, "but lots of people heard your father threatening Jim yesterday afternoon. Coincidences don't get much more brutal. If you're heading to the Dog & Gun then I'd leave it for now if I were you. Emotions are running very high in there."

***

Whilst the village was a hive of activity the usual air of tranquility pervaded up at Cock Hall. Lady Belton looked up from her writing desk as the door opened and Harrison walked in. "You have a visitor my lady."

"I heard about the fire," she said, looking up. "so I thought you'd show up sooner or later."

"Hello mother," said Jim Lightfoot.

"Harrison has made your room up James. No doubt you'll want to go and freshen up?" suggested Lady Belton.

"Thankyou," said Jim sitting in the chair opposite her, "I'll do that shortly. I hope I don't need to ask, but you didn't have anything to do with the fire did you?" asked Jim. "When I was here last we had such awful words between us that......" the hurt look on Lady Belton's tired and ancient face told him all he needed to know. "Of course not. Forget I ever asked you."

And so the mystery of the missing son that John Simmons had first discovered earlier in the year was about to come to light. As an academic man who was used to reading a lot of text very quickly John Simmons had perused the document that Lady Belton thought was lost several times, but most importantly he had failed to notice a detail that might have lead him to associate it with Jim much earlier, for Lord Belton's real name was Charles Alexander George Rhodes-Lightfoot. Belton was an acquired name from when the family seat was in the nearby village of Belton Felswick, at a time when the landed gentry could seemingly use whatever name they desired at will. When the Beltons struck the deal with a male villager to sire a child and Jim was subsequently born, he was sent out as a baby to distant relatives, a female cousin of Lord Belton and her husband in Yorkshire who bought up the child as their own. As a teenager Jim had been informed of this and was less than impressed with the news and had harboured a festering antipathy towards his real parents ever since, visiting Cock Hall rarely and never venturing into Allaways so that no-one from the village had ever seen him before until he turned up at Peony Cottage. In fact, he had not been back to Cock Hall for over fifteen years until that day, only keeping in touch with his mother in increasingly sporadic letters. Jim had never been told the true identity of his natural father despite repeated attempts to solicit the information from Lady Belton.

As Harrison poured tea for Lady Belton and Jim Lightfoot, who we must now assume to be none other than the present Lord Belton, the elder asked something that had been rankling for some time.

"I hear you've been cavorting with that Ecklethwaite girl? You do realise that you simply can't marry her?"

Jim's eyes widened and he leaned forward from his chair. "Not that marriage has ever actually been discussed mother....yet!......., but just out or curiosity why would Mary be deemed unsuitable?"

"Because I have strong suspicions that your father is her father!" came Lady Belton's bolt from the blue. "I found him with Mr. Ecklethwaite's wife one morning in a state of dishevelment when she was a cleaner up here, more or less nine months before Mary was born. I'd gone to meet a friend in Tithampton but had forgotten some papers that I was posting down to London so came back unexpectedly and found them at it in one of the guest rooms. I just looked at them and said when you've finished I assume you'll be sacking her, collected my papers and went back into town. It wasn't his first indiscretion and I expect there are others down there somewhere." Lady Belton waved her bony hand vaguely in the direction of Allaways. "Biologically of course there is no problem, but if it ever came out that technically she is your half-sister.....well, you can see how it might look can't you?"

As we have witnessed before Lady Belton, or Isabella Clarissa Rhodes-Lightfoot to give her proper names, was growing tired of life. She had been a constant in the life of the village for many decades, and her whole existence had been one of devotion to duty. She had gone through with Lord Belton's ludicrous plan to hire a man from the village to make her pregnant because he had convinced her he was unable to perform his conjugal duties, although as she found out in subsequent years he seemed to have no trouble rising to the occasion with other women. From quite early on in her marriage of convenience she had more or less lived a separate existence from her husband, only coming together on important family occasions or functions such as the village show.

"Did Harry know about this?" asked Jim

"I doubt it," replied Lady Belton, "even back then he was so preoccupied with the Show that he barely noticed his wife. No doubt she was flattered by the attention your father lavished upon her during his seduction. Mary may well be Mr. Ecklethwaite's daughter after all but she bears absolutely no resemblance to either him or his late wife. And he's too stupid to think she's anything other than his own flesh and blood."

Jim looked up at the painting of his father above the fireplace and could not help but compare him to Mary. She certainly had his thick head of hair and perhaps their noses were similar. She undoubtedly appeared to share his lustful desires for Jim had been fending her off since the day he had met her it seemed.

"Oh well, I haven't got time to think about that for now. I'm going up for a wash and a change then I'll have to get back down into the village to see if there's been any news," said Jim as he was walking away from Lady Belton, who wanted to carry on the conversation.

"It's not been easy for me you know James. Seeing you at committee meetings in the village, handing over trophies to you yesterday and not even getting a hug from you, knowing that you wanted to try and earn the respect of the village in your own way and that I couldn't yet acknowledge our connection. Not that everyone appears to have a total respect for you judging by last night's events."

"I appreciate that Mother," replied Jim, "but I'm here now aren't I. We'll have enough time to talk in due course. I'll see you at supper."

Jim was just about to leave when he remembered something else, "Oh by the way. I've got your old will. Or at least I did have before it went up in flames last night. You left it in that old volume you gave to the horticultural society. I was at John Simmons' house a few weeks ago for drinks with Mary. He had to pop out to Mrs. Dibble's on an errand and told us to make ourselves at home and I came across the volume on his desk along with your old will. Needless to say I quickly secreted it about my person and as far as I know he hasn't missed it. I think we need to talk at some point soon about the potential further consequences."

Jim's mother was thus left to ruminate. She had never really got to know her only child for as we have discovered he had been packed off more or less as soon as she had given birth in London. Times were different then. Despite the agreement with the mystery male villager the Beltons could never be truly sure that he would keep his part in their devious plan a total secret and so they decided they could take no chances. Jim always looked upon his adoptive parents as his true mother and father despite being told at quite an early age that his real parents lived at Cock Hall and that he would one day become Lord Belton. Lady Belton recalled the few times when the prodigal son was periodically whisked into Cock Hall in secret during his childhood years so that he could get used to the place but in truth he had hated every last minute of it. His relationship with Lord Belton was non-existent and the stress caused by her husband's affairs meant that Lady Belton was often confined to her room leaving Jim to rattle around the large house making his own entertainment.

If Lady Belton could have had her time over again she would have done things much differently. The secret would probably be out soon enough but she was now past caring she thought to herself, as she heard Jim descend the stairs rapidly, before slamming the large front door of the Hall aggressively on his way back down to the village. She felt almost as if there had been an unseen passing of a baton, for soon her son would become responsible for the upkeep of Cock Hall, and the incessant and worrisome involvement in the tribulations of the village folk. Her sense of relief was palpable.

***

It was now early evening but the Dog & Gun was as busy as it would normally have been towards closing time. It had become an information base camp for the villagers as they watched the comings and goings of the police from the village hall through the windows, and everyone had an opinion about what had happened. Most of them were exceedingly wild but it is fair to say they were far from conflicting. As was seen in the horticultural marquee the day before and with his terse conversation with Mary on the village green John Simmons was never scared of jumping to conclusions.

"I just collared one of the policemen as I was walking over the green and they haven't found him yet. I saw Mary too and told her she'd best find him before the rest of the village does after what he's done."

"Hear, hear," agreed Ted Grangeworthy, "the sooner he's caught the better. You can't go setting fire to folk's property just because they grow better vegetables than you. Imagine if his own daughter had been in that house, which as we all know would have been more than likely!" Ted nudged the side of his nose, content in being one of the first to have noticed Jim and Mary getting close after the show committee meeting back in July. Ted was still happily unaware that his daughter Molly was now several miles away setting about a new life with Pete Greensleaves' brother.

Bill Grudge now tried to bring his former policeman's calm procedure to the table, "Now then folk, let's not get carried away with too much conjecture before we all know the full facts."

"Absolutely right," concurred Mrs. Dibble. "Even the most seemingly open and shut cases often turn out to be nothing like you had ever imagined so let's all calm down and make ourselves available for anyone who may need our sympathy."

You always got the impression that Mrs. Dibble had seen many things in her life to the extent that nothing shocked her anymore, without ever being able to put your finger on why that might be so, and she certainly never gave anything away if that was indeed the case.

Bob Dillage had spent the last hour circulating amongst his regular customers to find out exactly what they had or had not told the police during their respective interviews, frantically worried that there might be a visit any moment with regards to his illegal lock-in the night before. Jane Tallboys was the latest to try and reassure him.

"Don't you go worrying yourself Bob. We all knew what to say. I said that me and Mary were assisting Pete Greensleaves home as he were much the worse for wear after last orders was called, and that Mary had noticed the flames and then phoned the emergency services."

Bob put his face in his hands. "You didn't mention anything about money going over the bar then? Did you Jane? Think carefully."

"No Bob, I did not!" confirmed Jane, "I said it was just a few friends having a private gathering and celebrating the show's success."

Bob had several more conversations like this with different people and started to grow more relaxed as the evening wore on.

The collective heads of the pub's occupants were suddenly turned toward the door as the figure of Mary walked in. She nervously scanned everyone's faces for a friend to turn to, for she was still frantically worried as to the whereabouts of her father, and concerned that Jim may have turned against her. She knew all too well how vitriolic village gossip could get. Some looked straight at her with disapproval in their eyes, some merely looked towards the floor, the dart board, the window, anywhere to avoid making eye contact. After an uneasy silence it was Mrs. Dibble who predictably came to her rescue.

"Dear child, come and sit next to me. Would you like a drink?"

Slowly but surely, everybody found the power of speech again, meaning Mary and Mrs. Dibble could talk without their conversation being heard by the whole pub.

"Are you alright darling?" asked Mrs. Dibble cupping Mary's hands tenderly, "Is there any news on your father?"

"No one has told me anything Mrs. Dibble. It's all very worrying." Mary started to lose control as tears welled up in her eyes. "He wouldn't do anything like that, I know he wouldn't. I know how bad it looks though."

Mrs. Dibble beckoned Deirdre Dillage across, "Brandy for Mary please Deirdre," she ordered.

"Oh no really," protested Mary.

"It'll do you good child. There's nothing like a stiff one to calm your nerves," Mrs. Dibble was not to be denied. "Here," she said passing Mary the glass that Deirdre had just poured, "get that down you and then tell me if I'm not right about it."

Mary threw the drink into her mouth and shuddered, closing her eyes and screwing up her nose as the tipple that she was entirely unaccustomed to slipped down her throat. After a few shivers she recovered her composure and looked at Mrs. Dibble. "Do you know what? That has damned well worked. I can feel myself calming down. Another one please Deirdre."

Over the next few minutes Mary threw another couple of brandies down her neck and wondered why she had never tried it earlier in her life. She felt emboldened with every gulp, and turned defiantly on her bar stool to see if anyone was looking at her, almost daring someone to challenge her about her father. Nobody had the guts to confront her it appeared.

At this point, and for the second time in a little over a quarter of an hour, the pub suddenly fell silent as the door opened and Detective Sergeant Feltham walked in. "Good evening one and all," he said in his customary patronising tone. "I thought I told you to stay at home young lady?" he said looking at Mary. "No news of your elusive father yet then I take it?"

"None sergeant," answered Mary, and with her recent anxiety now relieved by the effects of the brandy she ventured further, "If there was I'd have contacted you by now as you asked me to!"

Feltham looked taken aback but experience should have told him that insensitive questions delivered to people under the influence of alcohol invariably get batted back with extra boldness. He took a few moments to recover his thoughts, colour rising up his face to reveal his irritation at Mary's nerve.

"I've arranged to meet Lord Belton here. Has he arrived yet?" he asked somewhat bluntly, the question directed at nobody in particular.

Everyone looked at each other confoundedly. A few smirked and nudged each other, wondering how such an important investigation could have been assigned to such an idiot. Bob Dillage as patron of the premise felt he needed to speak first, although in truth he did not want engage a man in conversation who had always made his life difficult if he could avoid it. "I think you must be mistaken Sergeant, for Lord Belton's been dead for many years."

Barely had the words left Bob's mouth than there came another voice from the far corner of the lounge, the hidden one where Jim Lightfoot and Mary would often spend their evenings together and where Jim had plied Harry with drink. "Here I am Sergeant." No-one had seen Jim Lightfoot enter and seeing the look of confusion on everyone's faces he thought he had best make a quick statement, staring mainly straight at Mary as he did so.

"I realise this may come as a shock to you all but I am actually the current Lord Belton. I wanted to live amongst you and get to know you all without having the barrier of my birth title between us. I hoped to throw myself into village life and gain your respect before it came out. In time I hope you will all come to understand and forgive me for the secrecy and let me explain in more detail. In the meantime, Detective Sergeant, shall we?"

Jim ushered Feltham back into the quiet corner of the bar he had just exited and they sat together, on opposite sides of a table with their heads inclined so that nobody could hear what they were saying. It's fair to say that every villager in that establishment had a dumbstruck look of confusion as they all struggled to come to terms with what they had just learned. John Simmons was first to speak, the penny finally dropping in his head as to the documents he had found in Lady Belton's file on the village and which he still believed to be in his possession rather than burned to a crisp at Peony Cottage the night before.

"Well bugger me! He's a sly one isn't he?"

Bill Grudge picked this up. "Oh I don't know. Sounds like quite a noble gesture really. He's become one of us through him throwing himself into the village show and I dare say that wouldn't have happened if he lived up at Cock Hall. Fair play to him I say."

Several people nodded or hummed in concurrence and after a few moments the stunned silence gradually ended as conversations were struck up once again, although pretty much everyone was keeping an eye out towards the hidden corner where Jim and Feltham were conducting their tete-a-tete. The last few minutes had been a fuddled haze for Mary who still sat at the bar, the brandies contributing to her sense of bewilderment. It was all starting to become a bit much for her. She really needed sleep but with so many questions still to be answered and the alcohol preventing her brain from making any clarity of thought she felt as if she was close to exploding.

"Are you alright my dear?" asked Mrs. Dibble anxiously. "You look as if you're about to feint dear girl."

"I really don't know," Mary replied. "Did I really just hear Jim saying he was Lord Belton? I don't understand. What is going on in this village today?"

"You've had a long day Mary. And a very troubling one. Don't try to understand things now. They'll be explained soon enough I'm sure," Mrs. Dibble suggested soothingly.

Mary felt giddy, the alcohol making every thought in her head a hazy whirlpool of emotion. Bill Grudge helped Mrs. Dibble to get her seated before she fell down. "Where is my dad?" she suddenly wailed.

"Now, now, Mary," said Bill calmly. "Don't stress yourself. He'll be licking his wounds somewhere I'm sure."

At this point the door of the Dog & Gun flew open and two men in suits walked in briskly, surveyed the faces of all the now silent pub-goers looking at them before eventually finding the figures of Sergeant Feltham and Jim Lightfoot. They approached and one of them stooped and whispered in Feltham's ear, who nodded in turn and sent them away. The Detective Sergeant said something to Jim then got up and left himself, leaving Jim with a troubled look. After a few moments alone Jim got up and approached the bar slowly, his head down.

"What is it Jim?" John Simmons asked.

"Mm? Oh, err, I'm afraid I have just had some bad news. Terrible news actually," Jim said reticently.

Mary looked at him. She had never seen him look so worried before. And then it dawned on her that his bad news affected her somehow, before standing up from her chair and screaming "Noooooo!"

Jim rushed towards her just in time to stop her falling, several others helping as she lashed out with her arms and legs.

"What is it Jim? What's happened?" asked Bill Grudge after they had managed to calm Mary a bit.

"They have found a body in the rubble of Peony Cottage," Jim explained.

TWENTY SEVEN

<u>Mystery solved</u>

It was a sombre scene. The last light of the day was just fading. Barriers had been erected around the charred rubble of Peony Cottage and a forensics tent had been hastily erected over the recent discovery. A couple of dozen of the pub's regular customers had made their way over to wait for news, Jim and Mary among them. Mary was being supported by John Simmons and Bill Grudge, whilst Jim was talking to Feltham. After ten minutes Jim returned to the group of villagers.

"He says it's no use us all waiting here. Forensics will be working all night and they won't have any news for us until they've conducted all their investigations and filed full reports. In fact it will probably take days, so we may as well all go back."

"I need to know Jim," Mary asked suddenly, "do they think it's my dad?"

"I'm really sorry Mary," Jim replied, "but I'm afraid the body is so badly charred they'll need dental records to identify who it is."

Bill Grudge and John Simmons looked visibly ill at this last revelation. Nothing like this had ever happened in Allaways-on-Cock before. Harry may have been a nightmare most of the time but he was one of them and it now appeared that he was gone. Mary's legs buckled and Jim instinctively lurched forward to stop her from falling, John and Bill doing their best to help her up as well. Everyone felt sick to the pits of their stomachs.

As they all cried, hugged and tried to reassure each other, they failed to notice the dishevelled figure of a man with a banging hangover quietly approaching them, eventually standing in the middle of the group and looking at the pile of still smouldering ruins.

"What the blazing fuck's gone off 'ere then?" he enquired robustly.

Everyone broke embrace and looked up at the owner of familiar voice, some drying their eyes to make sure they were not deceiving them.

"Dad!" squealed Mary, flinging her arms around his neck.

"Harry!" shouted almost everyone else.

Detective Sergeant Feltham turned round and quickly approached Harry Ecklethwaite. "Harry Ecklethwaite, I'm arresting you on suspicion of arson and manslaughter. You do not have to say anything....."

Before Feltham could finish his speech Harry launched into full expletive mode.

"Who the fuck's this soft twat? You fucking clowns seem intent on harassing me don't you? Is some fucker gonna tell me what's going on or what?"

Undeterred Feltham swung Harry around and expertly applied handcuffs to his wrists before he knew what had hit him. "Johnson, take him away please," he ordered to one of his subordinates.

"What the........?" Harry was completely disorientated.

"Nooo, you can't do this," screamed Mary hanging on desperately to her father's jacket.

"You're a bloody murderer Ecklethwaite!" someone in the crowd of villagers shouted.

"Step aside everyone please," Feltham ordered as the villagers surrounded him. He was concerned the situation might get out of hand so he called over to a police van for back-up, and several officers piled out of it and approached the baying throng.

Suddenly a booming voice called out "STOP!" which caused all present to stop in their tracks and look at the figure of the normally mild mannered and silently nodding George. "Big prat was at my house all night," he continued. "He came round about ten last night to complain about how he'd been cheated at the Show. Couldn't shut the old sod up. Drank a bottle of my scotch then fell asleep on my sofa just before dawn, never moved all night apart from some snoring, farting and belching."

As they all stood around, aghast and open-mouthed, nobody could decide which was the more shocking revelation of the past few minutes. That Harry had nothing to do with the fire at Peony Cottage, or that George could actually talk more than a few words. It was the most anyone had heard him speak in decades. Feltham spoke first.

"In the light of this new information I am de-arresting you Mr. Ecklethwaite. You are free to go."

"What? Free to go? I haven't the first fucking clue what's going on," Harry raged. " I wake up on George's sofa less than an hour ago then make my way over here to see what all the commotion is and get assaulted by some jumped up little fucking…."

Bill Grudge and Jim Lightfoot quickly manhandled Harry away several yards so that he did not get into any unnecessary trouble. The DS was visibly embarrassed and it would not have taken much pushing in order for him to arrest Harry again for a breach of the peace. Mary followed and managed to get her father to calm down long enough so that they could all take several turns each in explaining the unprecedented events of the previous eighteen hours or so.

"So who's the stiff?" asked Harry after some consideration, rubbing his head which still raged with a monumental hangover from George's best whisky.

"We don't know yet dad, but the important thing is that it's not you." Mary said. "I've been frantic with worry all day."

Harry looked truly contrite. "I'm sorry lass. I should have let you know where I was, of course I should. But I was out of it. I only popped into George's for a quick drink and he insisted on pouring more into my glass. Honest."

Bill, Jim and Mary all looked at each other and rolled their eyes collectively.

"Well I'm off back to the pub. Is anyone else coming?" Bill Grudge asked.

"Yes I think I may as well join you Bill," John Simmons replied having just joined the small group.

"By eck, count me in if you're buying Grudge," Harry said, but Mary had other ideas.

"Dad! You're going nowhere. You're coming home with me this minute and you're going to have a bath. You stink!" Turning to Jim she smiled nervously, wondering how their relationship had been affected by the bizarre events of the last day. Jim rubbed her arm tenderly.

"Good idea Mary. Get him home. I'll see you tomorrow," said Jim.

Since Harry's sudden appearance Jim had not said much. As soon as Feltham had announced the discovery of a corpse, and in line with everyone else, Jim had assumed the deceased to be Harry in light of his vanishing act since late yesterday afternoon. He had felt a strange and terrible sorrow for Mary who would now be left on her own and was mulling over in his mind how best to deal with the situation. If anything Harry's revival left him feeling relieved that he did not have to come to any hasty decisions that he might have to care for Mary as more than just a good friend from now on. But these thoughts were now replaced by a feeling of unease about his spectral house guest of the past few months.

What if Dick was not a ghost after all, and the dead man had now died twice? Had Dick duped the whole of the village? Worse still, did anyone else in the village know and were they all having one huge joke at Jim's expense? What was indisputable was that somehow Jim had been tricked into believing the existence of a ghost at Peony Cottage, and as the others left him to his thoughts he suddenly realised he had been a complete fool, and there was no way he could own up to his gullibility, that much Jim was sure of.

***

It took nearly a week before the police could get back to Jim with concrete information. Feltham visited Cock Hall one morning to deliver the news, and sat in front of Jim in Lady Belton's spacious yet sparse drawing room, the old lady herself an interested and somewhat agitated witness. The faithful Harrison had handed his notice in and left immediately as soon as he realised Jim was about to become a permanent fixture around the place. He remembered him as a troublesome young boy and had no desire to run around after him at his age. Besides, he figured he had done more than enough for the family and it was now Jim's turn to take the reins. Lady Belton had still not come to terms with the news however.

Detective Sergeant Feltham took out his notebook and flicked through the pages looking for the relevant entries.

"The deceased man's name was Tallboys," he reported.

Jim gripped the arm of the chair he was sitting on but a bigger shock came next as the Detective checked his notebook.

"A Mr. Geoff Tallboys, identical twin brother of the gentleman who used to live there I believe."

"Geoff?" Jim queried, highlighting the name with the tone of his voice.

"That's right," Feltham affirmed. "Did you know him?"

"Err no, but I knew a Mr. Dick Tallboys lived there before me as you say."

Feltham took up the story again. "He was a merchant sailor. Came to the village twenty years or so back to live with his twin but here's the weird thing. It appears that absolutely nobody in the village has any knowledge of him, only his brother who lived in the cottage as you quite rightly say. However, there are records of him, Geoff Tallboys that is, using your previous address of Peony Cottage to forward all correspondence to once he left the merchant navy. It appears from our investigation that the twins may have lived there as one and the same person and kept this to themselves in all that time. Can't imagine why they would want to do that though."

Jim did however. It all suddenly dropped into place. Hadn't Mrs. Dibble once told him that Dick had boundless energy and seemed to be everywhere in the village at all hours of the night and day? He could just imagine the two old rogues hatching the plan by the fire one night after Geoff's prodigal return. It certainly explained why Harry Ecklethwaite always seemed to be surprised by 'Dick' whenever he entered the garden for dark and clandestine purposes. Had it started out as a joke that they just decided to carry on with and then could not escape from without a lot of awkward explanation Jim wondered?

"I do have one other piece of information that puzzled us," Feltham said, "and I was wondering if you could enlighten us."

"Oh? Fire away Mr. Feltham, excuse the pun," answered Jim, "anything I can do to help."

"Well, the fire was started by a candle setting alight some oily rags in the basement of Peony Cottage where this Mr. Geoff Tallboys was found. My guess is that he fell asleep and forgot to snuff the candle out, but according to the post mortem he had suffered a heart attack so he wouldn't have known much about it."

"Oh dear," Jim mouthed softly, shocked at eventually finding out what had happened that night. "I'm afraid I didn't even know I had a basement. It must have been very well hidden? It certainly wasn't on any deeds. And he must have been hiding there all the time I lived there do you think?"

"Indeed it looks that way Mr. Lightfoot. We found four hidden passageways, two of which came up into the house and two that surfaced in your garden. They really were quite ingenious," explained Feltham.

Jim took a few quiet moments to come to terms with the facts. When he had returned to Peony Cottage with the Cock Cup after the Show that afternoon and announced out loud his good news he had fully expected that 'Dick the Ghost' would soon appear to congratulate him. But he had not done so and he remembered feeling a bit miffed about that. Now Jim could only assume Dick, or Geoff as he now knew him to really be, had already suffered his fatal heart attack by that time and was lying alone beneath his feet, his candle slowly burning until it fell or was blown over thus starting the catastrophic fire. He remembered commenting on how 'Dick' had seemed paler than usual the night before the Show, and how his health must have been going downhill and felt bad about not being able to help him. He was stirred from his thoughts as Feltham cleared his throat and started to speak again.

"But that's not quite the end of it. You may remember that you gave us a sample of your blood, along with a few others in the aftermath of the fire at Peony Cottage, so we could eliminate you all from our investigations."

"That's quite correct," Jim concurred. "Is there a problem?"

"Well no, not for us," Feltham ruminated, "we've finished our investigations. This is a bit awkward I must admit, but I do have to tell you that in all probability, according to the DNA reports, the deceased man was your father. I'm very sorry."

If Jim had not already been seated he would have sunk into a chair, as it was he felt giddy enough to seek to compose himself in the aftershock of this latest piece of news. All these months not only had Jim been living with a ghost who was in actual fact very much a living, breathing person, he was also the mystery man who had impregnated his mother. Jim turned around and stared at her, his eyes imploring her for some answers.

"So now you know," she began to explain stiffly, "Geoff Tallboys came here a lot longer than twenty years ago. Over fifty to be exact. I found him poaching in the pond one morning and went to berate him, but he was a cheeky soul and I couldn't help but like him after a while. He made the occasional visit to the village to visit his twin between long trips at sea. When your father came up with his preposterous plan for me to get pregnant by a stranger I immediately thought of him. He was safe because he was hardly around and wouldn't be likely to cause trouble. I knew he had returned about twenty years ago as he used to visit me. We became companions and I would always tell him how your career was going and where you were in the World. It was like two parents discussing their child, just as it should be, and something I was never able to do with Lord Belton. You got your wanderlust from him I suppose. When his brother died suddenly a couple of years ago he was distraught and didn't know what to do. I made all the funeral arrangements for him and he was very thankful for my help. When you wrote to me, Jim, and said you were planning on returning to the village for good, but how you didn't want to live at Cock Hall it was Geoff who came up with the idea of you living at Peony Cottage so I got the estate agents to send you the details. Lo and behold you fell for it. However, I never saw Geoff again after you returned and just assumed he had gone away again. But now he's dead and that's truly awful. "

Lady Belton dabbed her cheeks with a handkerchief as a few tears fell from her eyes.

"Oh mother, I'm so sorry," said Jim supportively.

"Well then this is a tale and a half," said DS Feltham standing up suddenly. "But rest assured the matter is now closed and I will not be divulging any details as tittle tattle in future. I won't detain you anymore and will bid you both good day."

Mary Ecklethwaite appeared at the door and Jim asked her to show Feltham out. She had been a regular visitor to Cock Hall just as she had been to Peony Cottage, herself and Jim falling once more into their pre-inferno routine, although always with Lady Belton as a chaperone it seemed. When Mary returned Jim sat her down and explained the story from start to finish, how he was sired by the dead man nearly fifty years ago and how that same man came to be found in the burnt remains of Peony Cottage. Lady Belton sat impassively throughout the whole tale. At no point did Jim mention anything about a ghost, only how shocked he was to discover someone was living underneath him all that time. When he had finished Mary sat with her hands over her head.

"Are you okay Mary?" Jim enquired.

"Yes I think so. But it's a lot to get your head around isn't it? More importantly, are you okay? And what about you Lady B?" Mary asked of the old lady familiarly.

Lady Belton had started to become quite attached to Mary during her regular visits now that Jim was forced to live at Cock Hall, and especially in the absence of her faithful Harrison. In a quiet moment she had even told Jim she gave her blessing if things ever progressed to a more permanent union.

"Thank you child, I am fine. It's quite a shock to suddenly discover someone you had some affection for once upon a time is no longer going to be around. I'm ashamed to say we shared a bed on more than the occasion of Jim's conception in subsequent years. He kept me company and made me feel good at a time when Lord Belton was being positively beastly to me." Lady Belton suddenly felt a weight lifted off her shoulders with the admission of her feelings.

"Try not to upset yourself mother," Jim said calmly. "I don't think he suffered if that's any consolation to you."

"It is a bit I suppose," agreed Lady Belton with a long sigh. "I'm going for a lie down before lunch, all this bad news is giving me a terrible head-ache."

After Lady Belton had shuffled out of the room Jim and Mary were left alone for the first time since the day of the Show, and the atmosphere was a little awkward.

"Alone at last!" Mary said uncertainly.

"Yes indeed," Jim replied. "It's been quite a week. Thank you for keeping Mother company this week whilst I've been sorting things out with the police."

"You don't have to thank me Jim," Mary asserted. "I'd do more than that for you and I hope you know that?"

As usual Jim did not know quite what to say to a member of the opposite sex who had designs upon him, and reverted to his standard response of smiling nervously and mumbling, before changing the subject rapidly.

"So what mood is your father in today?" Jim asked Mary.

"Pretty cheerful I have to say," she replied. "Since all the excitement he appears to have calmed considerably. In fact, he says he'd like to meet you for a drink later if that's okay with you?"

"Oh? What on Earth for?"

"I don't think you have anything to worry about Jim, I think he just wants to apologise to be honest."

Jim was unconvinced. He had not seen Harry since he had suddenly and miraculously appeared from the dead, but had heard from John Simmons that Harry was still seeking retribution and claiming to have been cheated out of the Cock Cup. Jim was in no mood for a prolonged confrontation and resolved to see Harry that evening and have it out once and for all. He needed to show him that there was a new King on the block, one who would take no messing from now on.

TWENTY EIGHT

Truce

Jim arrived early at the Dog & Gun for his meeting with Harry, collecting a Gazette from Ralph Chubb's shop on the way. After acknowledging Bill Grudge, John Simmons and Ted Grangeworthy who were all enjoying a game of dominoes, Jim ensconced himself into his usual hideaway to read Daryl Bilkin's report of the Show. Bilkin's spelling and grammar had not improved any.

100th Alloways Show goes off with a bang – by Daz Bilkin

It was a pleasure to be at Alloways-on-Cocks's annual show last Saturday to witniss one of the most compeling vegatable contests your ever likely to sea. Perenial champion Harry Ecklethwait was beaten into second place for the first time in many years by villidge newcomer Jim Lightfoot. As you can see from the photographs some of the exhibits would not of looked out of place at the National Champianships, and it went right down to the wire before the result was announced at 4.30. Jim Lightfoote paid tribute to Harry Ecklethwate after collecting the cuvetted Cock Cup for most points in show. "Harry is a legend and it's a huge honnor to have beaten him today, but I think I got a bit lucky. I look forward to futur battles with my menter."

Jim vaguely remembered saying complimentary things about Harry in the aftermath of the presentation when Bilkin was interviewing him, having been prompted by the reporter who had seemed genuinely upset that Harry had not won. He also recalled feeling surprised that Bilkin appeared totally oblivious to the ranting going off only a few yards away when Harry was berating Bill Grudge, and that a proper reporter would surely have seen that as a more newsworthy story.

The rest of the one page report contained a few quotes from the likes of Bill Grudge on the record receipts attained during the day, from John Simmons who was also proudly pictured with his best vegetable in show exhibit and Jane Tallboys who was mentioned in despatches as the sporting participant on the dunking machine, saying that she had thoroughly enjoyed her regular soakings on such a warm day, or as Bilkin had written it, 'sokings'. Amongst the many photos, including one of Jim with his carrot cake and winning marrow, was one of Deirdre Dillage in the beer tent planting a kiss on Dave Preston's cheek whilst looking sideways at the camera, an otherwise innocent snap of Show day fun with sinister overtones for Pete Greensleave. Jim also could not help but notice in among the photos, mainly in the backgrounds were several images of the back of Mrs. Dibble's unmistakeable head and thought it unfortunate that such a stalwart of the village just happened to be turned away from the camera every time that the shutter went snap.

Jim spared a thought for the allotment holders over at Tithampton who must have been frustrated at the continuing lack of a culprit being named and shamed in the paper but hoped they took some comfort from Harry getting beaten at last. Jim had since heard that Bilkin had been sacked from the Gazette for completely failing to report on the fire at Peony Cottage. When his editor had asked him why he had not included the suspicious fire in his report on the day's events Bilkin had said "What fire?"

This caused Mike Jeffers to explode into a verbal tirade with the speed of a machine gun. "Biggest fucking story of the year and you fucking missed it you snivelling pile of useless skin and fucking snot shite, get the fuck out of my sight you hopeless little prick!" was apparently how Bilkin's editor had delivered the news to him, along with a not insubstantial amount of warm saliva.

Harry now appeared in the pub, and as soon as he noticed where Jim was sitting he broke out into a huge smile and waved at him cheerily as he approached.

"What are you drinking lad, a pint is it?" Harry asked, "I'll get them in, back in a jiffy."

Jim had insisted on going alone at first, and had asked Mary to leave it an hour before joining him in the pub. He had spent the afternoon mulling over various scenarios about how his meeting with her father might go, and thus far he was not experiencing one that he had prepared for. He watched as Harry merrily and pleasantly exchanged small talk with Bob Dillage, and wondered if he had perhaps been abducted by aliens, who had used his skin to cloak an altogether more amiable creature which they had now returned to Earth to live peacefully among the humans.

"There you go Lord Belton," said Harry jovially as he handed Jim his ale, before taking off his jacket and throwing it over the back of a chair.

"Now then this is nice isn't it? Damned shame about that business at Peony Cottage wasn't it? Have they identified the dead man?"

"Please call me Jim. I don't think they can Harry," Jim lied. "Poor chap was so badly charred I'm afraid. Poor fellow."

Jim had already agreed with his mother and Mary that there was no reason for the victim's identity to be divulged out of respect to him and Jane Tallboys' and her mother who was Dick and Geoff's sister-in-law. They had been informed of the deceased's identity and were quietly grieving, for so long being under the assumption that Geoff was either still at sea or had died in a foreign land somewhere having heard nothing from him in decades. In reality Jim merely wanted to avoid awkward questions about how he could spend the best part of a year living above someone and not know of their existence.

"Well it were indeed a bad do. But at least you were safe and sound, that's the main thing. I'm glad now I've got some decent competition at the Show each year, mighty glad I don't mind admitting," said Harry, revealing that he too knew how to lie through his back teeth. "Sorry if I were perhaps a bit offhand with you on Show day lad. It all gets a bit stressful when you know they're relying on you to put some good entries in. Shake?"

Harry held out his hand towards Jim. Jim looked at him momentarily, wondering if there was a catch, and then took it in his own and shook as if they were now the best of friends. Harry's motive soon became clearer however.

"My Mary says you're a grand chap and I've always trusted her judgement. I can't be going too hard on a potential son-in-law now can I?" laughed Harry.

Jim smiled as the penny dropped. Since the moment he was arrested and just as quickly de-arrested Harry had spent several days coming to terms with the developments in the village. That night Mary had got him back home and after he had washed the smell of stale whisky away, sat him down and told him all about Jim revealing himself as the current Lord Belton.

"I knew there was summat grand about that fine young man!" he had insisted. In the intervening days Harry had imagined Mary becoming the future Lady Belton, of spending grand Christmas dinners up at Cock Hall and mixing with the landed gentry on Boxing Day shoots.

"I'm sure that's not how most people perceive it Dad," Mary had counter argued. "In fact, I think you owe Jim a massive apology, not to mention the likes of Bill Grudge, John Simmons and many others that you've been horrible to over the years, this year more than ever."

"You're quite right Mary," Harry agreed, "although I'm sure there was definitely some cheating going on, but I'll turn a blind eye to it on this occasion. What's to be gained eh?"

"Oh Dad, won't you ever change?" Mary groaned.

"What do you mean? Just shows that even them toffs aren't averse to a bit of underhanded activity. Never mind that, has he hinted at marriage yet?" Harry was racing way ahead now.

Days later in the pub, Harry was now doing his level best to clear the way for Jim to ask for Mary's hand in marriage.

"You realise I'm joking about you being a son-in-law don't you, although I'd have no problem if you were that way inclined to act of course. I like you Jim Lightfoot, allus 'ave done. She's a fine lass is my Mary, don't you think Jim?"

"She is indeed a diamond Harry. And a total credit to you," agreed Jim

"Well it's not been easy I don't mind admitting. When her mother died I had to work doubly hard to provide for her and her brother, but she's the apple of my eye. Aye, she'll make some lucky chap a grand wife one day I have no doubt."

Jim felt a need to try and change the subject. "Was there anything else you particularly wanted to talk to me about Harry?" he asked.

"No, no, not really," blustered Harry as he downed several inches of his pint in one go. "Thought it would be nice to share a few drinks with you that's all. And to bury the hatchet once and for all, not that there was ever one on my side to bury you understand. I think some people just got a bit jealous about my success over the years and spread a few, shall we say, unnecessary rumours about." Harry almost sounded convincing.

"All water under the bridge as far as I'm concerned old chap," humoured Jim. "I've never been one to pay much attention to gossip. I like to look someone straight in the eye and take them as I find them."

"Ha! Indeed. I'm the same," Harry submitted. "You know Jim, I've always been one who likes to encourage other growers. Anyone asks me a question or seeks my advice then I like to tell 'em straight. None of this keeping secret growing concoctions to yourself. No point taking it to the grave with you is there?"

"I totally agree Harry," Jim assented.

"Good, good, good," Harry said over elaborately. "We're in agreement then. Between us we can make this show the best spectacle for miles around and learn off each other can't we? No point fighting is there? So tell me, how the fuck did you get a marrow that big then eh?"

Bill Grudge, John Simmons and Ted Grangeworthy were all watching this bizarre union of minds with increasing interest from their usual bolt-hole at the other end of the bar.

"What do you think it all means?" Simmons asked.

"Beggared if I know John," answered Grudge, "but whilst it's all smiles I reckon things are looking up. Looks as if they've decided to work together for the good of the show. Fair play to the pair of 'em I say. Harry even stopped me on the way back from the shop this morning and asked if we'd like him to do a talk to the Society next year on how he grows his veg. I must say he did seem very keen to help out."

"Well it all seems a bit sudden but I suppose all we can do is hope," Ted said. "We've had too much upset and argument over one thing and another in this village over the years. We all deserve a bit of peace and quiet from now on."

"Hear, hear," said Bill Grudge. "I reckon Harry's had the scare of his life over this fire business, and he's now seen the error of his ways. We'll be seeing a different side to him from now on, you mark my words."

At that moment, Harry slammed his fist down hard on the table that he and Jim were sat around and then pointed menacingly at him across it.

"Fuck oooooof, you're a lying twat Lightfoot. There's no way you grew them carrots that long and clean so who the fuck are you in cahoots with? You can't come poncing up 'ere and think you can take over my mantle without some help from somewhere." Just at that moment Mary walked in to the pub to see how things were progressing. "And you young lady, you can forget about marrying this cheating bastard. I didn't get where I am today………"

As Harry continued his tirade, Bill, John and Ted threw their arms in the air whilst Mary stood dismayed at her father's sudden return to blaspheming normality. All the while Jim remained seated with his arms folded, totally unruffled, and just smiled.

TWENTY NINE

And finally folks…..

Dear reader, as is often the case, you may have been left wondering what subsequently happened to the main characters in later years after the events of this novel ended, so just in case here is a brief piece about each of them to put you out of your misery.

Bob and Deirdre Dillage moved away from the village and retired to Bournemouth. Bob spent his days offending the locals in the various seafront pubs, whilst Deirdre began an affair with the town's crown green bowls champion, and got fingered a lot by visiting seventeen year old schoolboys at the local youth hostel where she helped out at mealtimes. When Bob died he left her absolutely fuck all in his will. Turned out he knew about her affairs all along.

Mrs Dibble died not long after the events of this story and left an absolute fortune to the local animal sanctuary and WI. The local press got hold of this and after some digging found out that she had actually been a porn star of some considerable repute in the late 1960's and 70's and got very wealthy from it. She was perhaps better known as Suzy Shagfast and her late husband Alfred was none other than legendary Randy Rudge, otherwise known as Rentacock who died of a cocaine overdose at a sex party in Los Angeles in 1979. Ralph Chubb always felt he had seen her somewhere before, and indeed he had, mostly smiling out from the front covers of several magazines on the top shelf of his shop, although gaping out might have been a more apt description.

Bill Grudge ran out of steam six years after this story and had to be sent by his daughters to live in a retirement home on the outskirts of Tithampton for his own safety and their own peace of mind. His mind became increasingly muddled and he would often startle the care assistants by shouting at the top of his voice "up against the combine harvester, banging away for all to see they were!" before falling to sleep with an erection protruding from his pyjamas and frothy dribble seeping from his mouth.

The Reverend Arsley was found dead in his study, a silver letter knife sticking out of his neck, to which had been tied a luggage label on which the word 'pervert' had been written, thus continuing the theme of Allaways vicars dying in mysterious circumstances. To this day no-one realises that the reason his predecessor was found croaked on Mrs. Dibble's front lawn was because he had died of shock having called round with an order of service for her to proof read, only to peer through her window and observe her in black stockings, suspender belt, high heels and leather bodice with seriously sharp metal boob tubes whipping John Simmons who was naked, on all fours, begging to be punished.

The learned John Simmons had been a student connoisseur of Suzy Shagfast's greatest films and had been the only villager to recognise her when she came to live there. In order to buy his silence Mrs. Dibble had reluctantly bought many of her stage props out of retirement and they had met up regularly to re-enact some of her more memorable scenes, which she did not mind as it kept her quite nimble and feeling young again. They also spent many holidays together visiting various porn conventions where she was often the guest of honour.

Jane Tallboys visited a pornography convention with John Simmons one year and signed up there and then for an agency who looked after aspiring actors and actresses wanting to get into the adult film business. She subsequently made her name appearing in several straight to DVD movies where she lusted after men old enough to be her dad or granddad.

Lady Belton continued living for another eighteen years to everyone's amazement, gaining a new lease of life now that her son had taken over the running of Cock Hall and its grounds. She travelled abroad extensively, her lavish lifestyle funded by her son who sold vast swathes of estate land to build new houses in the village, after figuring that if he could get new blood living amongst them the Show would flourish. Which it did!

If Jim Lightfoot really was the clever engineer he made out and not such a gullible wanker he would have discovered the secret trap doors in the house and garden of Peony Cottage, one behind the mock orange, one behind a large rhododendron and a couple of particularly ingenious ones in the floors of the lounge and kitchen pantry through which a surprisingly nimble Dick/Geoff either escaped to or appeared from. Jim eventually decided that he was actually quite gay and spent many years frustrating the living shit out of Mary Ecklethwaite, who continued to visit him on an almost daily basis in a variety of scantily clad outfits all to no avail. Jim won most points at the show every year thereafter, finally surpassing Harry's record of eleven on the trot before he fell out with the committee over their insistence that carrot cakes should be deleted from the next show schedule.

Mary continued her futile one-way relationship with Jim Lightfoot, happy to be lady of the manor albeit in an unofficial capacity, but every few weeks would pop round to Pete Greensleave's house now that he was single for a good seeing to in order to get rid of her pent up sexual energies. She continued to live under her father's roof, never married, and took over the running of the annual show from Bill Grudge in due course.

Pete Greensleave was just grateful to have occasional sex with someone who did not announce it to the wider World when she reached orgasm. His wife Molly got fed up with the sexual inadequacies of his brother and left him a few years later for a local schoolteacher called Sarah.

Harry Ecklethwaite decided he could no longer go around sabotaging other folks' vegetables in the run up to the annual Show and instead put all of his energies into growing quality produce and advising other growers on how to get the best from their plots. On Show day he would be found in the horticultural marquee assisting the committee and helpfully answering any questions the visiting public might have, divulging all of his secrets in the process. He was happiness personified if growers he had helped with advice managed to beat him in any of the classes, and would always be available to look after other villagers' gardens if they went on holiday. And if anyone believes that last crock of shit they probably believe in the existence of fucking ghosts too!

George eventually nodded off. For good.

Kindest regards

Author

If you have been inspired to try your hand at your local show then you could do much worse than joining the National Vegetable Society who are specialists in the art of growing to show.

http://www.nvsuk.org.uk/

My heartfelt thanks are due to a few of the Society's members for their advice, anecdotes and inspiration during the writing of this book.

Rest assured that Harry Ecklethwaite is a pure figment of the author's imagination and most growers are friendly souls more than willing and happy to help anyone out with advice.

Go on, have a go!

***

Enjoyed the book?

Why not email me and let me know.

cmorehead3@aol.co.uk

Didn't enjoy the book?

In that case email

Harrygeorgeecklethwaitejunior987654321@gofuckyerself.co.uk

***

Dedicated to my wonderful, beautiful, perfect wife, without whom I'd be nothing.

***

Printed in Great Britain
by Amazon.co.uk, Ltd.,
Marston Gate.